Life's Magical Moments

A story of true friendship

About the Author

Francesca Liacopoulos-Fawer, a Swiss citizen, was born in 1952 and has been living in Crans-Montana since 1981. Following the loss of her husband, she made a pilgrimage with her sister on the Way of St. James in 2009, where her first short stories were written. Three of these stories were published in an anthology in 2012. Further stories appeared in anthologies published by Novum publishing house. Her first book, *Jakob: Diary of an adventurous and emotional pilgrimage through Spain*, was published in 2014 by Novum. Her second book, *Magie des Lebens*, was published in 2017 by Paramon.

Life's Magical Moments

A story of true friendship

Francesca Liacopoulos-Fawer

Translated into English by
Michelle Nequette

ZORBA BOOKS

ZORBA BOOKS

Publishing Services in India by Zorba Books, 2019

Website: www.zorbabooks.com
Email: info@zorbabooks.com

Print book ISBN 978-93-88497-57-2
E-book ISBN 978-93-88497-58-9

Zorba Books Pvt. Ltd.(opc)
Gurgaon, INDIA

For Mumsi and Nicole,
Now you can accompany us from a different place
with all of your love

Contents

Part one
The Promise

1

*I*t is still early in the morning when the telephone rings. Sleepily, Francesca glances at the clock and with surprise realizes that it's only 7.00 a.m. "Yes... hello," she answers haltingly.

"Hello yourself, sleepy head, I'm already in Zurich at the airport and in about an hour I will be flying due south, to the heat...to the beach...to you...yay! I'm coming...don't forget to bring your swimsuit because we are heading straight to the beach. I don't want to waste a single minute of this precious week," excited chatter spills from the other end. Francesca is truly awake now and with no less enthusiasm replies, "I can hardly wait for you to arrive!"

On a dreary and rainy but warm September day, it's finally time. Francesca, who has kept the villa in Corfu after her husband's sudden death three years ago, is impatiently awaiting her dearest friend, Marlène. Back then, after the funeral, she had tightly embraced Francesca and promised to visit her every year for a week. To this day, she has kept her promise. These unique, magical weeks were the best medicine for Francesca, who had found it very difficult to cope with the loss of her husband.

For a while now, the guest room has been lovingly readied awaiting the arrival of her friend, whom she affectionately calls *ma petite fée.* The white curtains printed with tendrils of ivy, along with the matching bedding and three aquarelles of Corfu that a dear friend had painted, lend the room an air of fresh and natural charm. A colourful bouquet from the garden sits atop a small, delicate antique table in welcome.

Exceptional, Francesca pays more attention to her looks as she puts on an airy white, lightly flared strappy dress that reaches her calves. She pairs the dress with her new leopard print wellington boots, which she recently received as a birthday present from Vanessa, her English friend who is spending the summer in Corfu with her husband, Dino.

She quickly brushes her sun-bleached, medium-length hair and with faint irritation studies the strange, drawn face that stares back at her from the mirror. Suddenly, she hears the gentle voice of her husband in her head: *Haven't you forgotten something?* A sigh escapes her chest as she remembers the game she played almost daily with him. "Yes, yes, I know, never leave the house without lipstick," she whispers quietly.

In her handbag, she finds a tube in a shade of coral and carefully outlines her lips. After all, she would like Marlène to see how much she's been looking forward to this week with her.

Thirty years ago, in the spring, fate had led Swiss-born Francesca and her wonderful Greek husband George to the Ionian island of Corfu. Right from the start, they were both captivated and knew it immediately: *This is it! This is where we will stay...*

Their arrival could not have been more beautiful. Everywhere, wild flowers and orchids had been in bloom in a symphony of colour. Solitary aspen shone, clad in their purple buds. For the first time in her life, Francesca could pick oranges and lemons directly from the trees. And then there were the small, orangey yellow fruits of the kumquat tree that, when processed into a liqueur, were a Corfiot specialty.

Interspersed throughout the area were many tall, dark-green cypress trees, straight as candles punctuating the countless silvery-green olive trees typical of the picturesque island.

They both found a diverse and lucrative summer job in a fur shop. George, in his late twenties, tall, slim, curly blonde hair, very attractive and charming with an energetic chin and beautiful blue eyes realized early that he had a special gift when it came to customers.

Everyone appreciated the air of sophisticated elegance that surrounded him. He was also popular with the other sales clerks who welcomed his friendly and helpful attitude.

Francesca, a year younger, enchanting, medium-height, knockout figure, shoulder-length wavy hair and very dark, chocolate-brown eyes sparkling with vitality was his closest confidante, his girlfriend and soul mate. They were an amazing couple and complemented each other perfectly.

Despite the six-day work week and the long hours, they still had enough energy to go to parties and go dancing. They were young and outgoing with cheerful dispositions and soon had an exquisite circle of friends. They were crazy about each other and loved life. Where else could it be more beautiful for two young people who were madly in love?

The two lovebirds used every free minute to explore the verdant, multi-faceted island, characterized by its hilly and mountainous regions, on moped. They preferred to ride to the rather rugged, craggy eastern coast with its charming coves and bathe at sublime, idyllic beaches. They often spent Sundays with friends on the long sandy beaches of the west coast swimming, water skiing, windsurfing and of course, partying.

They roamed hand in hand through the beautiful historical town centre, with its distinctive Venetian style and visited the Agios Spyridon Church, where the relics of St. Spyridon, the patron saint of the island, were housed.

Several years later, they built their dream villa in Poulades. The beautiful property was situated at a higher elevation in the centre of the island. Bright yellow spring gorse bloomed among the cypress and olive trees along with myrtle, wild thyme and mint, which smelled heavenly when trod upon or rubbed between one's fingers. Rounding this out was a magnificent view of the north-eastern coast of Corfu and the mainland on the opposite shore with its high Albanian mountain range in the background.

Not a lot is happening on this rainy September morning at the Ioannis Kapodistrias International Airport. A few deserted buses are parked in their reserved spots. Taxi drivers are patiently waiting for customers as they smoke one cigarette after the other, their windows open while the air conditioning runs at full blast. Others are standing together in small groups, gesticulating wildly as they excitedly debate politics in loud voices. A bored policeman paces back and forth in front of the airport lobby, patrolling the area with an expressionless face. An elderly man stoically pushes a snaking train of interlocked luggage trolleys in front of him. The rain causes his sweaty, bedraggled clothing to cling to him as he slowly makes his way past the arrivals gate.

Francesca barely notices any of this. With determination, she enters the airport lobby in long strides. She stands still for a moment, surprised by how cold it is inside and shivers, rubbing her naked arms. Here too, not much is happening. A few young travel agents are standing around in small groups idly holding signs emblazoned with their agency's name, waiting patiently as they do every day for their new guests to arrive. A few more steps and Francesca is standing under the up-to-date arrival and departure board. With irritation, she notices that the plane hasn't even landed yet. *Oh drat! Today of all days they have to be late.*

Resigned, she glances about until she finds a sheltered corner and collapses into a chair. Since the death of her beloved husband she has let herself go and lost a lot of weight. Despite the tan, her face looks pale and sunken. Most striking though are her deeply sorrowful brown eyes.

Whenever Francesca is alone, which happens often, she withdraws into her own dark world where the warmth of the sun's rays can no longer find access. Her friends and family do their best to coax her back into the world of the living, but somehow everything just seems to bounce off her...

A loud scratchy voice suddenly rings out over the public-address system announcing in Greek and a mumbled, incomprehensible English that the flight from Zurich will be landing thirty minutes late.

Francesca feels an internal tension and restlessness begins to take hold and she takes one, then two deep breaths. *Ma petite fée has kept her word and is coming again this year. I promise you, I will pull myself together so that we can finally spend a few wonderful days with each other without me constantly bursting into tears. When I think back to the past two years...*

Twice already, they have spent an unforgettable week together in Corfu. Francesca is ashamed though when she thinks back to the time when she ran around with bloodshot eyes on a daily basis. Many tears had been shed and there had been many heart-wrenching moments. She had felt guilty for not having been able to offer her best friend a carefree holiday week. Nevertheless, Marlène had comforted her day after day with great patience, empathy and love.

Francesca had composed herself, and every day they drove to the same beach in Barbati on the east coast of Corfu. They reclined in practically the same beach beds and ate lunch at the same *taverna*, Piedra. Two years before, while walking along this beach packed with noisy, happy people, they had noticed a quiet place with large white umbrellas and solidly-built matching loungers.

The staff would immediately bring each new guest a full ice bucket and a bottle of water and place them on a small table. It was quite a service! Ideal for those who shied away from large crowds and preferred peace and quiet in addition to a more private setting. It was just the right ambiance for the two friends where they could have uninterrupted conversations without the fear of nosy neighbours. It was a place where they wouldn't be subjected to the carefree, light-hearted chatter of their fellow human beings. It was an oasis of quiet sophistication.

Unfortunately, each day was a repeat of the same scenario. Francesca paid no attention to this veritable paradise and throughout the exquisite meals – that would inevitably end in tears – she poured out her aching heart to her friend.

They didn't register the curious looks they received or the fact that the situation slowly became embarrassing. Marlène tried everything to calm Francesca down and explain to her among other things that it was pointless to fight against something that could no longer be changed. She tried to convince Francesca that she needed to learn to acknowledge and accept Fate. Marlène always insisted though, that her friend finish what was on her plate because she was down to nothing but skin and bones. Her swimsuit hung on her like a shapeless rag.

Francesca looks at the clock. A half hour has already come and gone, and still no sign of the airplane. Several people with disgruntled expressions are also waiting at the exit. Others are wandering about looking frustrated. Once again, the public-address system blares out a loud and unintelligible announcement that most likely means the flight is still delayed. Her back is slowly starting to ache, so she stands up to move her legs a little. She discovers a massage recliner with an *'Out of Order'* sign and carefully lowers herself into it. The recliner is actually quite comfortable and it doesn't take her long to sigh and sink back into her bleak and dismal thoughts.

Meanwhile, Marlène is staring in fascination out of the window of the airplane that will finally reunite her with her friend. She observes the landscape below her drift by until they approach Corfu's unusual runway located between the green hills of the eastern coast. It looks as if the landing strip is rising from the depths, an artificial runway, which has been built in the middle of a lagoon.

As the words *"Welcome Home"* come to mind, they affect her in a way that makes her heart swell. It's a familiar feeling, as if George were welcoming her to his home. It's also as if she were bringing him a part of herself from Switzerland to Greece.

One week of pure, unadulterated friendship and an exchange in spirituality awaits her. Precious days beyond the daily routine, time to immerse in the Source and create a deep connection. Time to open Francesca's eyes and heart and guide her towards a different Truth; a Truth other than the one she currently knows.

Marlène recalls the words of someone she had sought out a while back, when she had wanted to know her purpose in life, why she was here on this earth. "*A star wanders across the heavens. Then, at a certain point, out of love, Heaven sends this star to Earth. You are this star, Marlène, in all its purity, light and splendour; and your calling is to illuminate the Journey of Life of those whom you hold near and dear...*"

Finally, the plane lands an hour late. Francesca soon catches sight of her friend among all the travellers who, after clearing Customs, are charging towards the luggage carousel. Although Marlène is of medium height and rather petite, she stands out in a crowd with her long, straight blonde hair, her harmonious facial features and her beautiful, striking blue eyes that are now gazing around full of curiosity. She also makes quite a fashion statement dressed in her trendy attire – designer jeans paired with a colourful T-shirt and a short black leather jacket draped casually across her shoulders.

They start waving madly at each other as soon as they make eye contact. Finally, the moment has arrived. Pulling her pink suitcase behind her, Marlène strides briskly through the exit towards Francesca, a look of radiant joy on her face. Seconds later they are hugging each other emotionally, each filled with cheerful anticipation of their planned week together.

Marlène looks at her friend in surprise, who for once has not appeared wearing her typical dark clothing. She slowly walks around her and remarks happily, "You look great! I think it's wonderful that you finally had the courage to wear something cheerful. You look like an angel with leopard legs. I want to see this every day. This is the new Francesca, gone are the depressing colours. Promise me!"

"Oh, stop with the nonsense. You're embarrassing me!" Francesca replies bashfully. But now she's relieved that she was able to overcome her inhibitions when she sees how much it pleases her friend. It is true, though, these past few years she had only felt comfortable wearing dark clothes.

However, nothing can spoil Marlène's good mood, even though the weather has put a damper on her wish to head straight to the beach. She's in such a good mood that it's contagious. Francesca suggests they drive into town. Fortunately, by the time she parks her ancient Mercedes, which she lovingly calls "Merky", in the vicinity of the old castle, it has stopped pouring outside.

Marlène looks around enthusiastically. She recognizes the long *Esplanade* with its many cafés located along the vaulted archways.

"The open green space you see right in front of you is the cricket pitch, where they still hold high-ranking matches on a regular basis. I just get annoyed though, when I have to look at the large parking lot that surrounds it. It spoils the whole landscape," Francesca explains with a grimace.

The heavy clouds that still hang threateningly over their heads can't curb Marlène's enthusiasm, as she looks about happily soaking up her first impression of the unique city. *My God, Francesca, George and I are One, a unified Energy. I can feel it in every stone of this city. I wonder if she's also experiencing some of this. Will I be able to convey some of these things to her? Will she trust me enough that I can lead her into this other dimension?*

Francesca points to the impressive castle over in the east and proudly explains, "This old fortress is the *Palaio Frourio,* and over there, on the north end of the Esplanade, that beautiful, imposing structure is the Royal Palace, which is home to the Museum of Asian Art, the municipal library and the council art gallery located in the eastern wing."

It makes Marlène happy to see her friend's renewed vitality and the enthusiasm with which she's sharing her knowledge. Despite the dreary and rainy weather, it's still pleasantly warm. They stroll through the shopping district in the best of moods, past boutiques, shoe shops, monuments, banks and expensive jewellers in a town pulsating with life. Francesca is carried away by Marlène's exuberant joy. She feels like a tourist herself as she presses her nose inquisitively at every shop window.

They find a shop selling beautiful crystals, some of which have been processed into jewellery. Both women scrutinise one after the other until Marlène suddenly finds an unusually beautiful, 12cm long white rock quartz.

She reaches out and grasps it. Instantly, she feels a vibration that radiates throughout her arm. The power that flows from this rock has her completely mesmerised. She hears a voice inside her head: *I, Michael, Archangel of Strength, come with my Spear of Light to give you a little prod, so that you can pass on the Secret of the Star in the Here and Now.*

Right then, Marlène realized that the crystal has been waiting for her. But how can she explain what just happened to her friend?

"Look," she says excitedly while she holds the crystal up to the light admiring it, "can you also see it, how interesting the designs in these inclusions are?"

They suddenly find themselves playing a new and exciting game. Each wants to detect more shapes and forms in the crystal than the other. Francesca can feel her friend's elation and purchases the crystal for her as a keepsake. Beaming, Marlène thanks her with a huge hug.

However, this much shopping can make a person hungry. Unfortunately, it has started to drizzle again. They hastily make their way through the streets, some of them quite narrow, until they reach the main square, *Plateia Dimarchiou,* home to the town hall and quite a few good *tavernas*. A short while later, they are seated underneath a giant pergola of bougainvillea, hungrily polishing off a delectable moussaka and Greek salad with feta.

During the meal, Marlène admires the attractive town hall directly across them. Once Francesca has enjoyed her first sip of wine, she proceeds to explain in detail, "The town hall is one of the most beautiful buildings in town. It was originally the assembly hall for Venetian royalty. When the weather's good I'll show you the bas-relief sculptures that cover the outside of the building. In the centre of one wall is a carving of the petrified Phaeacian ship, which is on the municipal coat of arms of Corfu."

"It's beautiful", Marlène replies, and quickly swallows a bite, "I'm looking forward to it. Perhaps we can do a sightseeing tour in one of those vibrant, horse-drawn carriages that I noticed when we parked." She is happy that her friend is more talkative and also more outgoing than she used to be. Hopefully, it will stay that way.

"Of course. There's still so much to see. The picturesque market, the old town with its Venetian flair, which lies between the new and old fortress. The narrow streets and monuments, the whole atmosphere, will remind you of Venice. There's still quite a bit that I can offer you in the line of landmarks and things to see," Francesca says with a smile. *Actually, it's about time that ma petite fée gets to see something else on the island other than the beach of Barbati.*

The sky is still overcast with thick, grey clouds, but at least it has stopped raining. After their meal, they both stroll up to the *New Fortress*.

"From here one has a stunning view of the old town and the harbour, even in rainy weather. The castle is said to have a dense network of underground tunnels connecting it to the old fortress."

"How exciting, just imagine that." Marlène is impressed.

However, Francesca's feet are slowly starting to ache in the unaccustomed plastic boots. She hadn't expected to run around in them for hours. Her friend too, has had enough for today, so they quickly hurry back to the parking lot where Merky is waiting. They drive along the shoreline in a north-easterly direction towards Poulades, where Francesca has her villa.

It is a mild evening and the first stars after the rain appear in the sky. Following a delicious supper consisting of Rösti, baked in a heart-shaped form, served with a Greek salad prepared by Marlène, they linger outside on the terrace by candle light enjoying their first evening together.

"Tell me," Marlène asks reflectively, "How long have we known each other? Do you still remember how we met?"

Francesca settles deeper into the chair and folds her arms behind her head. The corners of her mouth crinkle in amusement as she studies her *petite fée*. "Almost 30 years ago...half an eternity!" she replies and laughs as she registers her friend's sceptical look.

Marlène shakes her head in disbelief and replies uncertainly, "Never! It can't be, we couldn't be thaaat old..."

"Well sweetie, time won't stand still, even for us...I remember everything perfectly, as if it were yesterday. It was the same year that George and I wound up in Corfu. Our former employer had recently posed the most unbelievable suggestion that I fly back to

Switzerland that very year and try to find a suitable shop in a ski resort. Of course, this was after he determined that with George he had hit the jackpot. Can you believe it! What a grand idea. Summer in Corfu, winter in a skier's paradise...we were so fortunate." Francesca takes a deep breath. She closes her eyes and transports herself back to the past. Marlène starts to worry that her friend has fallen asleep and lightly touches her hand.

Francesca collects herself, blue eyes imploring her to continue with the story.

"After I spent days travelling by train through various ski resorts, I was in luck. I found a suitable location, right in the centre of Crans-Montana. One day, I was just on my way home after discussing some problems with the architect. You walked towards me with long, graceful strides and the most dazzling smile ever."

"What," Marlène giggles from behind her hand, "I'm supposed to have approached with graceful strides?"

Francesca has to laugh as well. "*Mon Dieu*, you were so young, not even twenty...and me, I wasn't yet thirty," she smirks. "Even though it's been such a long time, I can still see you...strikingly pretty, petite and with a waistline to die for. You looked like an exotic butterfly amongst all the other pedestrians in your miniskirt and vivid rhinestone top, wearing loads of bracelets. You looked as if you were from St. Tropez, Malibu or a beach pulsating with life like the Copacabana, not from a small mountain village. Back then, you had very long blonde hair that reached all the way down to your bum in which you had braided colourful beads."

Marlène interrupts her friend's verbal torrent of compliments. "Oh no...seriously...was I really that bad back then?"

Francesca smiles at her affectionately. "Bad, no, just unusual in your lively and whimsical style that stated: "I don't care what all of you think, I'll do whatever I please." That really impressed me."

Marlène stands up and retrieves some iced tea from the refrigerator for herself and refills her friend's glass with some chilled white wine. "Yes, ok...and what happened then, did I speak to you?"

Francesca shakes her head. "A few days later I saw you leaning in the doorway of a jewellery shop looking bored as you kept an eye out for customers. I went over to you spontaneously. Although I'm somewhat older than you, you addressed me in an informal manner straight away. You were proud as a peacock as you showed me around the shop you had just recently opened with your boyfriend, Eddy – the two of you weren't married yet – showing me the precious diamond jewellery and other exquisite stones."

They cheerfully toast each other, then, Marlène continues with a laugh, "Now, I remember. I placed a gold necklace around your neck, which had been masterfully crafted from three different types of gold that you absolutely did not want."

"That's right," Francesca continues, "and all the while you were challenging me with your incredibly blue eyes. I really didn't want to buy a necklace, but then my cheeky mouth got the better of me and I said how lovely it was, though I would prefer if it were shorter...it's been a long time since I retreated so fast from anyone...I was just happy to have escaped without making a purchase."

Marlène's blue eyes light up. Suddenly, she too feels transported to a small Swiss village thirty years in the past. Both are overcome with a fit of laughter when they think back to the moment when Marlène stared in bewilderment as Francesca said a quick goodbye and made her hasty retreat.

"I remember I ran after you the next day," Marlène sputters.

"You darted down the Main Street totally out of breath swinging something over your head and calling my name. Oh my god, that was so embarrassing...in the middle of the street with all those people watching us with great interest." Francesca can't stop grinning when she thinks back to the scene. Again, she feels drawn in by the unusually large, radiant blue eyes of her friend, her bird of paradise. What a strong aura this girl has. What a considerable magnetic attraction. Back then, she remembers, she wore her hair pulled back in a long ponytail.

A radiant smile appears on Marlène's face and the candlelight illuminates a row of even, white teeth. "Right then and there, Eddy had shortened the necklace to the length you wanted. You poor thing, now you no longer had an acceptable excuse and had to buy it."

Francesca cuts in laughing, "You also offered it to me at a special friendship price. But the best part came the next day. Once again you came running after me screaming and...do you remember?"

"Yes, yes...I know, I know how embarrassing it was," Marlène replies, and shakes her head at the memory.

Amused, Francesca continues, as she remembers the scene, "At first, I felt really sorry for you, as you stood in front of me with clipped wings. You sheepishly explained that you had forgotten to calculate the customs charges and add them to the price. But I was unable to help you because I didn't have the funds. I had to raid my savings account in order to pay for the necklace. I was cleaned out."

"Yeah, after that you made me a great counter-offer," Marlène interrupts grinning, "You jazzed up my old wolf jacket by sewing fox tails onto the shoulders."

"Exactly. And then, with a delicate gesture that I barely registered, you breathed a kiss on my cheeks, hugged me, and before I could say anything else you were already gone. Never before had I met someone who was as light as a feather, so fragile, almost like a fairy...I still wear your necklace every day. It's my good luck charm."

With shining eyes, they look at each other. "Our story's pretty unusual, isn't it?" Marlène asks in a soft voice.

"Yes, it is...that day I thought I had reeled in a little fairy, who to this day has been loyal to me and never slipped away. What a wonderful friendship this has become, all from an accidental meeting."

Quiet and introspective they both gaze into the starlit night reflecting on fond memories. They would have preferred to spend all night sitting outside discussing and philosophising. But Marlène's eyes are falling shut. It's been a long day for her. She had to get up quite early in the morning. With a big hug, they wish each other "good night" and then fall sleepily, but very happy into their beds.

2

M arlène is awakened very early by the slowly advancing daylight while the villa is still deeply ensconced in the stillness of the morning. In the distance, she can hear a dog barking. Close by, an inconsiderate rooster is crowing in an effort to drown out the incessant chirping of the birds that grows louder by the minute. Slowly, she throws back the covers and rises. Yawning heartily, she stretches herself. She quietly tiptoes outside in her short, blue dress upon which two sleeping mermaids are printed.

On the horizon, behind the mountains on the mainland, the sun rises up high like a red disc. Barefoot, Marlène tromps through the garden grass that is still damp with morning dew. She stands motionless to absorb the earth's energy that rises up within her and envelops her like a warm embrace. She raises her eyes and feels how the energy from the heavens floods through her.

Moved, she approaches her favourite tree, a centuries old olive that is divided in the middle by a rock, something that makes it very special. She embraces it, whispering softly. She immediately feels the oscillation, the tree's vibrations that join in unison with her beating heart.

My God, everything seems so simple here. It's as easy as child's play to be One with Nature's forces. The adversities of everyday life can't touch me here. This entire week, I can simply be. I can listen to my innermost self without having to grapple with the usual rules of daily life.

A touch of joy overcomes her. A small smile plays on her lips as she slowly makes her way back to the house.

In the meantime, the sun is shining directly into Francesca's eyes. Blinded, she squeezes them shut. In her inner eye, small round dots suddenly appear. The larger one in the centre looks like an arrow. She immediately remembers the Way of St. James. Astounded, she shakes her head. *What's that supposed to mean?*

Just to be sure she wasn't mistaken she closes her eyes tightly once more. It doesn't take long, and the same thing happens again. This time though, the dot in the centre takes on the shape of a dove! It's the *same* dove that's chiselled into her husband's gravestone.

Overwhelmed, Francesca remains in bed quietly for a little while longer until she hears familiar sounds coming from the kitchen and the aroma of fresh coffee wafts into her nose. In a long lightweight t-shirt she hops down the stairs and greets her friend with a big kiss on the cheek. "Did you sleep well sweetie?"

She knows that as the hostess, she should actually be the one indulging Marlène and not the other way around. But her friend dismisses her concerns right away. For a few days, she enjoys mothering her friend who is still filled with grief. Francesca, of course, is delighted by all this care and revels in being pampered again because for years her husband had been in charge of this. He even used to bring her breakfast in bed!

Marlène has really thought of everything. Mountains of freshly toasted bread, jam, honey, coffee and tea are waiting on the table. First though, she returns to her room to retrieve the crystal. In front of her astounded friend she fills a small dish with salt into which she dips the rock. Following this, she carefully washes the crystal with clear water and places it in the sun so it can absorb the positive energy. Only then do both women take a comfortable seat on the sun-drenched terrace and enjoy their breakfast. Francesca recounts her early morning experience when the first ray shone in her eyes.

"You see, you are slowly recognizing the signs as well and are no longer closed to them. I'm certain that George was trying to send you a message that he's here with us," she replies, impressed.

Francesca retrieves the crystal and notes with surprise that the inclusions have turned blue. Marlène explains eagerly that they are now filled with energy and that the blue may represent George's eyes.

"Really? Wow!" Startled, Francesca notices an unusual tingling in the arm holding the crystal...

It's a beautiful, warm autumn day. Later, in the best of moods, they drive to the beach in Barbati located on the steep eastern coast of the island, Mount Pantocrator looming in the background, where their favourite *taverna*, Piedra, awaits them.

Last year they spent the whole week there. The crisp, artful décor and the polite and friendly staff had pleased them immediately. They had enjoyed it there right from the start. Each table under the large, white umbrellas was covered with a damask tablecloth and set with elegant porcelain, candles and small bouquets of flowers.

Soon the friends are sitting at the bar looking radiant. Soft jazz filters quietly from the loudspeakers, instantly making them feel like they're on holiday. Today, Marlène is wearing her hair in two long braids. She's gorgeous in her trendy light blue micro bikini trimmed with rhinestone appliqués. Matching fingernails, toenails and a large fashionable watch with a light blue wristband complete the look. To celebrate the day Francesca, wearing an inconspicuous black one-piece, orders an ice-cold Mojito. Her friend on the other hand, contents herself with a glass of fresh pineapple juice because she doesn't drink alcohol.

With a gentle sigh, Marlène casts her gaze across the calm sea until it reaches the fortress and Corfu's Old Town. Her brilliant blue eyes continue to scan the coastline of the mainland on the opposite shore until it disappears in a cloud of haze. "Ahhh, it's so beautiful here. I've been looking forward to this moment all year."

Francesca nods with a blissful smile, "Welcome *petite fée*. Here's to a wonderful week." They clink glasses in an unspoken promise. And then nothing can stop them. They quickly grab their beach bags and run down to the long pebbly beach. To their delight, they discover two empty loungers under one of the large white umbrellas directly by the sea, which they quickly occupy. Francesca races to the crystal-clear water. She dives in and swims out with a few brisk strokes before returning to Marlène, spluttering water. Her friend follows somewhat cautiously. "It's sooo wet and cold!"

"Oh, come on, the water's splendid. Just get in here. Now!"

A small shriek escapes Marlène as she finally wades into the water, then carefully and with deliberation swims parallel to the coastline alongside her island sister. *What a strange feeling,* she reflects, *everything in the water is in motion. I can no longer rely on anything. I've lost my self-confidence. Any moment now, one of the waves could devour me...*

Francesca knows that Marlène doesn't quite feel safe in the water and therefore matches her own rhythm to her friend's. Every now and then she floats on her back and with a touch of melancholy observes the small clouds serenely drifting through the sky, constantly merging into new formations. "You can't imagine just how much I miss him. All at once there's no more cuddling, no more touching and gentleness. There's no longer someone who can hold me and make me feel secure," she suddenly shares in a quiet voice.

"Doesn't the sea feel like a single delicate embrace today?" Marlène replies. "You must understand, George *is* the sea. It's a part of him that's holding you, carrying you so that you glide without effort. He's in the air; he *is* the air that you breathe. He's everywhere because now he's part of the Whole, part of you as well."

For a long time, there is silence, until Francesca huffily mumbles something unintelligible and swims away in a forceful crawl. Marlène understands that right now her friend needs a little time alone, so she swims the short distance back to the beach. She quickly changes into a dry, colourful bikini and stretches out on one of the comfortable loungers in the sun. While they have been swimming, a kind waiter has delivered an ice bucket with a bottle of water and two plastic glasses, which he placed on a small table between their loungers.

Meanwhile, Francesca keeps swimming with smooth, even strokes as she puts more distance between herself and the shore. She feels the water beneath her gently rising and falling, like a chest drawing in air... breathe in, breathe out... She continues to swim farther out into the open sea. She really wants to believe her *petite fée*. The concept is so sublime. She wonders if it's possible, if she can imagine her husband being part of these velvety, soft depths enveloping her body, caressing and carrying her through the gentle swell.

But then again...what wouldn't she give for *his* hands to be caressing her, *his* warm, soft lips that could send shivers coursing through her, *his* arms in which she would feel secure and *his* loving blue eyes in which she could lose herself. *I have to get used to the fact that George has become part of everything; I must learn to feel happiness and joy. If I can be connected to him in this different manner, I can still feel his presence even if it is in another form of existence.*

Out of breath, she turns to float on her back. A sigh rises from deep within her chest. *What happened to the promise to pull myself together and stop being so gloomy?* She fills her lungs with air and dives effortlessly into the blue depths of the sea to wash away her sad thoughts.

Half an hour later, Francesca stands shivering in front of Marlène after having swum away her emotions. "I'm going to change quickly. It's high time to do something about my growling stomach. You're probably hungry as well, right?"

"Well, finally!" Marlène's replies promptly. Quick as a wink, she wraps a pareo around her hips that matches her bikini then runs light-footed over to a charmingly set table. It doesn't take long before Francesca, who has also smartened up and looks lovely wearing a black swimsuit and an intricately wrapped red *pareo* with a colourful fish print, sits down and studies the menu expectantly. And there, once again Marlène detects a subtle change in her friend. Is she finally emerging from her depression?

A friendly young waiter arrives at their table to take their order. Instantly, he remembers the two, quite dissimilar, women and greets them beaming. After he leaves, they both grin at each other mischievously. "Oh my god, how awkward. It's our Adonis from last year," Francesca giggles bashfully.

"Do you remember...? The same thing happened every day. It was like we were caught in a time loop and couldn't get out. We had barely sat down and I would start to cry. I don't know why, but here in particular we would always have such deeply emotional and heartrending conversations that always ended in an emotional tsunami."

Marlène snorts and after calming down a little says, "How could I forget *that*. I'm sure everyone thought we were a couple of lesbians, and I was the evil witch who made you cry every day!"

They giggle and lark around as they imagine this, until the smiling Adonis arrives and serves them their meal. Now they really have to laugh, especially when he withdraws with a sulky expression.

Then, it's time for a short siesta. Not even the slightest breeze stirs. Soft music drifts from the loudspeakers. However, the lure of the turquoise, crystal-clear sea is far stronger than the desire to lounge around for a while longer under the shady umbrella. Dreamily, the two friends swim next to each other. Although Francesca is caught up in the infinite moment, she casts a worried glance over to her *petite fée*, especially when she notices that they continue to distance themselves from the shore. Marlène has never been a strong swimmer. The deep sea has always frightened her. It is for this reason she always swims along the shoreline. But today, it's somehow different.

George's voice is but a whisper in Marlène's ear: *Remember that we all originate from the same source. The sea is your friend. You are a part of it, and it is a part of you. Trust it...let it carry you...I will stay by your side and support you.* Then a miraculous thing happens. Her fear vanishes and after about 100 metres, they reach the final yellow buoy that marks the ingress and egress of the small rental boats. "Thank you, George," Marlène whispers stricken, as she gazes up at the azure sky. The blue reminds her of his kind eyes always watching over them.

Marlène hangs on to the buoy for a brief rest. A radiant smile spreads across her face. "Didn't you notice something?" she asks expectantly.

"Well, of course. Are you no longer afraid? What's come over you? Since when can you swim so well?" Francesca marvels.

In a serious tone, her friend explains that for a while George has been swimming alongside her giving her constant encouragement. Francesca looks at her incredulously.

"Really! Even now he's right here with us, and he's happy that we're both doing so well. How else would I have found the courage to swim so far from the shore with you?"

Francesca feels quite strange. *How bizarre is that! But how wonderful if it were really true. But why shouldn't it be? Ma petite fée has a gift and has already seen George several times. She knows that it no longer scares me when she shares these things with me. On the contrary, it makes me feel infinitely better to know that he's here, right now, with us.*

Abruptly, Francesca playfully splashes water in her friend's face interrupting this unusual moment. "Come on now, you still have to make it back."

But today nothing can disrupt Marlène's sense of peace. With even strokes she slowly swims back to the shore. At times, she rests and floats on her back, having learned how to do this somewhere along the line, then without hesitation she continues on steadily. Francesca is overjoyed for her friend and very proud of her. What an experience, what a success for her...

Francesca sets a lovely table outside on the balcony and lights some candles while her friend prepares a simple evening meal. It is a beautiful, mild evening. Silent and contemplative, they gaze at the sky ablaze with millions of stars until Marlène breaks the harmonious silence in a quiet voice, "Do you sometimes think back to the day when Aris, Eddy, Maël and I visited George in the hospital in

Crans-Montana? You were intent on me giving him a healing Reiki treatment, and you sent everyone else out on the balcony. Then you went and joined them so that I could be alone with George."

Of course, Francesca has not forgotten that afternoon. They had all arrived at the same time – her husband's cousin, as well as his godchild, Eddy and Marlène's son. She dips her head in silent acknowledgement gazing at her *petite fée* with melancholic eyes.

Moved, Marléne is silent for a while, as she is transported back to that poignant moment. "All I did was gently place my hands on his feet, and I knew instantly that there was nothing else that could help him. Marked by the illness, his face sunken, I saw it in his knowing eyes. At that same moment in a despondent, barely audible voice George whispered, *"this isn't going to change anything...I would so like to let go..."* It was then that I felt it. He was already drifting between two worlds, and he really was ready to let go. In a low voice, I carefully told him that he should go ahead, that everything was as it should be and he did not need to be afraid. With sad eyes, he followed you as you paced back and forth outside on the balcony. He wouldn't take his eyes off you, following your every movement, each and every step. It was then that I finally understood, finally realized. He couldn't leave because you weren't ready."

"Are you trying to say that he already wanted to let go back then? That he suffered all the pain far longer just because of me?"

Francesca feels her heart clenching in agony. Why had she stuck her head in the sand like an ostrich? Why had she pretended everything was going to turn out fine?

"No, no," Marlène replies quickly as she looks at her friend reassuringly, "It still wasn't his time. But when he looked me straight in the eye, *he* already knew that at some point he would contact me. I wasn't aware of it back then... but *he was...*"

Francesca lies on the bed un-showered and covered in salt and sun cream pondering the events of the day. *It's a wonderful feeling to know that Marlène can speak to me about George with such ease. She has a special, gentle way of explaining certain situations to me. In these moments, she takes away all my concerns, all my sad thoughts, my uncertainty about not having done things right. Belated remorse, things that I could have done, should have done better...for instance with George in his final days, I should have talked about our unspoken fears, his and mine...not tried to act as if everything was going to turn out well, even though I believed it right until the end...*

She shared something exceptionally beautiful with me this evening: "I saw all of your love, all of your devotion in your eyes when you would look at George, and he saw it and felt it. You caught each other's gaze and were able to silently communicate this knowledge to each other." *How unbelievably good that feels and sounds. I have finally got to get rid of my guilty feelings.*

Fortunately for Francesca, she is enveloped by a cloak of fatigue and falls into a deep and dreamless sleep.

3

$\mathcal{I}$t is still early in the morning. Yawning, Francesca pushes open her balcony door and observes her surroundings as she executes a long stretch. *My place is beautiful,* she muses with a joyous and thankful heart. Several years ago, George and I chose this exact spot for our home.

Goosebumps break out on her naked arms. One can feel the slow onset of autumn. A faint, almost transparent mist filters through the slender cypress and olive trees down to the sea. She can hear the pattering feet of dormice running back and forth on the roof above her. If only she could figure out how to get rid of those annoying pests.

During breakfast the sun manages to break through the fog. And once again an almost cloudless blue expanse stretches above the two friends. Francesca asks Marlène to wear something sporty and put on sturdy shoes because she would like to show her the island from an entirely different angle. The forecast calls for ideal weather conditions today – sunny but not too warm. – Francesca puts on Bermuda shorts and a t-shirt and swaps her summer sandals for a pair of sturdy hiking boots.

In the nearby village of Gouvia, Francesca's close Greek friend Despina, dressed casually in a white blouse and navy blue cotton trousers, is waiting anxiously for the two women to arrive. Francesca had called her yesterday to make plans for the day. Despina is well-acquainted with their destination and is looking forward to joining them on the outing. After an enthusiastic greeting, the trio drive off to the northeast in cheerful expectation.

The drive first takes them along the picturesque coastal roadway with a beautiful view of the sea and opposite mainland. A steep and very tight winding road takes them farther up, all the way to the peak of Pantokrator (906m), the island's highest mountain. They continue driving through narrow, scenic mountain villages, always with a view of the sea and the mainland. Not only is Marlène fascinated by the drive but the others also get swept away in delight at the beautiful scenery even though they have already seen it quite often.

In a craggy area reminiscent of a moonscape, Francesca abruptly hits the brakes after rounding the corner of a hair pin bend. Goats are challenging their right of way. They patiently wait until the last one has crossed the road picking its way slowly through the bizarre rock formations on a never-ending search for something edible. Finally, after the last steep leg they finally make it to the peak of Pantokrator – the rooftop of Corfu.

As if electrified, the three women run from one spot to another. The view from there is simply magnificent. The panorama of the Greek mainland and Albania as well as the vista extending across large portions of the island, in particular Corfu city and its airport, is breathtaking. From this vantage point one can even see both the east and west coasts simultaneously.

Deeply impressed, Marlène stands between Despina and Francesca. She cheerfully points her finger towards the city where three enormous cruise ships lie anchored in the harbour. Solitary sailboats float on the azure sea. Small motorboats glide through the water leaving a white V-shaped trail in their wake. One is tempted to almost block out the unsightly communications station. But then they are all shocked when they walk to the small priory and find that a giant radio tower has been erected directly over it. However, the stunningly beautiful interior is more than adequate compensation.

"Come on now, we still have a lot planned," Francesca calls out happily, hurrying them along. Marlène draws in another deep breath while taking in a final panoramic gaze in order to absorb all of this beauty.

A short while later, Francesca parks the car somewhere below the mountain peak.

"What's wrong? What are we doing here in this wasteland in the middle of nowhere?" Marlène asks completely aghast.

"Come on, come on, get out, this is where my surprise starts!" Francesca points silently to a sign that indicates the start of a trail that leads to *Old Perithia*. Marlène is an avid hiker and has gone on many mountain hikes. This is why Francesca knows she will be able to delight her friend with this outing. But that's not all. Lovingly she puts an arm around her shoulder, while at the same time looking over to Despina.

"Marlène found out in a phone call this morning that her newlywed niece who had been diagnosed with breast cancer, is going through her last round of chemo today. Since she started therapy, Marlène has organised daily hikes, varying in length, with friends and acquaintances. She asked each participant to send brilliant energy to her niece, so that she could draw the necessary strength from it to heal. So, I thought that today in honour of Romaine, we can walk to Old Perithia and together, with each step we take, we can send a combined force of energy her way, full of love, trust and courage."

"What a fantastic idea!" Marlène looks at her friend with moist eyes and hugs her affectionately. Despina too, embraces Marlène full of empathy. As a precaution, she had brought along water bottles for the three of them.

The rocky path winds in a gentle serpentine trail down the mountain. The view across the hilly landscape permeated with rocks is beautiful. Green patches of sparse, thorny vegetation hug the ground. Far below, nestled in between the hills is Old Perithia, of which almost nothing remains but ruins. The blue sea sparkles in the distance. A large white ferry slowly makes its way towards Italy. Small sailboats look as if they have been painted onto the deep blue sea. The late morning light casts everything in shades of ochre and brown.

The three women repeatedly stop and enjoy the magnificent view. Periodically, one of them bends down to pick up one of the many brightly coloured or interestingly formed stones, or detect a solitary flower growing from a rock, or they inquisitively study a lizard warming up in the sun.

After rounding a curve, they come to an abrupt stop and stare in breathless wonder at a giant eagle sitting only 40 metres away from them. It flaps its enormous wings wildly, while eyeing the intruders in equal astonishment. For a few seconds, it hovers close to the ground before it rises up with strong beats of its wings. The eagle circles their heads three more times before it majestically climbs higher in ever widening circles until it completely disappears from view.

"My God, did you see that? The powerful head with its giant glowing eyes and that terrifying curved beak?"

"Of course, you could see everything in detail. The most horrific thing for me was its powerful grasping claws and feathered legs."

"It must have dived down silently from above to grab its prey."

"Yeah, I'm sure it was mad that its lunch got away on account of us."

"Wow, what a unique experience, I have never seen such a large bird up close in nature before. That was just crazy. Brilliant!"

"The eagle, king of the heavens."

This bubbling excitement continues among them and it takes a while for the happy and enthusiastic temperaments to slowly settle down.

Marlène, however, has a more shamanistic interpretation of this raptor encounter, "He has a panoramic view," she explains to Francesca and Despina who are listening with rapt attention. "He can detect even the smallest detail from every perspective. When he is flying above us at this very moment we should open our eyes to everything that surrounds us. For Nature provides us with answers to most of our existential questions."

"Look, look, you've got to see this," Despina interrupts and points to the sky. All three shield their eyes from the glare with their hands and to their delight notice that there are now two eagles circling elegantly above them. Before they get stiff necks, the giant birds climb higher and finally fly away towards the Albanian mountains.

For the next hour, there is no lack of conversational topics amongst the trio, and while they chatter excitedly about their unique experience, they arrive at the abandoned village of *Old Perithia*. It is there, on the covered terrace of a cosy, newly renovated *taverna* that Spiro, Despina's husband, is anxiously awaiting them along with her niece Eleni and her *fiancée*, Paul.

"Where have you been? We're starving!" Ignoring the rather tepid greeting, each of the women wants to be the first to share their remarkable interlude and the unique gift they received from Nature. Of course, they were all impressed. But for some of them there are more important things at hand. To start with, food and drinks need to be ordered.

Everyone is talking all at once wanting to explain to Marlène the history of *Old Perithia* until Spiros, who is the oldest among them, raises his voice energetically.

"Would you all just be quiet and let me explain. So...*Old Perithia* is the oldest village on Corfu. Because the northern coast was continually under siege by pirates, the inhabitants built their village high up in a rocky canyon, so that at night no one would be able to detect the lights at sea. Quite clever...don't you think? For several years now, this village has been infused with new life. People who are looking for solitude have bought up partial ruins and restored them back to their original condition. *Old Perithia* is now a UNESCO World Heritage site. The few taverns here offer traditional dishes." With a pleased grin, he looks at the circle of friends, each of them listening to him with rapt attention.

"Didn't you forget to mention something important?" Despina challenges her husband.

"Yes, yes, I know, you are correct. The most unusual and special thing about Perithia is its almost 40 churches. There is no other village that has so many churches as this one here."

After their meal, they all ramble over well-worn trails taking a tour through the picturesque landscape characterised by its ruins of long ago. They encounter a friendly beekeeper, who invites them to sample his honey. When they leave, they each take home a jar of the incredibly tasty honey with its faint rosemary flavour.

Despina decides to drive home with Spiros and the others. "Traitor!" her hiking buddies call after her, laughing as they madly wave goodbye.

It is still pleasantly warm and the sun is shining down from a cloudless sky. Marlène and Francesca are still eager and looking forward to the two-hour hike back. They just shouldn't forget that at this time of year dusk falls very early. In unison, they stride in step with each other back along the gravelly trail towards Pantokrator. Francesca is very excited when alongside the path she finds a flat, very distinct rock in the shape of a cat's head.

"Look what I've found. This is unbelievable, it's as if someone chiselled the rock into this shape. It's so pretty...I'm taking it with me!"

"You're crazy, that rock's far too heavy. You can't possibly lug it back with you the whole way."

This time, Marlène's well-meaning words fall upon deaf ears. No matter what, Francesca wants to bring along this rock to commemorate her cat, Squeaky, who died the same year as her husband. She already has the perfect spot in mind, in a corner of her patio placed in between two planters with white gardenias.

With even paces they continue up the path covered in rock and scree until halfway up, Francesca suddenly spots a large colony of ants crossing the trail. The two friends take a seat on a flat rock and watch with great interest the busy and industrious insects moving to and fro. They observe how the ants instinctively head to their destination, at times hauling heavy loads over rocks and other obstacles, always headed in the same direction.

Full of admiration, Francesca says softly, "These tiny beings are real powerhouses. If you think about it, they haul fifty times their weight around with them their whole life. That's just amazing!

We look down on them and see nothing but little insects weighing about ten milligrams that slave away diligently and tirelessly their entire lives. However, these tiny ants probably can't discern us from where they are. Everything that we behold in our world they can't perceive because they're simply too small.

What if the same were true between God and us? What if he were somewhere out there in the infinite universe, then he too would have to see far, far more than we could ever imagine. Consequently, we have our limits too, just like these ants. What if there really was something out there that observes us just as we do these ants? And what if the dead were also able to observe us from their invisible realm?"

In silent fascination, both of them continue to study the ants until Francesca remarks with a small laugh, "Up until now I have always imagined it to be similar to a needlepoint tapestry that Aris – you remember him, George's cousin – once told me about as we sat in the garden philosophising. According to him, we are nothing but colourful threads. Threads, which are part of an immense, mysterious and magnificent tapestry. It takes all of us to compose a sublimely beautiful and supernaturally perfect picture. But all that *we* can perceive are the threads directly surrounding us. Some are intertwined, others have already been cut off at the very top and yet others hang down in differing lengths and colours. None of us can observe the picture from afar, not from the dimension in which we live, not from where we are standing.

These ants that we see here make it very clear to me how insignificant we are within the universe. We actually have the same problem they have. Our ability to perceive things is just as limited, and we can only guess what that picture might look like and hope that whatever happens to us in this world, the good as well as the bad, does ultimately lead to something indescribably beautiful."

A cold wind suddenly sweeps over the hills. As if wakened from a dream they both look around in surprise. They haven't noticed how the light has slowly changed. Quickly, Francesca collects her rock and with no further stops they both continue striding briskly. As they round each curve, they hope it is the last. Finally, they make it. Merky, abandoned and alone, is waiting for them in the same spot. Before they get into the car, Marlène hugs her friend. "Thank you, that was really great. Up until now, all I've ever seen of Corfu was the beach. I didn't know one could do such amazing hikes."

Although dusk has already set in, once they reach the coast Marlène spontaneously turns to her friend, "Couldn't we just for a moment, as a perfect ending to a perfect day, spend some time at this beautiful beach? I'd like to get in the water, so that I can say I went swimming every day in the sea."

With a laugh, Francesca stops the car. "Of course, go ahead. In the meantime, I'll go look for some fresh bread. It's too cold for me, and I think that after sixteen kilometres and four hours of walking I've had enough exercise for today." Among other things, she is exhausted and can feel her tired legs. *One can really tell the nine-year difference between us*, she sighs.

When she finally returns to the beach, a loaf of bread clutched under her arm, she finds Marlène still leisurely swimming in the fading daylight. The first faint stars having already appeared in the sky. *What a loon!* Francesca thinks. "You'd better get out now, or else you'll catch a cold!" she yells, waving her arms vigorously.

In the meantime, it has become painfully cold outside. Francesca and Marlène have pulled on heavy fleece jackets and are now sitting out on the terrace in the old but comfortable bamboo armchairs. Bathed in the warm light cast by a host of candles and lanterns, two cups of steaming hot tea are sitting on a small table between them. From somewhere close by comes the rhythmic call of a small owl. Countless lights shine from the small villages lining the eastern coast.

In the middle of this sublime peace and quiet Francesca suddenly asks, "Did you bring along your fortune telling cards?"

Marlène looks at her in sudden surprise and says astounded, "I didn't bring them. In all these years, you've never asked about them. And now all of a sudden..." Francesca gives a light shake of her head and reminds her friend of the one time at Easter when she had phoned her from the hospital in Geneva and asked her to consult her cards.

"Yes, you're right." Marlène gives a slight smile as she remembers this grave phone conversation.

"You had actually rung me and asked me to read George's cards. But I didn't want to because I had never read cards before from a distance. I didn't know if it would work without having the individual in front of me. It was only because of this that I didn't want to. But you insisted that I try because you wanted to know if you should fly to the States and if George's chance of finding a cure would be better there."

"Hmm...yes." Francesca replies softly.

"In order to be alone, I left Lisa and went into the other room," Marlène recounts. First though, she had to wade through the chaos that always reigned in her daughter's bedroom until she finally found a suitable spot on the bed for what she had planned.

"I am utterly certain that the first card I drew for George was *Death and Resurrection*. I didn't want to tell you but I felt I didn't have a choice as you were still waiting on the phone. It was imperative for you to get an answer. Your exact words were, 'I have to know!' To that I could only tell you to accompany him. 'All you can do is simply be by his side, always.' Do you remember?"

Moved, Francesca nods her head as she fights the tears. Only too well does she remember that moment out in the corridor where, behind a door, George was patiently waiting for her in his white, freshly made hospital bed.

"And while we're at it, do you also remember that afternoon in Crans-Montana? We had just returned from the clinic where we had spent the past two months. I went out to seek you whilst George lay sleeping. Also, I had been certain that ultimately everything would turn out well, I just wanted the cards to confirm it."

It breaks Marlène's heart to see how, even after three years, her friend is still suffering. "Do you still remember the cards that you drew back then?"

"Of course," Francesca replies in a tremulous voice. "It was a profound, incredibly important moment for me. Obviously, I have not forgotten those three cards. The first one showed the Devil, the next was a tree and the final one was of a seated woman."

"Okay, let me surround myself with the energy from back then," Marlène answers in concentration.

"The first card that you drew was *The Devil*, you say. A handsome man with red and yellow eyes, who is encased in a bell-like structure filled with smoke." In simple words Marlène tries to explain, "The red and yellow eyes symbolize George's illness, he is trapped in the bell jar with no hope to ever escape. He was afflicted quite suddenly by this illness. George wanted to live, but that was simply no longer possible."

Francesca swallows her welling tears and interrupts Marlène. "That's exactly how it was on that indelible day which changed our lives in such a brutal way. That day when George came home with yellow eyes, he was already marked by his illness. So often have I puzzled and pondered over this. Today, more than ever, I'm convinced that the Devil himself had somehow slunk into George's body. For how else could it be possible for a man in perfect health to be stricken without warning by such a diabolical illness from one day to the next." Francesca states angrily, but with great sorrow. "It just doesn't make sense, it's so unfair," she sighs in a trembling voice as she recalls the difficult, fateful time.

"The second card, a tree..." Marlène tries to distract Francesca as she continues her explanation, "It is complete. It's surround by a lot of energy, but it has no roots. The connection between it and the earth is disrupted. Though it's still a tree, it can no longer live in this world." Francesca can only nod in understanding.

"The third card represents Wisdom. It is a woman sitting in front of a closed door waiting. She carries two objects with her. One is a staff...hello! The Way of St James...does that ring a bell?" Marlène gives Francesca a sharp look. "The staff...for me that's unequivocally clear."

Francesca finally shows some animation as the meaning dawns on her. "Oh, oh my God, that's incredible...it's true. Back then no one knew that a year after George's death I would go on a pilgrimage travelling the Way of St James through Spain, all the way to Santiago de Compostela."

Unperturbed, Marlène continues, "and a lantern in order to see. It can mean a lot of things. Maybe all the things we have since experienced together. But that's not what is significant. What's important is that she is sitting there in all of her wisdom. That is exactly what you did. After George's death, you didn't try to move mountains, you just sat there. You didn't see a future for yourself. You stayed seated in front of that closed door, and you waited.

What *is* significant is the staff in one hand that urged you on, and the light in the other that slowly began to glow once more in your heart. You already had that light in you through George. Because the door remained closed, you had to learn for yourself how to light that fire without him. Until one day you noticed that the door was open; that it represented the link between the here and the hereafter, which is *always* open."

Francesca lets out a deep sigh, "I can still remember my shock when I chose the cards. Even without your explanation, I already knew that they were bad news.

Although I still had hope. They were just cards. We will beat this..."

"You asked me if George would get well again. In retrospect, if you look back, it should be obvious. The illness was there; he no longer had roots. He was dying, but he was still within the energy because even without roots, the tree was green.

And you, from a certain point forward ceased to be. You weighed 103lbs and had almost disappeared. But then something urged you forward; the staff, the Way of St James, the light...it had all been predestined."

Tears escape Francesca's eyes. She can't help it. She is overwhelmed by emotions. Everything is back, the loneliness, the sense of helplessness, the despair and the anger. "Why is it only those last days and weeks of our otherwise happy life that I constantly see with absolute clarity? Every minute has been carved into my heart for eternity. Why can't I just let go and remember only the happiest of moments?"

Marlène embraces her friend firmly. "Come on, let's go inside and have another cup of tea before we go to sleep. I'm sure it will make you feel better and it will warm us both up."

Marléne shudders...a chill runs through her. "Trust me. One day it will get better and you'll find peace. You will *never* forget George. But there will come a time when you too will get your life back under control. The scars that the pain has carved into your heart will always be a part of you. You will carry them like a precious treasure." Arm in arm they stroll back into the house slowly.

4

a fresh autumn breeze blows in through the balcony filling the bedroom with the scent of lavender and wild thyme. With a deep sigh, Francesca rises and shuffles barefoot out onto the balcony wearing one of George's old flannel shirts. Bereft of tears she watches the large red disc of the sun rise from behind the cypress trees into a cloudless sky. She doesn't feel the cold stone floor on which her bare soles rest. She only feels a solitary tear slowly rolling down her cheek.

She didn't sleep well. For the most part, she had lain in bed awake, analysing dismal thoughts. *Why did Fate tear us apart, separating us in such a brutal manner? I know that questions about how and why something happened are useless, but they simply can't be suppressed – Will you finally stop hurting yourself? – Actually, I feel as if the pain has become something of an ally because it makes me feel like I'm still alive...of course, it feels good to know that Marlène understands my fears, my despair and my anger and that I can constantly pour out my pain to her anew. It's so easy with her. She listens to me and each time explains to me lovingly and patiently that everything and all of us, are an integral part of the universe. That George too, is always there with me...but it's simply not the same...*

Marlène lies in bed pondering just what it is that ties her to Francesca for a lifetime. For years now, she has attended seminars on mediumship. She had spoken with George about this and he had shown great interest, encouraging her to search for new ways to communicate. She had decided though, that it was better to let the dead remain in their world without trying to find a way to contact them. This time though, it had been *him* contacting *her*, so that she could play messenger between him and his wife.

Not far from the villa, on a hill with a beautiful panoramic view of Corfu and the sea lies the quiet cemetery of *Agios Nikolaos*. After having breakfast in their usual spot on the sun-drenched terrace, Francesca places candles bundled in wrapping tissue, matches, liquid soap and a brush into a small backpack.

The friends walk beneath giant, ancient olive trees watching in fascination the play of sunlight on the large treetops until they reach the charming chapel sitting on a hill. The wrought iron gate and the stairs are entwined with blue morning glory. It is a truly beautiful sight that emanates peace and quiet.

Silent and reflective the two women hold hands as they stand before George's white marble grave. A simple chiselled cross with a dove adorns his final resting place. Then, Marlène gets to work and scrubs the gravestone slab while Francesca watches her, lost in thought. *How different it is, this third autumn. The way up here was somehow easier. My heart feels somewhat lighter. Could it be that time does help? Or is it simply the presence of ma petite fée that helps alleviate some of the sorrow? I wonder what she is thinking right now? What's going through her mind?*

Francesca hunches down pulling and cutting away the many weeds that have inundated the path, stuffing everything into a large, black rubbish bag. A short while later, the gravesite and its surroundings are once again looking clean and tidy. Marlène gives her friend a deep hug and full of emotion whispers, "The whole time I felt as if I were putting George's bed in order."

For a while, all one can hear is their sobs. Once the friends have collected themselves, they slowly leave arm in arm casting a final glance at the grave and the lovely little chapel in the cemetery. At the very moment that they walk through the gate Marlène discovers a feather lying at her feet, which she picks up with great care. "Oh...look here...one of the sides even has a blue shimmer."

The way she sees it, finding the feather is a sign that indicates the presence of an angel or a spirit leader who is by their side protecting and lighting the way for them on their life's journey. The feather is a present from a great spirit that represents the origin of the universe and all that it encompasses.

Shortly thereafter they discover yet another feather, again with a bluish shimmer. "In shamanism, this is a very good sign. I'm certain it's a present from George," she explains to her friend, deeply moved.

Francesca is happy and delighted. With Marlène she experiences something very special and magical each day. She just has to learn to discover these symbols for herself, when George places them in her way.

Meanwhile it is afternoon. Back at home they both quickly pack their beach gear and once again drive to the beach at Barbati, stopping first to dine on something delicious at Piedra. Today's menu features, among other things, homemade lobster ravioli, which Francesca pairs with an excellent ice-cold chardonnay.

In order to digest, they both stretch out on a large cabana bed underneath a giant umbrella that the *taverna* reserves for its guests. There are only a few people at the beach that day. Despite the pop music filtering out of the loudspeakers, one can still hear the waves' eternal melody. The sun is shining; it is deliciously warm.

Francesca is dozing when Marlène begins pouring out her heart in a quiet monotone voice. Not only does she talk about her vulnerability in her daily life, but also expresses her wish that all of the numerous difficulties suffered by her family, children and others would be solved. She talks about the expectations they have of her, and of her desire to be acknowledged for the help and care that she has given to her family. Somewhat surprised, Francesca opens her eyes and turns to her friend. Never before has she heard her always strong, *petite fée* speak like this. With concern, she looks into Marlène's sad eyes. How often does she make it unnecessarily difficult for herself? She's always putting others first and forgets herself along the way.

Francesca replies with a sigh and props her head in her hand, "Even you can't jump over your own shadow. It's not as simple as taking the theories you read in books, those that make sense at the moment, and then applying them to your own life. It's only when fate knocks you down that you realize reality looks a whole lot different. You become aware that feelings can't be controlled and that they don't always respond to even the best of reason. Unfortunately, I know what I am talking about, that it takes an enormous amount of energy to resist a problem instead of simply accepting it," and then she changes the topic. "Come on, let's cool down this heated conversation with a swim."

Francesca grasps Marlène's hands encouragingly and pulls her up from the bed. Together they slowly submerge themselves in the sea. After the initial cold shock, they shake off their melancholic mood and glide into the crystal-clear water and casually swim out to sea.

Tirelessly, Francesca dives below the surface into the still depths of the sea. *How wonderful it is to glide through the water at the same time observing some fish. I have to dive even deeper, so that it takes even longer for me to float back up to the surface motionless, with my eyes closed. Hmm...it's such a pleasant feeling to dangle suspended, float, fly...the cool water feels like a caress on my face.* She continues to enjoy this exquisite sensation of weightlessness. She can't get enough of it. This is exactly how an astronaut must feel as he drifts through space.

Marlène floats on her back allowing the surface of the water, which has been warmed by the sun, to envelop her in a gentle caress. *Is life a book,* she ponders, *where the story is being written from one moment to the next? Or is it a predetermined film that plays out before our eyes and we are the audience? Everything is in motion in our world. Only the present moment is important. What I do with it...to no longer agonize over an illusory future, not even that of my loved ones. To simply trust unconditionally...to open my eyes and heart to receive each day whatever gift life has to offer...*

Francesca is suddenly seized by naughtiness. She strips off her swimsuit and somehow fastens it around her head. She starts spinning in a circle faster and faster at first it is halting, but then, from deep within her it's released like an explosion. At the top of her voice one can hear across the water: 'I 'ave 'n onion on my head!' Over and over she chants this nonsensical refrain until, overcome with laughter, she swallows too much water and the ditty ends in fits of coughing. Sputtering, she gasps for air.

Finally, I get to see the former Francesca again. The one who could tell the silliest jokes. Who insisted that my children swap clothes for an impromptu photo-shoot in the garden – my son wearing his sister's flowered mini shorts and very tight t-shirt, while she wore a large shirt and military style Bermuda shorts. One New Year's Eve, she practiced ballroom dancing with them, another time she scoffed down a seven-layered crepe, as we looked on in astonishment.

When George fell ill unexpectedly that small spark of craziness, integral to her, was snuffed out. From that moment forward, she put on a smile and feigned happiness, but that smile didn't reach her eyes. And now, right here in the middle of the sea, wearing a swimsuit on her head, her face is once again beaming and her eyes are sparkling with mischief.

After Marlène has recovered from her surprise, she laughs and follows her friend's example, and, after some paddling around – and swallowing a great deal of water – she too winds up with her bikini in her hand. "And now...what do I do with it?"

"Put the bottoms on your head like a cap, and wrap the top around your neck!" They both have to pay attention amidst all the laughing and excitement, so they don't swallow too much water in the process. Marlène can hardly believe it. The sensation of swimming naked and feeling the water surrounding her body is indescribable. In high spirits, they splash around and let themselves slowly drift towards the beach. Right before they reach the shore, they each don their swimsuit in a civilized manner, which turns out to be quite a difficult undertaking, especially for Marlène. She is having some difficulty keeping her legs underwater. As soon as she has slipped one foot into her bikini bottoms, she loses her balance and falls onto her side. Francesca roars with laughter. Marlène looks like a beetle on its back, clumsily pedalling its legs unable to right itself. Finally, they both have had enough and climb out of the water shivering. Amidst laughter and grumbling, they crawl like two beached whales across the rocky beach to their flip-flops, which they have left by the shore as a precaution.

"We don't exactly look like two sexy mermaids rising from the depths," Marlène sputters.

Francesca runs straight to the cabana bed onto which she collapses with a satisfied sigh, while her *petite fée* fetches some refreshing cocktails for both of them. This is pure luxury. Both recline on the bed, relaxed. They scan the blue sea and the coastline, Marlène holding a glass of iced tea and her friend a delicious margarita. What a pleasure and such grace, to be able to enjoy this mild, late September afternoon with your best friend…

On the ride home Francesca stops at a small market to buy a wonderfully fresh fish and various vegetables that she wants to prepare on the grill that evening. Unfortunately, it's too cold that night to eat outside, so they sit indoors by the cosy fireplace that radiates a soothing heat and listen to the soft sounds of Leonard Cohen – one of George's favourite singers – as they enjoy the fish.

Suddenly, Marlène stops and stares at Francesca in open-mouthed disbelief as she notices her friend has taken one of the fish eyes and stuck it in the middle of her forehead and is now looking at her with an earnest expression. "You told me so much about the chakras that I wanted to show you my brow chakra, my third eye."

They can't hold it back any longer and both explode in unbridled, never-ending laughter. They laugh so hard that the fish eye on Francesca's forehead starts to jiggle. Marlène gasps for air convulsively.

"You are so crazy, off-the-wall demented!" Francesca holds her stomach as she wipes away her tears.

"Sorry, I apologize, I just couldn't help it."

Afterwards, bundled in blankets, they sit outside for quite some time in the middle of the lawn clutching a cup of tea while they observe the stars. Who knows, perhaps one will fall from the sky...

In a quiet voice, Marlène interrupts this unrivalled mood to recount an intense moment she had experienced a few years before.

"A friend of my daughter, who was six at the time, lost her father unexpectedly due to a traffic accident. Two days later, after school, Lisa and her brother invited this girl to come play with them in the garden. In the late afternoon, the child came to me and said, *"I would really like to eat outside tonight with your family under the stars."*

With Eddy's help, we prepared a barbeque on the balcony. When all of us were seated at the table it was nightfall. It was one of those beautiful, clear nights that you often have in the mountains. The little child sat on her chair and observed the night sky. It almost looked as if she were looking for something. We ate our dinner in silence all of us were deeply moved by this brave girl who was trying to overcome her pain. Suddenly, a smile brightened her little face. She pointed her finger at Venus and with complete conviction declared, 'Just take a look at this large, shining star.' We all turned our gaze to the night sky as the little one continued to explain, 'it's the most beautiful star in the sky. Right next to it is a very small one that doesn't shine quite as bright yet because it has just arrived...my daddy is sitting there.'

Since that evening, every time when I look at the sky, I search for Venus and greet the small star to the left of it because it embodies the power of faith and the love between the father and his daughter." Marlène whispers, her eyes shining with emotion.

5

$\mathcal{I}$t is early the next morning, and already the villa is buzzing like a beehive. Francesca has planned a major operation for the day. The gardener, already stressed out, is running around in the garden trying to divide up the day's tasks among the workers. Amongst other things, soil has to be filled in and grass seeds planted in front of the newly constructed wall of natural stone, which acts as a border around the entire lawn. At that moment, a lorry arrives with river stones that will be used to embellish the entrance to the villa.

Unperturbed, Francesca's irreplaceable and extremely diligent home help, Ermioni, busies herself with the cleaning. Marlène insists on contributing towards her fair share of the chores, and waters the various potted plants around the villa before breakfast.

Scattered white clouds drift by in the sky. The day, once again, promises to be lovely and warm. The two friends are not bothered by the industrious labour surrounding them, and with pleasure polish off their breakfast at their favourite spot on the terrace. Marlène is already spreading her third piece of toast with butter and bitter orange jam that Francesca makes from her own oranges when she suddenly asks, "Hey, tell me again what it was like on the Way of St. James because Nicole would like to hike with me for a section of the way. But to be honest, I'm not too enthusiastic. You know how I am…also, I can't carry a backpack or anything heavy due to my back problems. My sweet sister can't carry my load as well."

Francesca has to smile, "That is a blatant understatement. The only thing you carry along on a hike is a bottle of water and your good mood."

"Go ahead, make fun of me. But you walked almost 1000 kilometres through all of Spain with a heavy backpack weighing 8 kilos. Did the pilgrimage help you in taking those first steps out of your despair?"

Marlène looks at her friend in rapt expectation. With a smile, Francesca gives a slight shake of the head as she holds her hand up in mock defence.

"Don't exaggerate. I only walked slightly more than 800 kilometres. Because my feet had been reduced to compost, I had to spend part of the pilgrimage in a convent in *Santo Domingo de Silos*, which is located several kilometres from the Way of St. James. I stayed for five days until I was able to walk again. Then I took the bus in order to catch up with my sister and continue on the pilgrimage to *Santiago* and *Finisterre*."

"Alright, I know. But still, I could never have imagined you doing something like that, as sick and weak as you were. For weeks, you were walking constantly every day with that heavy pack on your back. That is an enormous, physical accomplishment. I really admire you."

Francesca is quiet for a moment trying to find the right words. "It's true. Every day I surpassed myself and became increasingly stronger. If with your question you wanted to know whether I had found answers to the *"why"* and *"for what reason"*, that would be a clear NO.

When I think about it, I truly believe that I had started to take the first steps towards *living* again. Thanks to my sister. If she hadn't shaken me out of my stupor a year after George's death, strapped a backpack on my back and squeezed me into a pair of hiking boots, I would have definitely fallen into a deep, black hole.

I also have to confess that before this, I had never heard of the Way of St. James and therefore had no idea of the hardships awaiting me. Straight away during the first few days, my feet swelled up and each of my toes were rewarded with a big, fat blister. Even though each step caused me excruciating pain,

I never complained to Doris because I soon noticed that the pain in my chest had lessened and somehow transferred itself to my feet. My heart became lighter, and slowly over time, as we walked for days through the beautiful landscape, it opened. Deep inside me something tender began to resonate. I am eternally grateful to my sister for helping me with the attempt to take the first steps back into life."

In the meantime, Marlène has prepared fresh toast for Francesca and poured her a little more coffee. After trying it and taking a sip, she continues with her story.

"Once my feet had healed, I honestly looked forward to continuing with my pilgrimage; opening myself to whatever each day had in store for me, learning to let go and discovering new things in the nature surrounding me. But the most important thing I learned in those not so easy weeks was that all the baggage we carry around with us our whole lives, this enormous burden that overwhelms us, such as responsibility, family, home, job, money etc., all that falls away, ceases to exist. You feel light and free, somehow cut off from the real world. You ramble with only a backpack containing your entire belongings, following the yellow arrows that at some point lead you to your destination. The estate problems here in Corfu, the sale of our boutique in Montana, all the new things that suddenly flooded into my life; instantly, all

71

of that became irrelevant. All of my troubles fell away. All I had to do was place one foot in front of the other."

Marlène interrupts Francesca's enthusiasm, and laughingly reminds her, "But I'm sure you didn't abstain from using your credit card, did you?"

Now Francesca has to laugh as well. "No, of course you're right. Just because you're on a pilgrimage doesn't mean you have to forgo all amenities." She smiles to herself, as she pictures the scene in the Jacuzzi in the newly renovated wing of an old hotel built of natural stone in *Santo Domingo de Silos,* close to the Benedictine monastery where she had rehabilitated her feet. She remembers how she almost suffocated in the bubbles because she had used two small bottles of bubble bath.

As they arrive at their usual spot close to noon, Marlène is pleased. "Take a look, right now we have the beach all to ourselves. And indeed, all the sun loungers reserved for *Piedra's* guests are still unoccupied. Only a few locals and tourists are splashing in the water or sunning themselves farther down on the beach. It's apparent that this spot exudes a certain exclusivity, and for that reason not all guests would feel comfortable here."

The two women stand motionless on the shore listening to the soft splash of the waves that swirl around their feet and leave behind trails of delicate, white foam on the beach. The stillness surrounding them is only pierced by the sharp screech of a lone seagull that dips in a low circular glide above their heads before executing a sudden plunge into the depths of the sea. A symphony of colour and delicate aromas float in the air. It is unbelievably beautiful. "Do you think others can see this as well?" Francesca whispers.

"Those who see with their hearts should be able to see as we do. Nature reveals itself to us each day in all its glory. But we are so often preoccupied with our daily stress that we don't take the time to admire it." Marlène replies just as softly.

Still caught up in the spell of this magical moment, Francesca sits down on the rocks and surrenders one foot to the glittering, azure-blue sea that swirls around it almost tenderly. *Will the small waves carry my thoughts to George beyond the far horizon?* she ponders. *Today the sea is like a promise, a sweet melody. I feel as if a very small piece of my pain is being carried out to sea with each wave.*

Francesca hasn't noticed that her friend has already changed into a swim suit until a stream of water hits her, yanking her from her daydreams. "Come on, hurry up!" Marlène calls out rowdily. "The sea's wonderful."

Before she gets as far as waist-deep, she runs back out shrieking, "Help! I've been bitten by a piranha, see how I'm bleeding!" and she points at a tiny bite wound just below her knee.

With great effort, Francesca controls her laughter and explains calmly that those were only small, but ravenous, fish that hang out by the shore just so they can nibble on the pretty legs of unsuspecting tourists, but they were otherwise perfectly harmless. In order to calm her hesitant *petite fée*, she takes her by the hand and together they wade back into the water. A school of the small fish launch an immediate attack. Amidst small cries of protest, the two friends quickly swim away from the shore.

Today as well, Marlène swims a long distance out. Her heart doesn't race and she no longer feels scared. She is so happy. It is a whole new sensation to swim and place trust in the sea, as if it were a friend. But even the most beautiful moment loses its attraction when a person is famished.

Quick as a wink they both change into dry swimsuits and wrapped in their colourful *pareos*, they swiftly make their way to one of the still vacant, charmingly set tables. They are surprised to see that almost all of the tables are occupied by tanned, happy guests enjoying glasses of chilled wine, as they wait for their meal to be served. One or the other of the guests has their face buried in a menu, studying it intently. A young Greek mother, who is also coming straight from the beach, tries to calm down her two loud and rambunctious, most likely hungry, children. Business is lively today in the *taverna*, and Adonis is sweating as he busily runs back and forth in between the tables. After an excellent meal, they decide to treat themselves to a delicious dessert of warm apple strudel with vanilla sauce.

Meanwhile, all the sun loungers have been occupied. A few of the guests have ordered club sandwiches and coffee frappes, ice-cold beer etc., and are following the paragliders and water-skiers with great interest; some are reading or sleeping. The childhood rule to wait at least two hours before swimming doesn't apply to the two mermaids. They disregard it completely and glide into the water contentedly. The sun is shining, it is pleasantly warm and the water is heavenly. This time Marlène surpasses herself as she exceeds her own swim record. She is overjoyed.

All the while Francesca is swimming parallel to the shore, ploughing through the smooth, blue sea with lithe, even strokes. She thinks of George as she glides through the water. All of a sudden, she can feel her husband swimming alongside her just like he used to. Every now and then she dives under, into a world of absolute silence, nothing else, gliding ever deeper until her soul is one with the sea. If it weren't for this unbearable pressure in her ears and her lungs, which scream for air after a while, she would undoubtedly lose herself in this unbelievable, hypnotic world disconnected from everything else.

Even though it's difficult for them, they have to leave earlier today. Francesca has summoned her courage, and, for the first time since George's death, invited her friends to a small cocktail party. Marlène greatly admires her for doing this because she knows how hard it is for Francesca to prepare for such an evening. In the past, it had always been George who sent out the invitations, organized the music and took care of his guests' wellbeing, making sure their glasses were always filled while his wife was busy in the kitchen preparing the food. Today, it's the two friends working together in the kitchen, side-by-side, ensuring that the evening will proceed smoothly.

Before long the table is filled with artfully arranged platters of cheese, grapes and small cherry tomatoes. To this Francesca adds some salmon rolls that she has prepared and then they are ready. There's just enough time left over to shower and primp a little, and before long, the first guests start to arrive. After a cheerful welcome, everyone takes time to admire the beautifications that Francesca has made to the property and in the villa. She is extremely proud to have found the courage to undertake these redesigns.

Unfortunately, Despina and Spiros along with their family are unable to attend. Francesca reckons the two brothers probably had another row. Even though the evening is running smoothly and harmoniously, there still remains a gaping hole. Francesca is constantly fighting away tears because now, with friends in the house who have all come with their respective partners, the emptiness she feels is more palpable than usual. She knows and can sense that her friends feel the same way. She can tell by the play of emotions on their faces that for them this evening without George is difficult as well. Every single person misses him and can feel the empty space he left behind in their lives. *He* is missing. Occasionally, Francesca can feel a familiar hand slip into hers and give it an understanding squeeze.

However, despite the powerful emotions the evening turns out to be a complete success. Francesca has proven to herself that she can get along without *him*, and despite everything he still lingers among them. They were able to talk and laugh about *him*. After the last bottle of wine has been emptied and all the appetisers have been eaten, everyone says goodbye, touched but happy that Francesca has finally been able to invite friends over just like she and George often enjoyed doing.

The two girlfriends appreciate the sudden quiet after this emotionally charged evening and collapse exhausted into the bamboo armchairs, which they have placed in the middle of the lawn. Silently, they marvel at the glittering stars shining mysteriously in the heavens.

6

*E*arly in the morning, Francesca is sitting on the low casing surrounding the balcony, where red geranium had once been planted. She lets her gaze travel far across the valley and down to the sea. It makes her happy, all this beauty that surrounds her. Delicate, white tendrils of mist creep through the high cypress trees throughout the entire area. Autumn really is showing its finest side. She can hear the loud quacking of ducks and the hoarse crowing of a rooster coming from the neighbouring property.

Smiling, she peers down to the window where the curtains remain drawn. Marlène is still cradled in the arms of Morpheus. Hopefully, the morning concert won't disturb her *petite fée's* dreams.

Gradually the sun rises, first only as a fine line slowly emerging from behind the Albanian mountains on the far shore, then growing until it swells into a large, glowing red disc. With open eyes and an open heart, Francesca soaks up this magnificent morning moment. Nature's opulence, so lavishly bestowed, is like a balm for her soul...

Propped on her elbows, Marlène leans out the window reflecting: *We all originate from the same Source, but as incarnations, different kinds of souls. Francesca must be a type of soul that is nourished by love. Day and night, always available to her loved ones. Helping them in a gentle way to master important chapters in their lives, and supporting them so they can fulfil their dreams. I, on the other hand, belong to a different sort, one that is there to awaken others, so that they can be reunited with the Source. Everything I touch, I can inspire, elevate to the Spiritual, bring it to a higher level. On the other hand, I don't possess great intensity, so I always run into problems when I try to put down roots in this world.*

After some time, Francesca hears familiar sounds coming from downstairs. *How sweet of her...I really can be envied! I'm going to miss having this abundant and pleasant breakfast every morning with my petite fée.* She races down the stairs to greet her friend.

Meanwhile, the sun has fought its way through the fog. A cloudless sky announces, once again, the promise of a glorious day. They both hurry and are soon driving to their favourite beach in the best of moods. Marlène wants to take advantage of her last full day and go swimming. And so, it doesn't take long before the two friends hurl themselves with whoops of joy into the water and glide side-by-side like two fish through the turquoise depths.

Francesca shows her *petite fèe* the perfect form for breaststroke, which is one of the most difficult swimming styles, and gives her helpful tips when she sees her having difficulty with her breathing technique. They also diligently practice swimming underwater, which until now had been completely inconceivable for Marlène. But today she is in really great condition. Without much thought, she copies every nonsensical thing that Francesca does. It's obvious that she is no longer afraid of the sea and its mysterious, impenetrable depths.

The absolute highlight and most fun part of the day is when the two loony chicks execute underwater dives without bikini bottoms. Marlène doesn't realise that she is sticking her white bottom, duckling-style, in the air. They frolic like carefree children. It's been a long time since Francesca has had this much fun. Some tourist or beachgoer is most likely watching their bold and uninhibited water games in amusement.

For one final time, they swim out to the farthest buoy. Francesca is extremely proud of her friend and impressed with her boundless exuberance and athletic performance. But then the body wins out, and

Marlène collapses exhaustedly onto the lounger so she can recuperate from her wild fun in the water.

While they are both gathering some strength with an exquisite risotto, it's inevitable that once again the conversation turns to deep subjects. Everything that Francesca understands very clearly at one moment, what makes sense and is good for her emotions and soul, is for the most part forgotten the next day much to her great frustration.

"It's stupid that we haven't recorded any of our conversations," she remarks and takes a sip of the chilled chardonnay. "How simple it would be to press a button and then be able to recollect all of our conversations when I need them."

She sighs and casts Marlène a gloomy look. "I'm fine. In fact, I'm almost happy. Of course, it's not the same happiness as with George, but I can't think of any other way to express how I'm feeling at the moment.

I can feel a warm, deep contentment inside of me. It's so wonderful that after such a long time, I am able to feel anything again. I'm also becoming increasingly aware that I feel the best when I'm in sync with nature, especially water, when I'm one with the sea."

Marlène reaches across the table to grasp her friend's hands and replies softly, "Time, maybe not today but at some point, will be your best friend."

Silently and lost in thought they continue with their meal.

After Francesca has slathered Marlène's back with sun lotion, she leaves her lying snug and content under the umbrella. Yet, before Marlène falls asleep, she puzzles over a way to organize all the important conversations and dialogues they have had up until now in order to not forget them. *When we're together, we blurt out the answers simultaneously, same as the questions. However, when we're apart, we just sit on our questions, they remain unanswered,* she philosophises before taking her well-deserved nap.

Meanwhile Francesca has a great desire to swim using strong strokes and with great speed along the coast to where the beach ends and the rocks begin. How incredible this feels to glide silently and without effort through water that is still quite warm and smooth as glass.

It's lovely, how far and deep I can see with no burning in my eyes whatsoever. There must be a lot of fresh water springs in this area. This is exactly what I imagine heaven to be like – to float silently, weightless...I wonder if this is how George feels in every instant, at every moment, just as I do right now? That's daft! What has Marlène been explaining to you constantly? George is the sea, he is heaven...therefore, he isn't floating; he's simply everywhere, even now, here with me.

She turns onto her back and folds her arms behind her neck. Relaxed, she lies there with her eyes closed allowing the sea to carry her. *What a wonderful, sublime feeling to imagine myself at this moment lying on George. He is the sea. I am lying on him. He is the water; he is carrying me. The small waves that gently play around my body are his hands caressing me tenderly.*

Francesca floats on her back motionless, caught up in this sublime and infinitely happy moment until a brightly coloured ball brutally tears her from her magical spell as it lands close to her head. With even strokes, and still somewhat dazed, she swims back at a leisurely pace.

Meanwhile, Marlène is awake and starting to pack up her miscellaneous things, all the while feeling an unmistakable lump in the pit of her stomach reminding her that the inevitable moment of her departure has almost arrived. She casts a melancholic glance towards the Albanian coast, its contours outlined on the horizon. The wind gently caresses her face as she whispers, "Goodbye, we'll see each other again next year." Tears slowly roll down her cheeks as she scans the surface of the water for her friend.

Francesca notices Marlène's concerned look as she impatiently waits at the shore, already dressed and holding out a towel to her friend as she leisurely steps out of the water. She wasn't aware that she had been gone so long and feels bad that her *petite fée* has had to worry about her.

After Francesca has showered and thoroughly rinsed the salt from her body in an outdoor shower, which has been provided for the guests she changes into dry clothes. They drive to Gouvia, so that Marlène can say goodbye to their friends Despina and Spiro, as well as to his brother Dino and sister-in-law, Vanessa. They don't linger because they want to spend their last evening in town.

While roaming the narrow streets and alleys, Marlène finds an enchanting white blouse fashioned in the Greek style that she simply can't resist. Arm-in-arm they stroll leisurely until they arrive at the large square by the town hall, *Plateia Dimarchion*. There, just as on the first day, the two friends enjoy a final, excellent evening meal under a flowering bougainvillea while they talk about trivial things.

They both feel as if everything has already been said. During this week, they have soaked up all the light, the energy and the love that they feel for each other. In a quiet moment when all that can be heard is the sound of knives and forks, Francesca muses,

"I just hope that I don't forget everything; that I can remember at least some of what we have shared, so that when I am once again in complete despair, I can bring to mind our discussions, which will help lift the darkness. At the moment, I feel a deep peace within me, and I hope that it stays with me for a long time." Without a reply, Marlène continues to eat in silence.

It's nice to know that she understands me without having to put it into words. It feels good to be able to talk to her about George, to know that she too won't forget him and that he has embedded a part of himself in her as well. For this whole week, she has had a strong sense of his presence. As a matter of fact, there were always three of us. I so wish that this feeling of being connected to what is 'up there' will always be present, even without Marlène. I have to learn that whenever I need it, I can establish this connection...it's my wish that one day it will be as easy for me to do this as it is for her.

At the same time Marlène is thinking, *I hope she doesn't notice how much Eddy and I are missing George; he was our best friend. As we see it, Corfu has lost a little of its shine since he left us. I can still hear the sound of his voice and his laughter. Right here in this very spot, we spent so many wonderful times as we listened to him tell Corfiot stories and anecdotes.*

7

ortunately, they don't have to be at the airport until 9.30 a.m. the next day, so they can enjoy another breakfast together on the terrace. It's obvious though that both of them have already set one foot outside the magical circle, or soap bubble, or whatever you want to call the place in which they have spent the past week. Their thoughts are already preoccupied with everyday things that will soon be confronting them such as washing, cleaning, school, shopping, post office, visits to the bank, problems at work etc.

Francesca is still in an upbeat mood despite the impending departure. She is convinced that she carries a piece of Marlène, just like the enormous piece of George, within herself. The memories of these very special, wonderful days filled with magic and mystery have to last both of them for a very long time, so that whenever they need they can recharge themselves with new strength and energy.

By the time they reach the airport, Francesca and Marlène are once again standing in the midst of reality and pulsating life. Here, they can no longer feel the wonderful magic that held them in its spell for a whole week. The many cars, the noise, the pushing and shoving of countless people arriving and departing to somewhere...

They stand next to each other lost and withdrawn in the middle of a horde of wildly excited yelling strangers and patiently queue up until it is finally Marlène's turn to check-in. It's breaking her heart to think of the upcoming separation. Not to see her best friend for months, especially now, when they have spent an entire week in perfect symbiosis, releases a wave of sadness. It's only with great effort that she can hold back the tears as she gives Francesca a brave smile.

The next hour just crawls by – It's as if time is standing still for both of them. In the cafeteria, they take the time to enjoy a glass of freshly pressed orange juice. Finally, her flight departure is called and simultaneously they stand up and join the queue to board.

When Marlène and Francesca arrive at passport control they are met with a long and extremely wide queue of colourful passengers. Crammed together, they stand in the midst of hundreds of impatiently waiting, sweaty people reeking of perfume and suntan lotion. They look at each other in this awkward moment, waiting to go through and not knowing what to say to one another. The two friends continue to get pushed about from all sides as they wait.

At first, there is only a small, stifled nervous giggle that very quickly grows louder increasing until it suddenly explodes into uncontrolled, unfettered laughter. A few of the tourists, those closest to Francesca and Marlène, are embarrassed and taken aback. Some are even frightened and step aside. In the midst of all these people the two friends stand holding their stomachs, doubled over with helpless laughter. In between they wipe away the tears rolling down their cheeks. Each time someone stares at them in irritation, it triggers a new bout of laughter. However, the two troublemakers slowly calm down and gain control over their hilarity.

"Come on, let's get this over with, it's no use," Marlène pants, breathlessly. "You're absolutely right. We've had our week and now it's over. *Ma petite fée,* I'm so delighted that you were able to be with me once again."

After a tender hug Francesca and Marlène finally say goodbye to each other. Neither of them wants to prolong the farewell unnecessarily. They whisper one last thank you to each other, a kiss on the cheek, and before Francesca starts to cry, she turns around and runs outside into the glaring sun and to her car.

Agitated, her emotions in a turmoil, she drives home. On the way, she recalls that in the early afternoon Eileen and Alan are hosting a farewell lunch for Vanessa and Dino, before they fly back to England for the winter. It is also an ideal opportunity for all the friends to get together one last time and say goodbye to the summer with a bang. *Going to a party right now is just what I need. I'm sure it will distract me from Marlène's departure. Meet later with my friends – this is exactly what I'm going to do.*

Back at home Francesca immediately throws herself into her chores. She pulls off the sheets and stuffs the washer full of towels and other laundry. She cleans and tidies Marlène's room. While the washer finishes its cycle, she heads to the garden and feverishly waters her potted plants, picking off their wilted blooms. Afterwards, she attaches the clothesline to the palm tree and the post on the terrace.

After the wash has been hung up, a quick shower, an attractive dress, a swipe of lipstick and a quick brush through her hair, and before long she's back in the car and driving off full of anticipation.

Just as she arrives at Eileen's, she receives a text message from Marlène:

I just arrived in Zurich and I'm carrying all the love you have given me. For this I thank you very much. It is a precious gift that I will save and withdraw small amounts from until you return in December. Your petite fée...

Francesca is touched and feels a solitary tear well up in her eye, then slowly roll down her cheek until it lands on her dress with a small 'plop'. Before she's completely overcome with emotions and another bout of tears, she gives an energetic shake of the head. She opens the car door with a flourish, gets out, and with determined strides heads off into the garden towards the welcoming sounds of music and laughter.

Francesca leans against an olive tree holding a glass of wine, watching the cheerful banter of her friends. A wistful smile appears on her face as she remembers how she too was once so carefree and happy. Suddenly, she spies Despina's sweet face among the merry gathering carefully watching her, a look of concern in her eyes. She gives her a sign with her hand to indicate she is okay.

Although Francesca makes an effort and doesn't want to be a spoilsport, but after the tranquil, sublime, week with Marlène, all the loud celebrating is simply too much for her. Despite noisy protests she bids her friends goodbye, sincerely, but firmly. She's had enough; all she wants to do now is go home.

Even though the peace and quiet at home is almost tangible, Francesca is still glad to sit in her comfortable old armchair on the terrace. She is watching the moon slowly emerge as a large reddish-orange disc between two cypress trees and then climb higher until it finally reaches its summit high up in the firmament. The night watchman casting its cold, pale light. *The moon and I...I wonder if he feels just as lonely up there?*

All of a sudden Francesca shudders. A cold shiver runs down her spine. She hadn't noticed how cold it had gotten. Quickly, she runs into the house and gets a warm blanket which she wraps around herself. She snuggles deep into her armchair with her legs drawn close thinking about the past week.

The days with Marlène were just wonderful. We experienced so many intense and special moments together. If I had it my way I would spend the rest of my days enveloped in this bubble of pure energy. She tears me from my dark reality and draws me into a world where everything is light and bright. With simple and plain words, she is able to explain things to me for which I myself don't have an answer. It's in such moments that I feel as if I understand everything, and that I can also accept and learn to trust once again.

It's a pity though, when I'm alone and try to reflect back on the conversations we had, it's as if there's a mental block in my head. Where did all the answers go? Where are the kind and well-meaning words, the patient explanations and clarifications? Why does this happen to me? Not even our talks remain.

Now, Marlène is back at home, in her world. Now, she must also face her reality. We can't constantly live in a fairy tale. But I am grateful. I know how lucky I am to have been able to find such a good friend, a soul mate. With her, I feel almost the same deep attachment and understanding that I had with George.

Well, I'll be seeing her again soon. In only two months I'll be flying back to Crans-Montana, to spend the winter high up in the snowy mountains. And then next autumn will be here before long. So, that's an enormous number of things I can look forward to.

Part Two

Miracles: Fascinating, Mysterious Power

*I*t is early on a Saturday morning and already bitterly cold at the beginning of September in Crans-Montana. Eddy, Marlène's dear husband, has driven her and Francesca to the train station in Sierre. Fortunately, it doesn't take long before the express train to Zurich arrives, coming to a screeching halt at track three. Eddy helps them with their suitcases and then gives Francesca a hug goodbye.

He embraces his wife especially tight because he knows how difficult it is for her to leave him and the children. He's happy though, to be able to give her this week of holiday, far removed from her daily responsibilities. For one final time, he wraps his arms around her tenderly before Marlène extricates herself from his embrace and hops into the train with Francesca. They are able to find an empty compartment. With beaming faces, the two friends wave out the window to Eddy. As the train slowly leaves the station he continues to get smaller and smaller until he completely disappears after the next curve.

Full of excitement and anticipation of their holiday together, they boldly execute a wild dance of joy. After calming down, they stow their warm jackets on the luggage rack above their heads and note in surprise that they look almost like sisters in their jeans and blue pullovers. "Now we're even dressing alike," Marlène grins, as she carefully notes the change in Francesca, who in the last few months has started dressing in a more flattering style. Her cheeks have filled out as well as the rest of her body, which has become more rounded in just the right areas making her look more feminine. Just recently she trimmed her hair to a vivacious bob, which complements her well-defined features and high forehead. Though it's a pity she still has those melancholic, vulnerable eyes, even if lately her laughter has been heard more often.

"Man, I am so happy!" Francesca exclaims cheerfully as she takes a seat by the window. "A whole week...our week, which will hopefully be as unique as the one last year."

With a contented sigh, Marlène replies as she seats herself across from her friend, "Don't expect anything. Just enjoy every moment and we'll open our hearts and eyes and see what happens. This is the only way we'll be ready for the surprises each new day holds in store for us."

At times, Francesca observes her travel companion sitting opposite her with a smile, eyes closed, listening to music on her iPhone while her foot taps rhythmically in tune with the music. But then her thoughts turn to Corfu. She really hopes that Ermioni, her cherished and trustworthy household help, has everything prepared for their arrival today.

The rhythmic rocking of the train soon lulls them into a dreamlike state. Marlène leans back relaxed, her head sinking deeper into the headrest as she gradually starts to daydream. *If I live in the here and now without looking to the past, or having expectations for the future, then I can turn my thoughts off for a moment and connect to my innermost self. I trust 'it' because 'it' will help me open my eyes to the many unique moments that certainly await me in the coming week. I just need to be receptive to what's coming and share it with Francesca, which should be easy during our week together.*

Meanwhile, Francesca is staring out the window lost in thought. She barely registers the towns and landscapes flying by noting them only in her subconscious. *How quickly time has gone by despite everything*, she muses. *I can hardly believe I've been alone for four years without my dearly loved George by my side. To think of all the things I've experienced, endured, overcome, learned and accomplished. I would have never thought I'd be able to continue living. And yet, everything has somehow worked out for me. Every time when I was lost and didn't know how to go on, help always came from somewhere.*

Just as she does now, she always remembers with a grateful heart a certain incident that took place at the right time, exploding into her life and taking a huge weight off her shoulders.

The best proof for me will always be, she continues to dream, *the fact that I was able to sell our life's work quickly and efficiently one year after his death. George must have felt that I no longer had the strength to open the shop each and every day and not see his loving face before me. I had used up all of my reserves having to tell customers the unfathomable truth daily and then having to look into their uncomprehending, shocked eyes until they stammered some consoling words and left the boutique completely distraught.*

This miracle happened the following year of her husband's passing on what would have been the anniversary of his birthday. While Francesca continues to stare out the window with a fixed blank stare, her face lights up with a blissful smile. *I will never forget that day. I had cried all morning, I was feeling really bad. Everything seemed to be more senseless and hopeless than usual. Later, in the shop when I was going through the post like I always do, I found myself holding a letter from an unknown solicitor. Full of curiosity, I opened it and read the sentence it contained at least ten times in disbelief. It asked if I was interested in selling the boutique because he had a potential buyer! All I could do was cry like a baby. How often the two of us had dreamed of having such a stroke of luck. Thank you, George!*

Francesca feels a gentle touch on her arm and turns her head slightly disoriented. Two large, light blue eyes study her in amusement. "Hey, come on, wake up! We just arrived at the Zurich airport, or would you rather ride back?" She needs a brief moment to snap back into reality, but then grabs her suitcase and hops off the train behind Marlène.

A lot of time remains until departure. They browse enthusiastically through the Duty-Free shops until Francesca stops in front of a Pandora display inspecting with interest the many beautiful pieces made from fine materials.

"A bracelet would be an amazing birthday gift for Despina, don't you think?" she asks, turning to her friend. "Look at these attractive pieces made of gold and silver." Francesca points to a display tray full of small charms. Soon, both heads are bent searching for the first charms to go with the silver bracelet Francesca has chosen. Marlène decides on a lovely silver heart and her friend fancies a charm in rose quartz. The bracelet still looks somewhat sparse, but one day, when it's full of keepsakes, Despina will be carrying her own story on her wrist.

Suddenly, Marlène gives a small shriek. She shakes her friend's arm and points excitedly to the departure board. And then, laughing and larking about, they dart down the long corridors of the airport.

"Corfu…here we come!"

It is splendid, sunny weather as the pilot lands with a few bounces on the runway of Ioannis Kapodistrias Airport in Kerkyra. As always, Marlène is overcome by a wave of joy whenever she sets foot on Greek soil, and she sends George and his homeland a greeting from the depths of her heart. There is not a lot of time for deep emotions though because Francesca is already dragging her over to the luggage carousel where, amidst grumbling and groaning, they attempt to wrestle their bags out from all the others. Finally they manage to grab their bags off the carousel. With radiant faces, they walk past the attentive customs official and at the same time discover their friend waiting at the terminal.

Spiro has been close friends with Francesca since she moved to Corfu – the helpful, trustworthy teddy bear, with his round belly and friendly bearded face, which always seems to sport a roguish smile. Right now, he has a grin stretched all the way across his face. He is waving at his friends with shining eyes. After an affectionate greeting Spiro urges them to leave quickly, "Come on girls, hurry up, I'm parked out front in a "no parking" zone. We don't want the police to be quicker than us."

Francesca has to laugh. *It's so good to be home again. Nothing has changed, not even the eternal game with the law.* While Spiro speedily loads the luggage in the car, Marlène asks in curiosity, "That bust on the plinth we just walked past, who was that?"

"Ahh...that is one of my ancestors: Ioannis Antonius, Count Kapodistrias. Born in Corfu and the first Greek president!" he announces proudly, as his already substantial chest expands by several more centimetres. Before he can continue with endless stories and explanations, Francesca resolutely shoves him into the car.

"Please not now, Spirouli," she says impatiently, "You can tell your family stories later on." How often she has had to hear this lecture, how one of his ancestors saved the Helvetians.

Shortly thereafter all three of them are sitting in the car. While Spiro eagerly chats, he manoeuvres the vehicle skilfully through town, past the impressive ancient fortress that dates back to the 1600's, which is a Corfu landmark. They continue to speed along the north-eastern coast until, in order to reach Francesca's villa, they turn off to the west to drive a short distance towards the higher central region of the island. After months of absence, Francesca is excited as she unlocks the large wrought iron gate that leads to her property. *Will everything be okay? The lawn and hedges trimmed, everything maintained just as I like it?* She turns to her friends and requests, "Why don't both of you drive ahead, I'd prefer to walk down to the house."

Slowly and deliberately she takes in her surroundings, enjoying the panoramic view of the sea and the Albanian coastline. Francesca inhales the mild September air deeply with all of its mysterious scents. She notices instantly that the wild thicket growing alongside the drive has been trimmed by her Albanian gardener and looks tidy. She slowly strolls along, one final turn and she sees it, her home, built in typical Corfiot style.

This sight always moved George and me, each time we would see it, returning after the winter season to spend some carefree summer months here. Each day in our spare time, we would drive up to the property to see how the builders were coming along, with our self-designed house. It just looks so lovely... how good it feels to be back home again, to feel closer to George.

While they wait for Francesca at the front door with the luggage, Spiro remarks to Marlène in French, a language he has a good command of since childhood.

"You can be sure that she will monitor and inspect every little detail. But I can understand why. It's her pride and joy, to have her property kept in immaculate condition."

"Fortunately, she can count on your help. For I can imagine that the things that need to be maintained here are not always easy for her, and she doesn't know the ins and outs like you do." Marlène replies laughing.

Happy to be home again, Francesca runs down the last few steps and finally unlocks the door. She quickly enters the darkened house and with her friends' help opens all the doors and windows. Her worries this morning were unfounded because she can immediately see that Ermioni has prepared and cleaned everything perfectly for their arrival. Then, full of expectation, she flings open the door to the terrace and steps outside into the open.

Her breath catches. All she can see is knee-high grass and weeds. *Why hasn't Thimios mowed the lawn? He knew we were arriving today. My God, what would George say to all of this? I'm sure Marlène is surprised at the unsightly condition of the lawn as well. How embarrassing.*

Deeply disappointed and frustrated, she turns around after this downer and stamps back into the house. "Spirouli, would you like something to drink? Campari and soda is in the fridge!"

But Spiro can see that the lawn, which has not been mowed for weeks, has really spoiled Francesca's arrival. With a few encouraging words and lots of love from his wife Despina, he hands Francesca a bag of groceries. With a genuine smile, he invites the two of them out to Greko's for a welcome-home fish feast that evening. He turns to leave and gives Marlène a commiserating goodbye wink. After such good news, a small smile appears on Francesca's face as she looks forward to meeting up with her dear Corfiot friends.

Also, Marlène is happy and excited to be seeing Despina. Since George's passing, they have become much closer. Despina, who likes to uphold her Greek heritage and traditions, shares her knowledge and feelings with Marlène even though she is normally quite standoffish with people who are not within her circle of friends. Marlène is delighted, as she perceives that the bond developed between them is slowly getting stronger.

While she unpacks her suitcase, Francesca puts fresh, clean sheets on her friend's bed. Though she avoids looking out of the window, her gaze is constantly drawn to the unsightly nuisance outside as if by a magnet. Never, in all the years has the grass grown this high. Her husband had always made sure that the lawn was mowed regularly and never failed to neaten the sides meticulously with a small edger. Hopefully, nothing bad has happened to the gardener?

Amused, Marlène watches the play of emotions on her friend's face. She can tell by the vertical line between her brows that she's quite bothered by the condition of the lawn. She knows exactly what Francesca must be feeling and wants to deliver her from this rotten mood.

"You know what, let's start by having a picnic on the terrace. Don't let a little bit of grass muck up your holiday. Look how sweet and caring it was of Despina to have Spiro bring us such delicious food."

"Of course, you're right. I'm sorry, and Despina really is an angel. She has been carrying out this ritual for years. Even when George and I would return home, there was always something edible waiting for us in the fridge, 'a welcoming care package' is what she called it."

Before her friend can get upset again, Marlène continues, "And after we're finished, we are going to manicure this nuisance with dedication." Now, Francesca has to laugh after all. Even though she really doesn't want her friend to work on her first day, she is relieved and very happy about the spontaneous offer.

An hour later she has calmed down. In answer to her industrious *fée's* request, she fetches the electric lawnmower from the garage and plugs the cord into the wall socket on the terrace. Marlène, needing no encouragement, moves off and starts to mow. However, she doesn't pay attention, and in her exuberant excitement drives right over the cord...the mower dies abruptly – it's dead.

"I can't believe it! Right now, when we need it the most the cord gets severed!" Francesca grumbles disappointedly.

She had so hoped to find not only the villa, but also the garden in perfect condition. She also wanted to impress her friend a little and show her that even during her absence she had everything under control, and that she had diligent helpers tending to the property.

Marlène lays a comforting arm around her friend. In the past Francesca had never been so bothered about the lawn because that particular chore had been her husband's. She had preferred to relax and sit in her old bamboo armchair with a drink in her hand, watching him mow the lawn stoically, dressed in an old shirt and trousers with a baseball cap on his head.

"Do you have insulating tape in the house?" Marlène asks, interrupting her melancholic thoughts.

"What?" Francesca replies, choking back the tears that threaten to start.

"Don't you worry, I'll fix this. Did you forget that my father was an electrician? So, something must have stuck with me."

Francesca quickly runs into the house, and in a small cupboard under the stairs finds the required tape in a box along with a hundred other things. Just in case, she brings along a knife as well. In a matter of minutes, her *petite fée* exposes the two severed wires, reconnects them, winds insulating tape around them and with that the project is done. The lawnmower springs to life once more!

Marlène runs into the house on nimble feet swapping her jeans for shorts and pulls on an old t-shirt. With a very self-satisfied smile she continues to mow the lawn with enthusiasm.

Happy with her friend's success, Francesca finds the strimmer in the garage. She doesn't want to stand around any longer grumbling and doing nothing; instead, she wants to help by trimming the grass along the edge of the lawn. But then...oh no...not again! The strimmer doesn't buzz to life...

Marlène turns off the lawnmower and walks over to her friend who is sitting on the ground in a little heap of misery, staring at the edger angrily. In a calm voice, she asks Francesca to fetch a screwdriver.

"And what do you plan to do with a screwdriver now? That'll never work!" Without another word she gets up and, after a pointed look from Marlène, returns to the house to locate the wanted item. Silently, her friend starts to take apart the strimmer.

Before Francesca has another crisis moment, watching the individual parts accumulating on the lawn, Marlène sends her off to buy a new spool of nylon line because she couldn't find an extra roll for the strimmer in the garage. Only with great reluctance does Francesca leave her enterprising *fée* alone with all the mess. But after her insistent request, she opens the boot of her old Mercedes in order to reconnect the battery after months of not being used. She gets into the car with hesitation, inserts the key into the ignition and turns it, as her heart thumps loudly in her chest. It takes two tries, but then the motor springs to life and starts to purr like a kitten.

Francesca almost starts to cry due to her frazzled nerves, "Good old Merky," she sighs from the bottom of her heart. She drives away to fetch the spool of nylon line for the damned strimmer.

Meanwhile, Marlène stands alone on the terrace staring at the individual parts of the machine that are spread out before her. After several attempts to repair it she's no closer to completion. So, she says out loud, "George, this is your job. Seeing you can't do it yourself, could you at least give me the necessary tips to reassemble all the parts, so that I can continue with my work? You've seen how Francesca freaked out about the untidy lawn."

And the magic works...her hands find the right motions to tighten every last screw, wind the nylon line on the spool and reattach the cover to the base. To Marlène's great joy, the strimmer starts to buzz again. *Whew, saved! Now all I have to do is finish my work.*

When Francesca arrives home more than an hour later she can hardly believe her eyes. Freshly showered, wearing shorts and a top with a hand-drawn design, she finds Marlène, lying in the hammock underneath the palm tree reading a book. At first, she gingerly stalks across the perfectly mown grass, even the edges have been trimmed, shaking her head in disbelief, until she finally starts to dance on the lawn spinning in exuberant circles.

Out of breath, she stops in front of Marlène staring at her as if she were a miraculous being. "I don't believe it, it can't be! How on earth did you manage to do this? You've always been such a princess. I've never seen you holding a hammer or changing a light bulb in a lamp; and now this...all of a sudden you can perform wonders!"

"George was watching over me from above and lent me a helping hand. Thanks to him, everything is back in order," Marlène replies innocently. "Come on, after this emotional arrival we should go up and visit George. I would like to thank him for the help he gave me."

"That's a wonderful idea," Francesca agrees, grabbing her *petite fée's* hands as she pulls her out of the hammock. "I had secretly hoped you would ask me. I'm going to call Despina and Spiro right away and postpone our dinner until tomorrow night. I'm sure they'll understand."

With the help of some garden shears she nips off a few branches of prospero, rosemary and evergreen myrtle. To her great joy, she finds one last white rose, which she adds to the bouquet for her husband. She runs and fetches matches and votive candles for the grave and shortly thereafter, they leave the property on foot.

Even this late in the afternoon, the sun is still shining and it's pleasantly warm. Slowly and leisurely, the two friends stroll up a narrow, worn path beneath high olive trees as they enjoy the play of sunlight filtering through the immense treetops. Beneath an ancient, gnarled olive tree Francesca suddenly stops and places her arm around her friend. In a faltering voice she admits, "I'm really sorry that our move-in today didn't go the way I had wanted it for us. I should also have had my emotions under control and not overreacted the way I did. Thank you very, very much, again, for everything. You have no idea what it meant to me. Now the lawn is just as beautiful as it would have been if George were still here."

"You don't have to apologise. I'm the one who should be thanking you. Every year you take me in and together we experience all these unforgettable moments," Marlène replies with heartfelt sincerity.

Silently and lost in thought they continue walking in a single file. Only the chirps and twitters from a few small birds can be heard. At one point the loud braying of a donkey interrupts the silence. As they emerge from the olive grove, they can hear the sound of a small, battery-operated airplane in the distance, buzzing in circles above the green hills. Shortly thereafter, they arrive at a gentle rise and the unique location of the small cemetery, *Agios Nikolaos*.

The wrought iron gate is overgrown with climbing vines blooming with blue, cup-shaped flowers. It is a beautiful sight. From up here the panoramic view of Corfu all the way down to the sea, and the town with its two fortresses and marina is simply fantastic. No wonder Francesca and George swore to have their final resting place here, when they accidentally discovered this special location years ago on a ramble. No one could have known then how soon this wish would be granted.

Francesca is happy to see that everything is in order and that the small cemetery looks well-tended. She arranges the bouquet with the white rose in a marble vase full of water and places it together with the candles that Marlène brought along next to the photo of her husband. Then, according to Greek tradition, she lights a vigil lamp – a glass filled with water and olive oil, in which a cork with a wick attached to it floats – and places it at the foot end of the grave slab. After all the preparations have been made, they stand at the grave very close to one another in deep reflection.

Even after four years, Francesca still finds it difficult to believe what happened. She wants to be strong, and when they arise, buries the melancholic feelings deep down inside. But often, when she's alone, she no longer has the strength to fight them. It is then that she asks herself the pointless question, *Why?* Why was her husband torn from her in an instant, like a flash of lightning that came out of nowhere? They had wanted to grow old together. And today, all that remains for her is this cold resting place of white marble and an abundance of wonderful memories. *But memories can never be a replacement...*

Marlène studies the photo of George that appears to be staring her right in the eye. She is gripped by a wave of melancholy. They will no longer be having long, late afternoon conversations in his fur shop in Montana while they wait for the last customer of the day to arrive; they will no longer argue over games of chess or laugh themselves silly over word games they used to play. He had even promised to introduce her to Kabbalah, but had run out of time.

A sigh escapes her, and she is not able to hold back the tears that ultimately end up dripping on the grave. *No, I don't want Francesca to see me in this condition. When George died, I swore I would always support her, help her find joy in life again. The way I am right now is a far cry from that.* But it's impossible to contain the wave of sadness that washes over her and she stands motionless, overwhelmed by her sorrow.

All of a sudden, she feels an arm placed gently around her shoulders. Side-by-side, through a veil of tears, the two friends silently gaze at the sun lying deep on the horizon, painting the sky in many shades of red. Even after it sets, the afterglow still lingers. Slowly, the first stars appear in the twilit sky. Comforted, they walk back to the villa.

That evening, while they enjoy a drink out on the terrace, Marlène suddenly produces a piece of paper from her handbag and holds it out to her friend. Surprised, Francesca looks at her and asks, "What's that?"

A little awkwardly Marlène replies, "Years ago I received a communication from an archangel via an extraordinary woman, whom my friend Isabelle recommended. I never thought that I would ever show it to someone. But this time I brought it with me because I'm convinced that you, who believes more in me than myself, will be able to understand these lines."

Full of curiosity Francesca takes the page and reads:

'I, Gabriel, Archangel of love, communication and announcement, would like to gently part the curtains that life has drawn in front of you, to thank you for what you are Marlène, for the swiftness with which you evolve. If you hadn't had love for others, you wouldn't have this look full of life which you bestow on each person you meet.

Today, I would like to fill you with divine love, so this power you already sense and approach, can spring in the heart of your being, of your life. I want to announce a future in which you are called to strengthen your power, this power of action within you, this power to help those who desire to transform themselves.

Your word will give truth. Not absolute truth, but truth for the one who needs to be beside you, to meet you.

Behind this strength, lie magnificent actions. The times you felt such moments of grace and absolute magic within yourself, conscious that your own wings had opened briefly, letting in a world of sweetness wherever there was sadness, suffering, war and hate.'

Francesca can no longer sit still and stands up. She takes another deep breath before continuing inquisitively:

'I, Michael, Archangel of strength, liberation and forgiveness, by my sword of Light, bring forth what still needs to spring within you as you may be a little doubtful.

The more you will become conscious of it, the more the power we sense within you will burst out. I thank you for showing so much respect to the injured and the weak you have met along your path of life. For giving them a helping hand, and allowing them to awaken without rushing them.

Dare to open the sky's hatches, this will let you set the star's secrets within the material, tangible reality. By giving you my strength, I give you my sword to defend and support you in all you undertake to always be closest and truest to your innermost feelings.

I give you a quill and invite you to write the path of heaven on earth, your path of heaven on earth, so that the best within you may be manifest.'

With large, astonished eyes she looks to Marlène, who with a silent nod encourages her to continue.

'I, Uriel, Archangel of protection and achievement, accompany you and help you realise all that your spirit can perceive. By unfolding my wings, I give you protection, the ability to feel supported, loved and safeguarded in all you do.

I invite you to never lose sight of your dreams, never cast them aside nor forget them. May you simply accomplish what you know is right. I admire your ability to know. I remind you that knowledge lies deep within each person. It is not only intellectual knowledge, it is intuitive knowledge arising from one's innermost feelings.

By working with you, I want to manifest your angel essence through your hands. The shape of angel wings is inscribed in your hands, because it is through them that you can move your wings and bring this magic onto the Earth. In this manner, you will always choose the correct and adequate path in your relationships with yourself and with others. A fairy is awakening within you, it is your magical side.'

After she has read the final word, Francesca collapses into her chair. Confused, she slowly raises her gaze. In silence, she refolds the piece of paper and hands it back to Marlène, who by now is watching her friend uneasily and waiting intently for her reaction.

Hesitantly, Francesca replies, "Wow...that's quite something! It's not easy to process it all at once. To be honest, I don't know what to say to all of this. It's all so fantastical, so unimaginable for me." A nervous laugh escapes her as she continues somewhat abashed, "Actually, that is the biggest understatement if you ask me..."

Marlène's expectant expression changes briefly, as if she were not pleased with her normally open and understanding friend's answer.

For this reason, Francesca continues more carefully, "Look...I know that you're someone very special. Forgive me though, and don't be angry, but this here is just too much for me right now. To start with, I've just digested the whole unbelievable fiasco this morning with the lawnmower, and now this wondrous letter talking about archangels!"

"Come on, let's go to bed. It's already late. You don't need to respond to anything right now," Marlène continues in a light tone of voice, "I'm just happy that you're not kicking me out because you think I have schizophrenia or psychosis."

Then, Francesca has to laugh as well. She's relieved that her *petite fée* isn't insulted by her, most likely, disappointing answer. Arm-in-arm they go peacefully back inside the house.

9

B old rays of sun that have found their way between the slats of Marlène's closed window shutters tickle her face until she yawns and stretches leisurely. Her first thought this morning is to teach Francesca how to communicate with Nature's elements. *Because she completely blocked out the message from the angels I shared with her last night...*Marlène ruminates, *she's not ready for that; it's too soon. But Francesca loves Nature; she feels as if she is one with it. I think she will be more open to the experiment I have in mind. I will show her today how to connect with a tree.*

She has barely completed this thought process before she hops out of bed. The weather is far too nice to be spending such a glorious day lounging about. While the enticing aroma of coffee, mixed with the smell of freshly toasted bread wafts through the house, nimble hands are setting the breakfast table out on the terrace.

At the same time, one storey higher, a sleepyhead lazily pokes her nose in the air and deeply inhales the aromatic scent. *Hmm...that smells tempting. My industrious fée is already busy.*

Now it's Francesca who, quick as a wink, runs into the bathroom and splashes cold water on her face so that she becomes fully awake. After a couple of swipes through her hair with a comb, she runs down the stairs in an airy, medium-length white summer dress. All these delicious smells drifting up from downstairs are making her hungry.

The two friends are sitting comfortably at the table, gazing dreamily past the many olive trees, whose silvery leaves are glittering in the sun, all the way down to the blue sea. A large white passenger liner heads almost imperceptibly in the direction of Italy.

A pleased sigh escapes Francesca, "I sometimes forget how beautiful everything is here. The amazing view, the cheerful call of the songbirds. And all of it enveloped by a gentle, aromatic breeze, and this beautiful, warm weather. That I can share this moment with you, for this I am deeply grateful."

"Of course, this picture is made far more beautiful by the immaculately tended lawn." Marlène adds mischievously, and they both burst out laughing. This is when Marlène notices her friend's toenails, which have been painted an aubergine-red. The big toes in particular she finds most appealing, each one flaunting a large daisy painted in white.

"You have no idea how happy I am that you can once again find enjoyment in even the smallest and most trivial of things."

While they both enjoy their coffee and tea along with crisp, toasted bread and Spiro's homemade marmalade, Marlène reveals how she has already walked around the property this morning and greeted her favourite olive tree.

Not very surprised at her friend's statement, Francesca simply looks at her evenly and continues to enjoy her meal.

"Would you be interested in learning how to fuse with a tree?"

"Sure," Francesca replies enthusiastically, and quickly swallows down the last bite.

They leave everything there on the table and run over to the olive trees. Francesca will have to choose one and then embrace it. She finds an old tree with gnarled branches and half-heartedly puts her arms around it.

Marlène, who is watching her, notices a sceptical, tell-tale pout form on her face. "You really have to embrace it you know. It has to feel that you want to become *one* with it," Marlène admonishes.

"I can't, there are tons of ants and other insects crawling around!" Francesca looks around until she spies another, younger tree with a relatively soft bark and heads towards it, hesitantly placing her arms around its trunk.

"Do you feel anything?" Marlène asks curiously.

"Actually, no! Perhaps I'm doing it wrong. Show me how you do it, so I can see how to go about it," Francesca requests.

In between rocks and thyme, Marlène leads the way to a more than one hundred-year-old olive tree, which she had already selected last year to help with her meditations. With a soft caress, she places her hand gently on its satiny, light-grey trunk.

"I can feel its energy, its regular pulse. I can feel its life force. While you are touching the tree, place your feet the way I do, slightly spread, on the ground. Imagine how they transform into roots that travel deep within the ground and blend with the roots of the tree."

Francesca leaves Marlène to herself and searches for another tree. She really wants to try again. But for some reason, absolutely nothing happens, even though she is mimicking exactly what her *petite fée* does. Disappointed, she slowly makes her way back to her friend, who is still leaning against the olive tree with a blissful look on her face.

"Do you think I could try it with your tree?" Francesca asks somewhat hesitant.

"Of course, come here. Greet it with reverence and ask it if it will allow you to feel its energy. Do this with an open heart. Simply concentrate only on the tree and your feelings. Don't expect anything, just be there, in the actual moment and surrender yourself to it."

This is exactly how Francesca wants to do it. Standing, in the same position as Marlène, leaning against the ancient, gnarled olive tree feeling completely relaxed, and after a while even believes that she hears its pulse. She almost attempts a smile, it's probably her own pulse she hears beating. However, the rhythmic beating doesn't stop. At first softly, but then increasingly louder, her ears start to roar. Suddenly Francesca has the strange sensation that, like a vacuum cleaner, she is being sucked in through one of its many holes. She feels that for a moment she has become *one* with the ancient tree, that she herself is a tree.

This sensation has suddenly and unexpectedly overcome her, insomuch that at that same moment, out of fear, Francesca frees herself from the tree with a forceful jolt. Still dazed from her extraordinary experience, she sits down on a large rock. Marlène slowly approaches her and asks in concern, "Is everything okay?"

Two, three times Francesca clears her throat until finally, in a halting voice, she can tell her friend about her unusual, phenomenal experience.

"My God, that's truly weird," she blurts out excitedly. "What would have happened if I hadn't pushed away from the tree immediately? It makes me feel quite odd to think I might have been imprisoned in the olive tree for the rest of my life!"

Marlène is surprised and also impressed by how quickly Francesca was able to carry out this exercise. Calmly, she explains, "You just experienced a fusion with a tree. And by the way, you can do this with all of Nature's elements – blend together and reap their soothing benefits."

However, Marlène also knows from experience how much practice and study it takes until one is capable of establishing such a deep connection. She congratulates Francesca from the bottom of her heart on this first, meaningful experience.

"Still, you should have warned me and told me that something like this could happen," Francesca remarks, still agitated. "Have experiments like this never scared you?"

"No," Marlène replies, "because I've learned how to open myself to these other dimensions incrementally. But I'm also aware of how lucky I am that I can make contact with my environment. Actually, we are all able to do this. You just have to take the time to listen and not doubt your abilities.

For years I've taught myself how to do this through seminars. You, on the other hand, have just received a free sampling. You felt something; experienced it, and it shocked and scared you. That's completely normal. You merged with the tree. You both were, for a brief moment, a complete Whole. We are all interconnected. If you can accept the concept that there is no distinction between two living entities, you'll realize that you can communicate with anything alive," Marlène explains, and puts an arm reassuringly around her friend's shoulders.

With empathy she continues, "If I had told you beforehand what could've possibly happened, you would have never had such a spontaneous experience and the result would definitely have not been the same."

Unable to reply in that moment, she simply nods her head in silence. Afterwards they head back to the terrace side by side in harmony. As Francesca tries to talk about her experience again, for it has got her very excited, Marlène interrupts abruptly, "Stop, not now. It's high time to finally cool off and go play in the sea after this very eventful morning."

As they do every year, since there's no place more picturesque than Barbati Beach, they head to the beach bar at Piedra with its white sun umbrellas and comfortable loungers.

Francesca's heart beats faster when a half hour later she stands barefoot in her swimsuit on the wet sand with small waves lapping around her toes. She inhales the salty air deeply and, as always, takes pleasure in the beautiful view across the sea to the fortress of Corfu and the rocky coves where the water shimmers a turquoise blue.

Meanwhile, Marlène has changed as well. In her colourful bikini and with her long blond hair she stands next to Francesca, light as a feather; a delicate butterfly. She gives her friend, who is still wearing last year's same shapeless black swimsuit, a critical look.

"So, really, this isn't going to work. I thought you had gotten rid of this impossibly dull dreary thing a long time ago and traded it in for something newer and brighter. The next time we go into town, I'm forcing you to buy a bikini!"

Unperturbed Francesca laughs and splashes Marlène. "Last one in the water stinks!" With an elegant dive headlong into the sea she swims away with strong swift strokes. *How good it feels again. It's wonderful to glide through the shimmering water, which is still pleasantly warm.*

Francesca is filled with a sense of infinite freedom as she draws an enormous breath into her lungs. Forcefully, she plunges beneath the surface swimming like a fish down to the sandy ocean floor before, with eyes shut, she lets herself drift back up to the surface. *So lovely...*over and over she dives into the azure blue water that shimmers in the play of sunlight. Here and there, lone clusters of sea grass sway gently in the current. Several fish dart past her startled.

At one point, when she is once again holding her head motionless under water, she notes that the sun is projecting its large shining disc onto the sandy seafloor and her own oversized shadow is reflected in the middle. Francesca spreads her arms and legs so that it now looks as if an enormous star has fallen from the heavens and landed at the bottom of the sea. Suddenly, another dark shape approaches and floats next to her shadow in the centre of the disc. When she surfaces to draw in another breath, Marlène is swimming alongside her.

"Look how wonderful the play of the sun is today. Dip your head under. Come on, try it!" Francesca encourages cheerfully.

Motionless they both float on the water, their faces below the surface. They watch as the sun casts its golden rays through the depths all the way down to the fine sand coating, the seafloor presenting them with its wonderful play of light.

It is always something special for the two friends to treat themselves to a delicious meal at this absolutely charming place that always reminds Marlène of the Côte d'Azur a little. The tables covered in white cloth are set with linen serviettes. A small olive tree in a blue flowerpot has been placed in the centre. Rhythmic salsa music plays softly in the background at the bar which is filled with an assortment of bottles, where even the most outlandish or exotic drink request is honoured making the friends feel even more as if they were on holiday.

They are a little disappointed though when they are not greeted by Adonis at lunch, but are instead welcomed by a new waiter who takes their order. Amidst lots of giggling, they both reminisce about their 'lesbian affair' in his honour.

Languid like a cat, Francesca stretches on her lounger after the meal as she relaxes into her well-earned afternoon nap under an umbrella.

Meanwhile, her friend, younger by several years, is full of energy and prefers to take a stroll along the beach instead. Slathered up with sun cream and a straw hat on her head she ambles along the shore when an idea slowly forms in her mind. Tonight, after supper, she is going to help Francesca receive a message from George.

The waves lap rhythmically on the shore and a small stone that looks as if it has an eye in its centre washes up at her feet. Marlène immediately recognizes its significance. *The eye.* In Greece, it is a symbol of protection. George is there with her to show her the way and assist in her plan. She bends down and picks up the stone. She thanks George's spirit and heads back, her heart full of gratitude. Without making a sound, so as not disturb her friend's afternoon nap, she stores her treasure deep inside her beach bag then creeps away quietly and heads towards the sea to go for a refreshing swim.

Still very sleepy, Francesca squints into the sun and notices with surprise that the lounger next to hers is empty. Then she spies her normally timid *petite fée* swimming quite far out heading towards the last yellow buoy of the boat rental service.

While she had been lulled into sleep by the gentle rush of the waves, the beach has filled with people. She slept so soundly that she hadn't noticed any of the comings and goings. Amused, Francesca observes two small children who are being thrown in the air by their father and shrieking with joy as they splash down into the water. Young people are playing a loud and spirited game of water polo. Not far from them lie a couple who couldn't be bothered by the noise of their arguing in a language that no one can understand. A considerably rotund, young lady in a conspicuous bikini with silver appliques attempts to climb onto a red airbed that is far too small for her, much to everyone's amusement.

Amongst all the sun-tanned beachgoers she notices a pale, extraordinarily thin Englishman who is pulling on plaid trousers and packing up his swimming things. His white shoulders and slick, hairless chest are showing advanced stages of sunburn. *It's got him really bad,* Francesca thinks with pity, as he walks past her with the hint of a smile.

Then her heart feels a small stab as she observes a young, good-looking Greek man devotedly massaging sun cream onto his attractive girlfriend's back. With a sigh Francesca jumps to her feet determinedly. Due to her burgeoning emotions, she forgets to put on her water shoes and painfully stumbles the few metres across the pebbles to the shore. She barely suppresses a curse that wants to escape her mouth before she glides, with relief, into the refreshing water.

Before she reaches her unsuspecting friend, she dives into the depths and swims right underneath her. Then, Francesca turns onto her back and slowly drifts upwards until only a small film of water separates her from Marlène, as she gapes at her with wide, bulging eyes.

"Yikes! Are you bonkers? You startled me..." she shrieks loudly and with a strong push plunges the culprit underwater.

Francesca can't help it and bursts out laughing when she sees her friend's startled face. This causes her to choke and promptly break out in a fit of coughing, which placates Marlène immediately. As they both swim slowly back to the shore she makes tireless diving attempts under the tutelage of her patient trainer.

Much later they both crawl, out of breath, on their hands and feet from the sea and lie for a moment on the warm rocks with their eyes closed and their legs dangling in the water. They smile contentedly as they listen to the soft rush of the sea and feel the warm sun upon their skin.

Twilight has set in unseen. Far out at sea the faint sounding of a ship's bell can be heard. They are both surprised to see the beach has emptied and they are some of the last remaining guests, who are enjoying the evening's peace and quiet.

The hours at the seaside, under the sun, have filled the friends with a languid sleepiness. They allow their souls and hearts to flow free and hear only the soft splash of the waves or feel a slight breeze that caresses their skin tenderly. They hear a cheeky seagull close by picking between the rocks hoping to find a tasty morsel. Caught up in this unique mood neither of them has remembered the invitation from their Greek friends, who are impatiently waiting for the two of them to arrive for supper.

When a wet-nosed dog starts to snuffle at Marlène's toes waking her from her daydreams, she suddenly remembers Despina and Spiro. She gives Francesca a vigorous shake and anxiously reminds her of the fish dinner with their friends, which immediately gives her a guilty conscience. However, in the meantime the mermaids have lost their desire to go out. They would rather spend a cosy evening at home. So, all Francesca can do is call her friends and sheepishly postpone once more.

Although Spiro and Despina are disappointed at this second cancellation, they show a lot of understanding and still look forward to the following evening.

"But there will be no more excuses!" Spiro remarks moodily.

"You're a treasure, Spirouli...we are truly sorry. But we are so worn out, we wouldn't be good conversationalists," Francesca replies, then returns her mobile to her handbag in relief. She is so glad that her friends aren't angry or offended.

On the way home Francesca stops at a simple tavern and purchases supper as she used to years back, a grilled chicken and chips with tomatoes. Right before the turn-off onto the gravel road leading to the property, Marlène suddenly bursts out laughing.

"What's wrong, why are you laughing?" Francesca wants to know.

"George is sitting in the back seat of the car," she giggles. "He's putting his arms around our shoulders, and now he's swinging a grilled chicken leg in his hand back and forth and his whole face is beaming."

Still laughing, Marène glances over to her friend to see how she's taking in this news. She can't understand why her eyes suddenly light up like a child who has just received a present. And all of this because of a piece of chicken?!

However, this piece of bizarre information does not surprise Francesca in the least. How often had it been that she and her husband had stopped at this roadside tavern after spending a wonderful, harmonious day on the boat and picked up a grilled chicken for supper. Or they had met up with friends for a carefree get-together to scoff down chicken or *kontosouvli*, juicy pork on a skewer. Along with this they consumed copious amounts of cheap table wine that almost stuck in their throats. George must have surely been happy to see that she found the courage today to buy chicken at this place so full of memories.

After supper, the girlfriends sit on the terrace companionably and listen to the wonderful voice of Rod Stewart. With eyes closed Francesca hums along softly to the song, *When I Need You*. She can feel a hot tear slowly roll down her cheek.

In the meantime, night has fallen. The light cast from candles and lanterns shining in every corner of the terrace creates a warm atmosphere.

Marlène retrieves the stone she had found that day in Barbati from her beach bag. She clutches it tightly in her hand and explains to Francesca, who is looking at her in curiosity, "I can extract energy from this stone in order to contact George. I actually find it hard to believe myself that this connection has established itself so quickly and distinctly here in Corfu. I've never experienced such a powerful symbiosis."

Francesca thinks back to how often her friend has assured her that she can see George. *Can she really see him now? How on earth is that possible? Perhaps it is only her intense wishful thinking that makes her imagine she can see him. But that can't be either, she would never pretend for my sake, even if it were to help me. We have far too much respect for one another.*

"Is George here with us now, are you really able to see him?" she asks breathlessly.

"He's standing right behind your chair with that typical smile on his face. I can see him as clearly as I see you. You're making a doubtful face. It's okay, I understand. But not only do I see him, I can also see him in the smallest of detail."

Images continue to appear in Marlène's mind as she tries her best to relate them to Francesca, who is completely surprised when her friend tries to describe George's "funny face" to her but is simply unable to do so. For this reason, Marlène attempts to imitate him. She juts out her chin as far as possible and rolls her eyes. Then she stands, lifts up her arms and shakes them wildly above her head in the same manner that George always did to make his wife laugh at his funny dancing.

Francesca has to smile. Overwhelmed by this glimpse into her *petite fée's* arcane world she asks quietly, "What does he look like now? Is it how he looked towards the end?"

"Not as young as when we met, but around 40 or so, with short hair," Marlène replies. "He's wearing beige trousers and is pointing out his brown shoes to me."

"What do they look like?" Francesca asks in fascination.

"They're brown leather moccasins."

"I don't believe it...those were the ones that he always liked to wear in the summer."

Astonished, Marlène watches as Francesca abruptly stands up and marches back inside. In the entrance, next to the wardrobe is a piece of furniture where she has stored her husband's shoes. Shortly thereafter, she is holding a pair of damp, mouldy green moccasins in front of her friend's face and asks excitedly, "Do his shoes look like these?"

"My God...yes!" Marlène peals out in laughter. "Now I'm seeing double; a pair of shoes in your hand and the same pair on George's feet. Now I understand why he was so intent on pointing out his shoes to me. Don't you agree that it's high time you got rid of them?"

Francesca gives her an unsteady smile, "If I think about how he's using you now to get me to throw out his mouldy shoes, it's somehow quite eerie."

"George's message is very clear. It doesn't help, you hanging on to all of his things. You need to finally get rid of them, give them away. You're only hurting yourself."

For a long moment, they are both deep in thought. Rod Stewart has stopped singing and the only sound they can hear is the steady screech of a small owl nearby.

Marlène pierces the silence and whispers, "This is a very unique moment for me as well. Up until now I've never seen the same thing twice. What I mean is

I haven't seen something in the spiritual realm and physical existence at the same time. He projected this image of his shoes to me so clearly that I actually could see two identical pairs, his and the ones you were holding in your hands. And once again I have proof that there are no boundaries between the visible and invisible world. There is only a veil that at times one can push aside."

A bright smile appears on her face. This amazing experience, this one-of-a-kind present she has received from George has touched her deeply.

"Tell me, can you also see or feel if he's healthy... does he look happy?" Francesca asks deeply moved.

"Up until now George has always shown himself with his own distinct smile and his joy at being together with us," Marlène replies, "In this other realm where he now exists there's no longer pain and illness, for they can only affect the physical body."

Even though it's extremely difficult for Francesca, as it still costs her a great deal of effort to come to terms with the loneliness and abandonment, she believes fully that a part of her husband still exists with her. This certainty helps her to continue on with life each and every day.

10

*O*n this warm and sunny autumn day Francesca would definitely like to show her *petite fée* a little more of Corfu and suggests they venture outdoors to explore the remote sandy beach of Halikounas.

Soon, they are driving away towards the south in the best of moods. The soothing vocals from a Yiannis Parios CD, Francesca's favourite Greek pop star from the 70's, drift from the car's speakers, which she accompanies enthusiastically off-key. This causes Marlène to break out in fits of laughter every time. She's looking forward to this afternoon and the opportunity to gather new impressions of this beautiful and eclectic island.

A small squeal of delight escapes her as the enchanting little island *Pontikonisi,* also known as the Mouse Island, suddenly appears. Behind the high cypress trees, a shining white Byzantine monastery stands from the 12th century or earlier.

After leaving the city behind them the girlfriends enjoy the drive along the narrow, winding coastal road, until they reach *Kaiser's Bridge*, over which the German emperor Wilhelm II would stride with his court on his way up to *Achilleion Palace*. In earlier times the bridge had been connected to the beach and the private mooring area of the royal fleet. The emperor had purchased Achilleion Palace from the Austrians and then had the bridge built so he could have direct access from the gardens on the lower palace premises, across the street, to the beach. Ironically, it was the German Wehrmacht that destroyed the middle section during WWII.

Marlène is thrilled by the story and wants to stop and get out. Together, they stroll to the end of the bridge, where a small marble dolphin sits on top of a pedestal where it has survived through all these years. A few steps lead down to the crystal-clear water where tiny fish dart in between the rocks covered in sea urchin and minute snails.

After a few loony photos, they both make their way to the palace up the old cobblestoned walk lined with cypress and oleander. To their dismay, after 100 metres a large, ornate wrought-iron gate bars their way.

Disappointed, they press their faces against the cold bars. With their eyes, they follow the trail as it leads first under a small bridge then up a steep incline to a charming pavilion, through the beautifully manicured gardens until it ends at the palace. In order to lift their dampened spirits Francesca suggests that they drive to Gastouri, where the official entrance to the palace is.

Half an hour later they both find themselves in front of another locked gate. Today, of all times, the palace is closed to visitors. It's such a pity. Francesca would have loved to show her friend this enchanting beautiful palace with its glorious park and amazing marble sculpture of a dying Achilles.

While they are admiring this architectural gem from the outside, Francesca explains that this was once a retreat for empress Elisabeth of Austria. It was built expressly for her between 1889-1892.

"I'm impressed. How do you know the exact dates?"

Amused, Francesca points to a brass plate that is affixed to the wall at the entrance to the palace. As they make their way back to the car she remarks, "By the way, I'm not sure if you still remember, but when we came to Corfu in 1981, this was where the state casino was located before it was turned into a museum several years later."

"Of course," Marlene replies cheerfully, "Even though it's been a while, I remember that Eddy and

I were here one evening with the two of you. I can also recall the magnificent atmosphere that the place had. You felt as though you had been transported to another time and place. It wouldn't have surprised me if Empress Sissi herself had appeared at the top of the majestic landing to welcome us. Just the thought of it, to have been acknowledged by her, would have thrilled Eddy and George."

Francesca laughs and gives a nod as she unlocks the car. "Sometimes, for fun, George and I would drive out here for the evening. While he enjoyed the gaming tables, I spent most of the time outside on the terrace in the company of the nine muses of Greek mythology."

A small smile plays across her face before she continues, "The gaming chip I was able to sneak away from George I would always exchange at the bar for a glass of champagne, which was usually the only winnings of the evening."

While Francesca is concentrating on the winding drive that leads back down to the coastal road, Marlène enjoys the spectacular view of the sea on which are scattered a few shining white sailboats and some large yachts of the very rich. Spread out before them lies Corfu in all its splendour, the airport and the mainland on the opposite coast that stretches far to the south.

They pass by several idyllic fishing villages until the road in Moraitika veers to the west. Shortly thereafter, Francesca turns onto a side road that takes them through a grove of olive trees directly to Lake Korission, where a narrow strip of sandy dunes separates it from the sea. The entire region is an important wetland as well as a winter habitat for many bird species.

Francesca is glad that she can show Marlène the long, pristine sandy beaches of southwest Corfu instead of only the mountainous region in the northeast. She steers her car a short distance down a sandy path between the lake and the dunes and simply stops Merky right where they are. They quickly grab their beach bags and plough through the dunes for a few metres until the endless blue sea spreads out before them in all its immensity. They are surrounded on all sides by dunes and kilometres of Halikounes' sublime, untouched beaches.

The friends drop their bags and rush gleefully to the shore where the waves splash gently around their feet. They are quite fortunate today. Francesca knows from experience that even without much wind the open sea can sometimes be quite rough and large waves break on the shore.

"It is so beautiful here," Marlène exclaims brightly. "This is how I've always imagined the sea to be. It's so incredibly wide, without boundaries, eternal. There's nothing that interrupts the infinite blue expanse, only where it unites with the sky on the horizon. Amazing!" She reaches for the sky in a long stretch and for a moment closes her eyes, overwhelmed with emotion.

Meanwhile, Francesca sits next to her and deeply inhales the spicy tang of the sea. Only too well does she understand her *petite fée's* enthusiasm, for she can also feel the infinite freedom and energy that radiates from this place, where the only things that exist are heaven and sea.

How many times had Francesca and her husband spent carefree hours here with their friends; or the times when she would come here alone with him on a Sunday. She scans the shore reminiscing: *Hand in hand we'd walk along the beach, searching for seashells and talking about our future. At times, we would jump in the water and splash about like kids. We would swim for long stretches along the shore, fall onto the warm sand and I would kiss away the salt from his sun-warmed skin. We were so happy and infinitely in love...I can still hear his melodious, joyful laughter.*

Francesca doesn't notice the fat tears rolling down her cheeks. She feels a soft touch on her arm and turns to look at Marlène's anxious face. "Come on, let's go swimming, do something crazy!" she encourages.

How empathetic my petite fée is. She always seems to sense when I'm not doing well. One could almost believe she has the ability to inhabit my body and experience my feelings, so that she can coax me out of my melancholic mood.

Marlène looks around in interest, and it's only then she notices they are practically alone on the long beach. Only a few bright beach towels lie far apart from each other on the sand. But then her plucky spirit takes over and she splashes her friend playfully. A split second later they find themselves in the middle of a water battle until, out of breath, they both jump into the water.

It is simply sublime to walk on the soft sand and not stub a toe on a single rock. In a playful mood Francesca dares Marlène to swim between her legs. To her great amusement Marlène gets stuck quite often. Of course, Francesca has helped this a little as well doing her best to trap her friend a few times just for fun.

They continue to think up new forms of mischief. In order to bump up the fun they tear off their swimsuits amidst a great deal of laughter and larking around! The two mermaids completely lose track of time until Marlène's stomach makes itself known.

Because there is no food available at the deserted beach, they quickly pack up their belongings and drive to a small cove nearby.

Presently, the two lovely women sit in the rustic tavern at Prassouda Beach and hungrily attack delicious grilled fish, locally harvested greens, chips and tzatziki with a Greek salad. In between bites, they dreamily gaze out at the azure-blue sea and along the steep rocky coast where today, in the distance, one can even see the cliffs of Glyfada. Directly below them three giant rocks emerge from the water. One of the rocks takes on the curious form of an elephant with its trunk.

After their meal, the two friends climb down a flight of cement stairs that lead to the small sandy beach. Instead of swimming, they prefer to stand knee-deep in the water and wade along the sheer rock wall to the next cove. After a few metres Francesca discovers a thick layer of clay in the rock from which she easily breaks off a few chunks. Once they reach the small cove, she dips the chunks of clay in the sea then spreads the wet mass evenly over her arms and legs. And while she explains the beneficial properties of the clay to her friend, she smears the rest of the mud on her face.

Marlène is all for it and does the same, covering herself from head to toe in clay. After the mud has dried, they look at each other and amidst raucous laugher prance about like fearsome African warriors covered in white markings.

Out of breath they flop down on the sand and gazing in the water discover some beautiful blue stones that immediately remind Francesca of her husband's eyes. While they are each occupied with selecting some of the most beautiful specimens, Marlène suddenly says, "George is here; I can see him again as clearly as I can see you. He, who has always valued friendship, is happy to be here with us and he's glad that we are spending such a lovely, carefree time together."

Francesca is always overwhelmed at how easily her husband and friend are able to communicate with each other through thoughts and images....that her friend is a channel between George and herself. She is very envious of Marlène's ability and considers it a magnificent gift.

With a deep sigh Marlène taps her watch and waves it under her friend's nose. Neither of them wants to keep Despina and Spiro waiting this evening.

Playfully, they splash each other washing off the war paint. Once completed, their skin is smooth and soft like a baby's. Before they make their way back along the cliffs to the beach, Marlène breaks off a few more chunks of clay to bring back for her friends and family.

Because the autumn evenings in September are already quite chilly, Francesca pulls on long trousers and a light cotton jumper after taking a long, hot shower. On her feet, she's wearing fashionable open-toed sandals, so her aubergine painted toenails are visible. She chuckles to herself, *I wonder what Despina will say when she sees the kind of nonsense I've been up to again?*

As she skips lightly down the stairs, she finds Marlène already waiting impatiently in the kitchen. She is completely en vogue wearing trendy, light blue skinny jeans, and a pink jumper with rhinestone appliqués. *As always, she looks fantastic with her long blonde hair and large eyes made up in blue*, Francesca thinks proudly as they leave the house together.

They arrive at the fish *taverna* even before their Greek friends. They have barely taken their seat at a table on the terrace before Spiro and Despina arrive, grinning like two Cheshire cats rushing to embrace them. The joy at seeing one other is mutual as they greet each other wholeheartedly.

However, Despina can't let it be and turns to Francesca still somewhat offended to remark, "It's great that we actually get to see you because we weren't sure if you were going to cancel on us again." Francesca is silent after this pointed, but well-deserved statement, and gives her Greek friend an extra loving hug.

In contrast to her burly, jovial husband Despina is a vivacious, delicate little thing. Her intelligent, topaz eyes shine in an even, well-proportioned face. Her light-coloured hair is cropped short in an attractive style. The most striking thing though is her flawless, light skin that makes her look unnaturally pale and wan in the summer.

Companionably, the four of them finally sit at the table together immersed in lively conversation. Spiro orders, Greek style, a variety of platters full of scrumptious dishes. Wild-grown greens, chips, Greek salad, calamari and an especially tasty grilled fish; all of this accompanied by water and a jug of wine. Suddenly, he remembers that he has to tell Marlène about one of Corfu's most important men, who also happens to be his maternal second great-grand uncle. He keeps clearing his throat until finally he has everyone's rapt attention. It is only after being assured of this that he begins his story.

"As I already mentioned at the airport, Kapodistria was born in Corfu and became the first Greek president. It is he who rescued Switzerland and secured your country's independence. As a result of his contributions to the draft of a new constitution in 1814, which went into effect the following year, that Switzerland's federal constitution came to be!'

"Ugh...here he goes again," Francesca laughs, rolling her eyes. "We'd better get this over with as soon as possible."

With a large grin Spiro sits unperturbed and glowing with anticipation, as he is finally able to pass on his knowledge to Marlène. He knows this is annoying Francesca to no end. When he sees that everyone, including her, is looking at him with interest and curiosity, he continues awkwardly, "Kapodistria, who was full of liberal ideas, was deployed by the Russian Tsar for all important and sensitive missions, including the time he was sent to Switzerland as a Russian envoy. He was able to secure Swiss accession to the alliance against Napoleon I at the Viennese Congress in 1813. As Russia's representative, he signed the second Treaty of Paris in 1815."

"I can't remember if I ever learnt about him when I was in school," Marlène interjects in surprise.

"And I'm not sure what's a figment of his imagination and what's real," Francesca concludes and gives her friend a challenging look. "But in Lausanne, at the Quay of Ouchy, there is actually a bust that was erected in honour of Ioannis Kapodistrias in 2009. I was there with friends and saw it with my own eyes. It appears he also aided in the accession of Geneva, Neuchâtel and Wallis, to the Swiss Confederation."

Spiro and Despina laugh in amusement. Never had they thought they would hear this uttered by their dear Swiss friend because for years Spiro has tried to explain Russia and Greece's special relationship with Switzerland with only tepid success.

"What I'm trying to say," Spiros continues, "is without help from Russia or Kapodistria, Switzerland, which back then was on the brink of civil war, would probably have never survived."

"I think it's wonderful that Greece has such a deep relationship with Switzerland. And to think that we are friends with one of the ancestors of this legendary Greek man, that's just brilliant!" Marlène replies excitedly.

She stares hard at this aficionado of Greek history with his red cheeks and eyes shining with joy, who knows how to tell stories and anecdotes about the country which he is so proud of.

Although Spiro's history lesson is very interesting and informative, all this concentration so late in the day soon has everyone yawning. The three girls can barely keep their eyes open.

"Hey now...don't go sliding off your chairs, the most hilarious thing is yet to come!" Spiro looks with a challenging wink over at Francesca, who at first tries to ignore him, but then realizes that it is far better to let him have his fun and tell his story to the end. Otherwise, he will never give it a rest. Meanwhile, even Marlène is looking at her with expectant eyes. Despina, on the other hand, sits back down on her chair with a resigned sigh.

"Okay, imagine this...years ago, a "person" waved a document under my nose. It was written in French in about...I don't know, the 1800's or so, and it states that all descendants of Kapodistria have the right to Swiss citizenship and may also obtain a passport." Every time Francesca has to tell this part of the story she has to roll her eyes in capitulation at the foolishness of the Swiss back then. It's always the same game between the two of them that they enjoy with each retelling.

"That is amazing!" Marlène exclaims in disbelief.

Spiro giggles like a schoolgirl.

"And get this, it gets even better," he teases Francesca as he bursts out into uncontrollable laughter.

"The document states, amongst other things, that when a descendant enters Switzerland, all the church bells are supposed to ring! Can you imagine such idiocy! And the funny thing is that a few years back the impossible happened as Spiro travelled back to Switzerland with George and me in late October. We had just driven through the Gotthard Tunnel, and you won't believe it but the church bells started to ring! But never fear, they were only sounding out the hour, so nothing strange or supernatural has anything to do with it!"

Spiro just chuckles as he continues to tell how he purchased a map of Geneva when George stopped at a filling station for some petrol right after passing through the border, and how, after a short while, he was actually able to find a street named *Rue de Ioannis Kapodistria* on the map. For hours during the drive he pestered them until they finally capitulated and agreed to search for the street with him the following day.

"Yes, yes, I know all of this is true. But then your street turned out to be no longer than a rubbish bin!" Francesca interrupts sarcastically.

Amidst laughter and teasing the foursome finally stand and say goodbye with a *'kali nikhta.'* As Spiro steps into the car, he yells after them, "And it is a proper street, at least three blocks long!"

Giggling, the girlfriends watch as he gives a thumbs-up sign out the window and quickly drives away into the dark night. As if he were afraid that Francesca could still have the final word!

11

*O*nce again Francesca emerges from a restless and dreamless night. She had strongly hoped that during the week with her friend the powerful energy, which they generate when they are together, would go to work at night as well as when she was asleep. Her deepest desire is to be close to her husband, at least in her dreams. But even this wish was not granted. Why doesn't he reveal himself to her? Marlène can see him. She is connected to him in a very special way. Francesca doesn't think it's fair at all. But there's nothing she can do about it, so she has to let it go, even though she desperately wishes it were possible.

Depressed, she rises, and wearing only George's old, faded t-shirt steps out onto her balcony. She doesn't feel the crisp, early morning air. She doesn't see how, slowly, a thin, light strip of red appears above the Albanian mountains; doesn't notice the white wisps of fog spreading through the cypress and olive trees announcing the slow advance of autumn. She neither hears nor takes note of the dormice scampering on the roof with abandon.

Naturally, Francesca is glad that every now and then, with a little help from Marlène, she is able to be close to her husband. She gives a deep sigh, *but it's not the same having to converse and convey feelings through a third person.*

She realizes how ungrateful this sounds and how she should be happy that, thanks to her *petite fée*, she has the certainty George is doing well in the place where he now exists. She should pay more attention to the tangible evidence he sends her each day, which is supposed to give her courage and show her that he is always by her side and doing his best to stand by her and support her as she goes about her daily life.

It's hard to believe how Marlène always seems to find the right words and arguments and can envelop her friend, who is so often in despair, with her warm empathy. In such magical moments, Francesca strongly believes she has taken in and understood everything with her heart. Unfortunately, it happens quite often that when the time comes to recollect those talks, the words and sentences seem to dissipate like smoke. Where did all the answers go? The explanations, statements and interpretations? What remains are the loving, comforting words of her *fée*. All the rest is gone!

But she is thankful for her life. She knows not to take such an empathetic friend for granted, a soul mate to have at her side, who has never given up on her and who has led her back into life with great love and patience.

Dejected, Francesca heads to the bathroom and splashes water on her flushed face. Because she hasn't heard noise coming from downstairs yet, she retrieves her laptop from the office to read her emails. *What? No Internet?* She tries to call the phone company and stares at the dead receiver. *Nothing, not a sound. Blast it, what's wrong now?*

She tries her luck with her mobile. Calmly, a friendly official at the telephone company explains to her in coherent English that repairmen had been sent out yesterday afternoon to inspect all the old lines. She should look to see if a rodent has unfortunately damaged a line.

What on earth does Francesca know about telephone lines? Nothing, except they are necessary for making telephone calls and supposed to function all the time. A quick look at her watch tells her it's far too early to call Spirouli and ask him for help.

In order not to wake Marlène, she sneaks downstairs and carefully opens the front door. Following the line with her eyes, Francesca tracks how it runs from one telephone pole to the next across the entire property until, to her great dismay, she spots the severed end of the cable lying on the ground. *How could this happen? What did those idiots inspect? Not only did they come onto my property uninvited, but now they've also severed the line because I'm sure that rodents haven't gnawed through it!*

Indignant, Francesca stomps back to the house, where in the meantime Marlène has already set the breakfast table.

"Where did you come from? I thought you were still sleeping," she asks surprised and looks at her friend's grumpy face. In agitation, Francesca recounts the newly discovered annoyance and how the telephone company wants to place the blame on pesky rodents. She's too irritated to enjoy breakfast this morning and jumps up from her chair apologizing for her surliness and finally goes to ring Spiro. He is a treasure and calms down his agitated friend offering his help right away. As she shares that she will have to meet Spiro in town, Marlène welcomes the change and immediately offers to accompany her.

Spiro is already waving to them impatiently as they arrive at the car park on the esplanade. Marlène quickly says goodbye to them and they promise to ring her later on so they can meet up for a bite to eat.

While Marlène is strolling through the narrow, picturesque alleys admiring the countless small shops and charming cafes, Spiro and Francesca are running about like crazed chickens from one office to the next trying to fix the phone line mess somehow. The whole ordeal ends in a typical Greek back and forth, where, ultimately, nobody knows anything, and after two hours they are right back where they started.

Unlike Francesca, who is soon overwhelmed by all the bureaucracy and whose tolerance has reached its limit, Spiro, in his stoic way, is already used to situations such as these and does not get flustered. If anything, he's annoyed by the constant whining and wants to end this debacle by himself. With a firm goodbye he dismisses Francesca, who wants to give her friend moral support and assist him as he wades through the infernal paperwork. But Spiro shakes his head resolutely and with an encouraging smile promises her that everything will be back in order by the next morning, "And don't forget, the party at Vanessa and Dino's is at 3p.m," he admonishes, before he finally heads off.

Francesca is still feeling guilty about Spiro when, a short while later, she meets up with her friend at an elegant bistro in *Platia Agios Spyridon* for a small bite to eat. Marlène's ears are ringing as she is subjected to Francesca's lamenting and retelling of the ordeal over and over again while she tries in vain to enjoy the delectable beef carpaccio in front of her. The hothead, on the other hand, can't eat a single bite. Her stomach is one giant knot, which she tries to loosen with a glass of chardonnay.

Marlène has her own idea of how to combat Francesca's frazzled nerves and decides to take her on a very special shopping excursion. After paying the cheque, she takes her hand determinedly dragging her balking friend from one shop to the next hoping Francesca will find an elegant, fashionable and colourful bikini. But she finds something she doesn't like about each one she looks at. Marlène's efforts to find something suitable are beginning to look futile. With a despondent look at her reflection, Francesca views the pitiful result and tries to suck in her stomach. This does not improve the look even with the most ambitious efforts. How could this have happened? How is it possible that in the course of a few years her body could change in such an unflattering way without her knowledge?

But Marlène remains stubborn. She doesn't want to see her friend running around in that impossible black swimsuit any longer, so she won't give up so quickly. After more than an hour of sobering and hopeless dressing and undressing, Francesca has finally had it. Marlène can't believe that not a single flattering two-piece can be found for her friend. After hunting through most of the boutiques in Corfu and turning them upside down, she insists on trying one final endeavour.

Reluctantly Francesca follows her dear tormentor into the next shop where together they select a few appealing styles. Again, she finds herself in a changing room surrounded by a mountain of bikinis and chooses a red one to try on first. Only then does she notice that the room has mirrors on all sides, and she stares stunned at her reflection, which taunts her from all sides screaming out the naked truth and forcing her to confront each and every unbecoming inch of her body.

"Argh...that's it...I've had it...I'll never survive this... this can't be me!" Marlène hears her wail.

"What's wrong, come on, show me...it can't be that bad." And quick as a flash she slips into her friend's changing room.

"What are you in such a stew about, it looks great."

"Are you daft or something. Don't you have eyes in your head? The straps are digging in everywhere and making little fat rolls swell up where there never used to be any. And just take a look at my back. Instead of two muscles on both sides of it, I now have two floppy things that look like bananas. My back already looks like my mother's, and she's thirty years older than me!"

Now Francesca has really had it and throws everything in a heap. She's had enough of this horrid chamber of truth. Completely disappointed and demoralised for not being able to find something as simple as a bikini, she trots along next to Marlène, who tries everything to cheer her friend up again.

While walking they come to the shop selling crystals, which they know from the previous year. They cheerfully greet the same distinguished gentleman as he recognizes the two women. While Marlène browses through the considerable assortment of fossils and minerals searching for a gift for her son, a very beautiful lapis-lazuli ring with a large white pearl catches Francesca's eye. Contrary to the bikini-disaster, this fits her like a glove and right away stays on her finger. She's very happy about the ring with its unpolished blue stone, and it helps compensate for her injured self-confidence.

Marlène has also found something – a unique fossil for her son, Maël. But now they have to hurry so that they are not the last ones to arrive at Vanessa's.

Gouvia is a very touristy village and is located in a small cove on the eastern coast. A typical pink Corfiot house which was built by Spiro and Dino's grandmother, Maria Dessila, for her five grandchildren, lies directly by the sea with a gorgeous view of the Kommeno peninsula across from it. Below the house, a short narrow bay leads to a small island where the romantic chapel, *Ipapanti,* stands. North of the property lie the ruins of the Venetian harbour that date back to the early 1800's, and a little farther south, lies the impressive marina with its hundreds of white sailboats glinting in the sun. Before Francesca and George built their house in Poulades, they had also lived there in one of the flats. Back then everyone simply called the place the *Kibbutz*, or *Pink House*. Steadfast friendships developed here that had grown even stronger with the passing years.

As the girlfriends step out of the car, they can already hear music and laughter coming from the house. Dino and Vanessa have taken great care and decorated the tables festively. The party is well underway. Lights have also been strung up between the trees for later on. Both are greeted exuberantly from all sides. Despina is already there, waving at them cheerfully. Francesca spots Eileen and her husband, Alan, close to the barbecue where they are helping Dino prepare large platters of meat.

Vanessa takes Marlène by the arm and leads her to her guests of honour, Bob and Brenda, her parents. Born charmer that he is, Vanessa's father's eyes almost pop out of his head when he sees Francesca's dainty and fashionably dressed friend, "Mademoiselle, I am dazzled by your beauty," he stammers and gives her a mischievous wink. Vanessa's mother has to laugh as she gives a quite astonished Marlène a heartfelt greeting.

Although Francesca has spent many unforgettable moments in the pink house, she is always impressed anew with the beautiful view and picturesque surroundings where, like now in the afternoon, individual sailboats keep on puttering slowly into the marina.

An excitedly chattering group of people cluster around the long table heavily laden with appetising salads, grilled hamburgers, sausages and large amounts of souvlakia with pita and tzatziki. Everyone is focused on getting a small sample of all the delectable food on their plates. The mood is festive and all are glad to be together once again. "Only Spirouli is still missing!" Francesca remarks, and immediately feels guilty.

Meanwhile it has turned into late afternoon and is still very warm outside. Marlène soon feels out of place among all the high-spirited guests, most of whom are strangers to her. Even though she knows it would be rude to leave the party so early, she would much rather go to the beach in Barbati but would not like to disappoint Vanessa.

Francesca, on the other hand, would like to celebrate a little longer, but doesn't want her little spoilsport to head out alone either. Discreetly, in order not to bother the other guests at the party, they say goodbye only to Vanessa. She, however, understands only too well how Marlène is feeling, and, after a big hug, sends them both on their way. She didn't mind going for a refreshing swim either.

Only a handful of people are enjoying the last hours of the evening, as the two women glide into the calm water and start to swim leisurely. A young woman with very short black hair, a pierced nose and eyebrows sits by the shore, arms encircling her drawn up legs, and observes the sea with a dreamy expression. A middle-aged, deeply tanned man is reading a book, another, lies peacefully, eyes closed, on a light blue air mattress. The sky slowly changes colour and the atmosphere softens. A fairy tale mood envelops the beach of Barbati.

Later, after Francesca and Marlène have tired themselves out swimming, they stroll along the shore to dry off searching for unusual stones. At one point a stone catches her interest and Francesca bends down to examine it. Shocked, she examines the stone from all sides then shows it to her friend, "Do you also see what I see?" Marlène can only nod her head then looks at her earnestly.

"It's really weird, I've never seen anything like this before!" Francesca continues breathlessly, "How on earth can you stay so calm?" Confused, she holds out the stone, which is about the size of an egg and has the likeness of an evil, grinning devil.

Calmly Marlène explains to her puzzled friend, "If you study any stone carefully, you can always detect something unusual. It doesn't matter how large it is. In your case, it's reflecting the illness that tore George away from you quite suddenly."

Francesca continues to examine the curious rock, unsure if she should keep it or if she had better toss it away. All at once she feels very uneasy. But then she resolutely drops the stone into her beach bag where it disappears to the bottom.

Marlène also collects a stone and turns it around slowly from one side to the other. "Take a look," she says and hands it to Francesca.

"What do you see in this stone? And don't say "nothing", just take a close look."

At first, she really doesn't notice anything unusual. It is simply a stone like any other. But after turning it over in her hand and examining it a few times from all sides, with a lot of imagination she can detect the likeness of a dog. As she rotates it more slowly she then perceives a face. Soon it becomes a fun game, when suddenly she lets out a small cry.

"I can't believe it. Now I'm seeing the devil again."

Astonished, Marlène smiles. She is surprised at how swiftly her friend has caught on to this exercise.

With irritation, Francesca hurls the stone back into the sea and sits down on one of the sun-warmed rocks. Leisurely, she searches for other specimens in order to practice this new activity.

"Go ahead and choose two stones that you like and bring them along. Then, at home, I'll show and explain to you how to recognize images in rocks, and how you can use them to receive answers to your questions," Marlène encourages.

Francesca is looking forward to learning something new–and probably exciting–from her *petite fée* and promises to find two exceptionally beautiful examples for the evening. "Go and wrap the pareo around your shoulders," she remarks in concern, "you're getting quite red from the sun."

Marlène unwraps the colourful fabric from her hips and places it around her shoulders. With a smile, she raises her hand in salutation and continues her stroll by herself along the shore, pausing every now and then to examine the occasional stone.

The sun has disappeared and dusk has long set in. The devil's face is lying in the car between them staring at Francesca maliciously. It makes her feel somewhat uncomfortable. Several times during their game of finding stones she had stumbled upon rocks that bore the likeness of the devil, which made her feel very unsettled. Before she turns onto her gravel drive, she stops the car abruptly at an old rock wall alongside the road, flings open the car door and quickly grabs the devil stone depositing it in a small hollow in between the masonry. "Are you feeling better now?" Marlène says, amused.

It is a magnificent, mild evening. The exterior lights cast a bright light illuminating the surroundings. After showering and changing into something comfortable they both sit with a cup of tea in *Mumsies Corner* – a cosy outdoor section sheltered under a covered pergola that Francesca's mother had always loved when she had still been able to visit her daughter. Marlène has armed herself with writing material and looks at Francesca invitingly.

"So, go ahead and take one of the stones you chose on your beach walk today and examine it carefully. Ask it a question that's close to your heart. You will receive an answer through the shapes and images in the rock."

Curious to see what is about to happen, Francesca places one of the stones in her hand and asks, "Devil, what do you want from me? Why am I seeing you everywhere all of a sudden?"

Shortly thereafter, Francesca points to the stone and whispers in a stricken voice, "I can see a coffin lid with a cross on top."

"Answer only with a single word. What does it look like, what does it mean to you, what do you feel?" Marlène asks.

"Death," she replies in an empty voice, "And right next to it, I can see a small profile of a devil with horns."

"And what are you feeling?"

"Injustice, anger!"

Francesca turns the stone around and tries to see something else.

"Right here, look...I see a man, slightly bent with his arm outstretched wielding a hammer as if he is going to use it."

"And what are you feeling?"

"He is going to use it to smash and destroy us?"

Marlène encourages Francesca to continue. She is very impressed at the ease with which her friend perceives forms and images in the stone.

In a strained voice Francesca continues. "This image here looks like an otter. It's kind of comical."

"And what do you notice about it?"

She ponders this for a moment and then replies, "Perhaps, concern?"

"Why is the otter concerned?"

"Because he has to protect his family."

"Okay. Now, we just have to formulate a reasonable sentence from all the prompts I've written down," Marlène explains eagerly as she deftly jots on a piece of paper:

"Death is unjust; it has destroyed our lives. I could not protect George from its power. Does that answer your question?" Mute, and with eyes brimming with tears Francesca can only give a slight nod of the head.

They both retreat into deep silence until Marlène urges her friend to retrieve the other stone. She wants to try out a different approach, a more direct one based on intuition.

Francesca tightly grasps the second stone and says out loud, "From this one I would like to know what my further life has in store for me?"

She rotates the stone in her hand for several minutes with concentration, examining it from all sides before she states, "I can see an angel with long hair and wings. Will it protect me from all that I fear in life?"

"It's George. He's already sent you so much evidence and has shown you that he is always there by your side," Marlène explains, "Go on, continue!"

"I see a woman, in a long dress with long hair and an egg! Next to her someone is sitting in a round circle with their head bent and knees drawn into their chest," Francesca replies, her cheeks flushed with excitement.

Marlène looks at her friend in admiration.

"It's the two of us, a fairy helping a foetus – a new born – to grow a little bit more each day."

She takes the stone from Francesca's hand and holds it for a moment in deep concentration. After the stone has spoken to her she places it back on the table and begins to write:

Knowledge and clarity through the quill. The story will take place in Greece. A female warrior, who moves forward with strength, suppleness and elegance.

Francesca peers over her shoulder glancing at the page, "I don't quite follow you, or should I say, I don't get it! Please explain this to me."

"The story that takes place in Greece will be told through writing. You are a fighter – so, a warrior – hiding behind armour, but moving forward day after day with dignity and strength. The suppleness represents your openness towards new ideas, even the most unconventional ones."

"The most beautiful proof though," Marlène continues, "is that you are following me into this other awareness and are understanding my arcane thought processes that, up until now, were completely unknown to you."

She looks at Francesca ponderingly, then says in a raw voice, "When we are together, everything brightens. You are the light that illuminates my path, and I am the staff that supports you as you make your way through this world."

Full of emotion, they both embrace. What a mind-blowing experience...

12

*m*arlène is awakened by the crowing of the rooster who begins his day at 5 a.m. It would be unthinkable in Switzerland, but here on Corfu one doesn't need an alarm clock. Between barking dogs and the incessant "cock-a-doodle-do" of the rooster, there is no way a person can keep dreaming and sleep away the day. Lying stretched out on the bed, she dozes for a little while longer, on the day that Francesca will celebrate her 60th birthday.

Her friend had believed she would grow old at George's side. But now she must learn to forgive life for this awful blow of fate that tore him away from her far too soon. *Forgive life?* She muses. *Strictly speaking, life never makes promises. We may imagine that somehow life owes us something, but in reality, every person paints their own picture of how they envision their future, with all of its expectations, values, emotions and dreams.*

And what does forgiveness really mean? It stems from feelings of guilt. One believes it is necessary to forgive the guilty party. Who do we think we are to believe that we are in a position to judge the actions and thoughts of another? There is nothing to forgive, if no one has been judged. It is only through someone else's actions that we become aware of the things we can change in ourselves.

If I view life as it is, like a film that plays out before my eyes. If I stop being a performer and become the audience, then I can better understand that there is a difference between acquiescing to events that take place and accepting them, no matter what they are. What I consider to be good or bad is only my way of looking at it, not what it really is. And if I am able to distance myself, gain a little more perspective, just BE...that is what my innermost self knows, what it has always known, what it has constantly known, what has always been...

Francesca is awakened by the cheerful chirping of birds and listens to them with her eyes closed. *My own small, private early morning birthday concert, just for me, how wonderful...but again, it's a birthday without George. No surprise hidden under the pillow. No "Happy Birthday" whispered into my ear before breakfast is served in bed...stop it, right now! You're only hurting yourself.* She feels her eyes start to fill with tears and the pressure increasing in her heart. With a determined swipe, she dries her eyes.

For a long while Francesca stands motionless in the shower, as the heavy jet of water washes away the last of her dismal thoughts until her mind is empty. It's her birthday, and not one dark thought is allowed to cloud this day. Today she wants only to be happy and treat herself to good things.

Wrapped in a large, fluffy towel, she opens the closet and takes out a sizeable parcel wrapped in colourful paper. Doris, her younger sister by three years, insisted that she bring along this present in her suitcase, so she would have a gift from home on her birthday. Up until this point she has been able to contain her curiosity and leave it in her closet. But now her fingers are itching and she would really like to tear the parcel open right away. But she controls herself. She quickly throws on a blue and white striped sleeveless dress, grabs the parcel and runs down the stairs in joyful anticipation wanting to open it in a more dignified manner in the company of her *petite fée*.

Meanwhile, Marlène has found an ABBA cd and is singing along softly to the unforgettable song, *Mamma Mia* while she sets the table on the terrace with care, decorating it with a vase of freshly picked flowers that she selected from the garden that morning.

She lovingly embraces the birthday girl and says in a celebratory voice, "I wish you the most wonderful birthday, for the best friend in the whole world, full of magic and love. May all your plans, expectations and dreams come true."

"Thank you, *ma petite fée*, for your well-meant wishes. However, I'd be happy if one or the other of my wishes would come true," Francesca replies with sincerity and smiles.

Even the weather is in a holiday mood. The sun is shining down from a cloudless sky warming both their hearts with its rays. Francesca has supressed all her dismal thoughts from that morning and is simply looking forward to her day.

Much to Marlène's delight, for she has been watching her friend fidget for quite a while now, Francesca becomes even more restless, and starts to slide back and forth on her seat full of tension and curiosity. The entire time her eyes remain fixed on the parcel. She can't wait to see what her sister has come up with this year for her birthday present and just wants to rip off the paper.

"Hey, stop, not so fast," Marlène cries out, and just in time manages to grab her arm. "You have to guess what's inside, only then is it fun. I do this with my sisters all the time. First you have to feel the parcel on all sides or shake it gently. Perhaps a sound might reveal what's inside."

Doris has often delighted her with something very special. For her 50th birthday, she surprised her sister with an authentic white Carousel horse made of wood with a mane of real horse's hair, which she transported by car all the way to Corfu where it now proudly stands in the entryway of her villa. This years' present will definitely be something quite unique as well.

"Perhaps she found an antique candelabra at some rummage sale or purchased a silver butter dish." Francesca replies as she carefully shakes the parcel, but is unable to detect a sound.

"There's no way...it's not very heavy, so it can't be a candelabra."

"You're right, and that wouldn't be unique," Francesca muses.

"Perhaps an antique make-up case?"

"Well really, you don't seem to have a very active imagination. What would I do with it? Anyway, the parcel is far too large."

"You're right. It doesn't have to be something antique. Perhaps it's a bikini?" Marlène says with a cheeky grin.

"I give up. I don't have the foggiest idea of what could be inside."

Giving it one more shake, Francesca, who is too impatient to discover its contents, rips the paper off her sister's mysterious parcel!

One would need to film the expressions on the two friends' faces. They both stare perplexed at a pink, 3-tiered imitation birthday cake, about 25cm high topped with four decorative candles. The cake is surrounding by large, vivid letters that spell out the words *Happy Birthday.* The entire cake is decorated with fake white icing and colourful flowers.

Gingerly, Francesca takes the cake, which has a very strange feel to it due to the soft, pliant material. By accident, she touches a small lever that sets the cake in motion. While the friends gaze in astonishment, the cake starts to rhythmically move to the music as it sings the *Happy Birthday* song.

Simultaneously they burst out laughing. Never before have they seen something so crazy and outlandish.

"That's so typical of my sister. She's always up for some kind of nonsense." Over and over they have to laugh while they watch the cake sing and dance.

Finally, Marlène stands up to take the dishes into the kitchen. "Come on, let's not lose any more time and head over to Barbati for the day."

"You're right because we have to be back by 5 p.m. for my small birthday gathering. But aside from looking pretty, we don't have to do anything. Do you remember Hillary, my friend, who is also a chef? He has offered to organize and take care of all the work."

If Francesca had her way, she would have preferred to spend her very special day quietly, without all the hustle and bustle or the need to DO anything. But today is her 60th birthday. She would like to celebrate and do something nice for all her friends who have stood by and supported her. It is the first birthday since the death of her husband where she has found the courage to celebrate. In addition, Hillary has promised to take care of everything and put together an unforgettable buffet. Therefore, they are both as free as can be for almost an entire day.

On the way to the beach, they pass by the spot where Francesca had placed the devil's head the prior day, and she suddenly decides to stop. "I'm sorry, but I can't stop thinking about that stupid head. I'm going back there, and if it's still there then I'm taking it with me."

Marlène can only laugh at her friend's irrational actions. And, true to her word, a few minutes later she is once again holding the stone that has caused her so much consternation. Francesca can't understand why she's doing this to herself because, just like on the previous day, she is overcome by the same, eerie feeling. She will have to dwell on this later. Now, though, they are going to head to the beach to go swimming.

On the glorious, warm September day more people and children than usual are romping about on the beach; proud parents, who watch as their children roughhouse in the water; grandparents avidly filming their *amazing* grandchildren with newly purchased cameras. A group of pretty young girls stand together with their heads in a huddle. Some young men are playing ball close by trying to get the girls' attention through deft and agile manoeuvres. Others are attached to their mobile phones or paging through a fashion magazine drinking *café frappe* – a favourite summertime drink in Greece. In order to tan quicker, new arrivals continue to bake in the glaring sun regardless of the fact that they are starting to burn. Rhythmic music flows from the beach bar's speakers.

After a refreshing swim—Francesca still wearing her dowdy black swimsuit—they both lie side by side and gaze at the clouds that slowly float across the sky. They try to outdo each other by identifying the most imaginative and fantastical shapes. But despite this relaxed atmosphere, Francesca slowly starts to get restless. At first haltingly, but then increasingly, she starts to feel a faint hammering in her head until it finally forms coherent, solid words. *"I'm waiting in the bag, I'm waiting in the bag..."*

Aggravated with herself, she retrieves the stone shaped like a devil's head from her bag and once again examines it closely from all sides. She knows if she doesn't, she'll never be at peace with herself. On the one hand, she is fascinated to have found such a stone in the first place. On the other hand, it sends a shiver down her spine when she holds it. She is also overcome by an eerie sensation, as if a black cloud were trying to envelop her.

For a while now Marlène has been studying her friend, reading the emotions that play across her face like an open book.

"If this stone is causing you so much discomfort, why don't you just throw it into the sea?"

Francesca shakes off her unease and replies astounded, "But it's only a stone that happens to be in the shape of the devil...I don't understand how it can make me feel this way. It's quite extreme, don't you think?"

But then she stands up decidedly and hurls the stone as far as she can into the sea, where it will hopefully remain hidden somewhere forever, in between the sea grass. *What does that mean, forever? It has already lain where I found it for such a long time. What does it care, if it has to wait thousands of years until perhaps someone, or something else, stumbles upon it in surprise? It has proven it's resilience.*

Although she is relieved to have rid herself of the mysterious head, a faint feeling of regret continues to trouble her. Despite everything, the stone was still something very special.

Today, Francesca is in a playful mood. She applies her coral-toned lipstick with care. She wraps her vibrant pareo around her hips with some intricate twists. She dons a fashionable sun hat and glasses before heading over again with Marlène to their favourite beach bar taking a seat at a charmingly set table.

Marlène, who has adeptly wrapped a scarf matching her bikini around her hips and braided her hair into a long plait, surprises her friend with a delicious menu. Raw tuna fillet, pastry filled with giant prawns, a delectable salad paired with an excellent, chilled white wine and sparkling water. For herself, she orders giant prawns with green asparagus and broad noodles. For dessert, the friendly waiter brings a small chocolate cake with a single lit candle in the middle. Cheerfully, Marlène sings "Happy Birthday" while she looks at her friend's joyful face.

"What a truly nice surprise, thank you *ma petite fée,*" Francesca replies, moved.

Marlène hopes she can help relieve that feeling of loneliness, which has been weighing on her friend's shoulders, and she can re-light the small fire in her eyes that was extinguished when George died. To have a nice meal together, to be by her side, to be there for her and strengthen their friendship is the present she would like to give her today, on her birthday.

Marlène is unable to fill the void that opened after George's passing. But she tries to make Francesca aware of the countless opportunities that life has to offer, so she can find joy as she continues on her path, so she can share the immense love which she is not always aware of, which burns within her heart. No one can hope for a better friend

Nonetheless, the way Francesca sees it time is relative. One rarely sees her glancing at her wristwatch, and she is always astonished and caught off guard when someone confronts her about how quickly time has passed by. One could say that time is no longer important to her. She simply lives in the moment, in the here and now, not caring in the least about what might happen later.

This is a completely foreign concept for Marlène, who has mapped out her life like a checklist, where she can daily plan and cross off all the things she wants to accomplish. Impatiently, she jumps from one activity to the next, already looking forward to what will happen in the following hours. During her holiday week with Francesca, she experiences, as she does every year, a different rhythm to daily life; living in the moment, embracing the opportunities that arise without a lot of organisation. This is a completely new world for her, but a welcome one.

As they turn into the drive of Francesca's property, the car from the OTE – the telephone company – is just leaving. Full of hope, Francesca exits the car. Two friendly young workers explain something to her in Greek, constantly repeating the same words: '*Endaxi, olla endaxi!*' As she waves to the disappearing men, and in response to Marlène's unspoken question, she replies laughing, "Okay, it means everything is okay!"

And indeed, as she holds the phone receiver in her hand a short while later the phone is making its usual sounds. In her mind, she sends Spiro a big "thank you" and immediately rings her mother.

A loud call comes from outside as Hillary and his girlfriend Dawn, heavily laden with bags and a plastic storage container, stumble in through the open front door. They are met with cheerful greetings. After everything has been unloaded in the kitchen and stored in the refrigerator, Hillary presses a glass of champagne into everyone's hand, and they happily propose a toast in honour of Francesca's birthday.

"Come on, come on, it's high time you got lost and take a shower, then make yourselves pretty. We still have quite a few things to prepare in the kitchen so that everything is ready for the party. So, get a move on…" Hillary commands, and sternly shoos Marlène and Francesca out of the kitchen.

Familiar rhythms await the first guests, who trickle in around 6 p.m. with a big "Hello, Hello". Meanwhile, Hillary and his girlfriend are in the kitchen preparing an exquisite buffet with great concentration, their faces reddened from the effort. They have already distributed a few platters of tasty hors d'oeuvres around the terrace on small tables with flower arrangements.

A sun-tanned, beaming Francesca receives her friends with a deep embrace wearing a silk summer dress with a bird and flower print and white sandals on her feet, embellished with Swarovski crystals.

Marlène stands by her side—like a beautiful butterfly— with her long blond hair wearing a designer dress made entirely of sequins in a striking shade of turquoise that emphasises her shining blue eyes. Though nobody knows just how much elbow grease it took her friend to help wrestle this tight, somewhat heavy, dress over her head.

Even though Francesca is relaxed and enjoying herself this evening, there is still a small drawback. *George should really be here by my side greeting our friends. I wonder if they notice this as well? Do they feel the same way?*

Marlène is doing her best to fill the empty place by Francesca's side. Still, each and every person is thinking of George, their friend, who should have been here tonight as well and whom everyone is painfully missing. But after the first glass of champagne the mood lifts, and everyone wants to help the party become a great success.

Before long, everyone is in a celebratory mood. The birthday girl is overjoyed when she finally discovers Despina and Spiro, who are among the last of her guests to arrive, gently guiding their 90-year-old aunt, Marie, as they make their way slowly towards the terrace to join the others. After a heartfelt greeting and congratulations, full of gratitude, she tells Spiro that the telephone line was repaired that day. He beams and gives her a cheerful wink, "All you need is a little bit of patience."

Francesca laughs, "Yeah, yeah, you mean spending a lot of time and using all of your charm to chat with the pretty young ladies in the offices." She gives Spiro's beard a teasing tug. Then she claps her hands and announces in a loud voice, "My dear friends, the buffet is open!"

Before they storm to the lavish buffet, each takes a plate and with many "Oohs", and "Ahhs", walks around the table to admire the delectable selection that Hillary and Dawn have displayed like a work of art.

The two hobby chefs have outdone themselves today and are praised from all sides for their efforts.

In the meantime, it has grown dark outside. Millions of stars shimmer majestically in the night sky with an incredible intensity. The evening is sublime and still pleasantly warm for that time of the year. While everyone is filling their plates with delicacies Francesca, with Marlène and Despina's help, walks around the terrace lighting all the candles and lanterns.

Francesca looks at the beautiful scene before her and feels content. Enveloped in the warm light of the many candles and lanterns, her friends sit at various tables that have been placed around the terrace conversing animatedly. Cheerful laughter fills the night. Meanwhile, Francesca has also filled her plate with some of the culinary delights and goes over to a small table underneath a palm tree where, at that moment, Aunt Marie is sitting by herself. The old lady takes Francesca's hand, and her kindly eyes look at her with understanding.

"How are you feeling, darling? You must miss George more than usual today. How often have I sat here looking at the beautiful picture the two of you made and listening to your lively conversations. I miss his cheerful, warm laugh."

Francesca can only give a silent nod, fearful that she might burst into tears. Just at the right time, an exuberant trio approaches them interrupting the sombre mood. Francesca replenishes their glasses with wine, Eileen places a platter full of delicious titbits for everyone on the small table and Despina brings a bowl of bite-sized fruits and grapes. They all notice that their dear friend is sad and sit next to her and Marie on the ground or on empty chairs. Unprompted, they start to tell funny anecdotes of earlier times; tales of the many parties that had been celebrated at the villa, and of course, tales of George. They are all thinking of him. For them, he will always be present here at the villa.

The circle of friends gathered around Marie keeps increasing. Marlène seizes a spot next to Francesca and listens in fascination to the stories. The men suddenly notice that politics are their only companions and that most of the women have gone to sit with Francesca and Marie. So, they all grab a chair and join the women under the palm tree.

What a singularly beautiful evening, with all the friends sitting together companionably conversing in quiet tones, listening to Leonard Cohen while they gaze up at the night sky where millions of stars shine down upon Francesca wishing her a final "Happy Birthday". Everyone can feel the energy and magic of this extraordinary moment. Francesca looks up to the starry sky, moved, and whispers, "Thank you."

13

*G*roggy with sleep, Francesca opens her eyes and immediately notices by the light filtering in, that it must still be very early in the morning. Since the balcony doors remain wide open most of the time during the night, she is rewarded this morning with a magnificent sunrise. From her bed, she observes how the Albanian mountains beyond the sea slowly change colour, darkening from a pale light blue to varying shades of purple. The sky too has taken on the same shades of blue, almost blending in with the mountains.

She notices with fascination how suddenly, seemingly out of nowhere, two elongated white clouds develop and glide along, one floating closely on top of the other. *That could be the two of us right now, floating in the sky.* Very slowly, as if they do not want to be torn apart, the clouds take on the shape of a cat's head, which immediately reminds her of her little cat, Squeaky. In astonishment, she continues to follow the clouds as they continually gather into new formations, until the perfectly formed head of a man appears in the sky. Her heart racing, she stares at the sky where the now classic profile of her husband appears to be looking down at her. The same high forehead, the proud nose, the slightly jutting, strong chin and the open mouth as if he wanted to say something to her. Moved by this morning present, she remains in bed lying there quietly.

Suddenly, the sun pierces a path through the clouds and Francesca can feel the way its warming rays make their way deep into her heart. The moment is indescribably beautiful. She is thoroughly convinced that her husband has sent down this special morning greeting. *I have never experienced anything as beautiful, or am I perhaps more sensitive and receptive today than I usually am?*

She slips on a pair of lightweight slippers, grabs a cardigan, which she pulls on over her t-shirt and hurries out onto the balcony. Still overwhelmed from what she has just experienced, she lets her gaze drift across the area noting that a thin, wispy fog has developed in between the cypress trees. She smiles as she thinks about how autumn has secretly crept in this year. The only thing she has noticed is that the warm, sun-filled days have slowly become shorter and that at 8 p.m. it is already dark outside.

By now the birds are twittering in mad competition. The bees are buzzing, and one can even hear the crickets chirping. Without any particular reason, a dog lets out a bark or two before lying back down to sleep in its sheltered spot. In the distance, a donkey is braying loudly hoping to gain attention, so that soon someone will bring it fresh water. One could think it was a warm summer morning, not an early autumn day in September. Marlène has really had luck with the weather.

It is already quite warm. Both of them have light t-shirts on. Marlène is wearing a frayed sun hat. These past few days, her skin has taken on a golden-brown shimmer, Francesca's is a glowing dark brown. She is wearing a baseball cap for protection from the sun. The past few days have worked wonders. Now, her melancholic eyes light up every once in a while, and her hearty laugh can be heard more often.

While Marlène clears the breakfast table, Francesca stretches out her legs and closes her eyes, *I feel different these past few months since I've discovered the value of writing things down. I feel more alive and I have more energy. I can't wait to see what my petite fée thinks of my manuscript, which, up until now I have kept from her.*

It is actually an uncomfortable memory when she thinks back to her panicky escape at the end of February, when she had stuffed whatever clothes she could find in a bag and driven off. She had no idea where she was going. She just needed to go. It was already early afternoon when she realized with shock that it was one of those damned leap years with its blasted 29 days. It was on this day, four years ago, when her existence had been irrevocably changed in a brutal manner. Her husband came home from work in the afternoon with yellow eyes, and two and a half months later, he had ceased to exist. In an inexplicable way, his life had simply been extinguished.

Because Francesca had left rather late, her escape ended a few hours later in Upper Valais, in a simple and friendly bed and breakfast. Sitting in her room in despair, she had an idea to write a short book for her sister on the adventures they shared on the way of St. James - a pilgrimage they went on following her husband's death. She started hesitantly, but her writing picked up, and soon she was completely immersed in the story. Step by step she mentally retraced her journey, experiencing the challenging route with her broken feet and wounded soul.

And then something happened to her. Something deep within herself began to resonate once more. For days, she sat alone in her room. She was a prisoner of the Way and wrote from morning till night. When Francesca drove back a few days later, excited and ready for action, she told Marlène on the phone—although somewhat ashamed—what she had been up to and what she had planned, and Marlène had not made fun of her, instead, she had found the idea fantastic and with great enthusiasm had encouraged her to continue.

After Marlène has tidied the kitchen, she returns and sits down with two glasses of freshly squeezed orange juice next to her friend, who is still lost in thought and staring off into the distance. Francesca suddenly mumbles an apology and runs back into the house with an enigmatic smile.

Two blue eyes follow her retreat in irritation. A short while later, Francesca falls back into her chair and hands her *petite fée* a manuscript.

"What's that?" She asks, astonished

"Do you remember when I suddenly took off at the end of last February without telling a soul?"

Marlène nods her head in silence.

"Back then, I confided in you that I wanted to write a short book for my sister as a way of saying "thank you" for going on the pilgrimage with me to Santiago. You are now the first one who gets to read it. These past few months I have been writing like crazy, nonstop for days. It would really please me if you read the draft and tell me what you think about it, and I want to hear your unbiased opinion. If you think what I have written is pure rubbish, then I'll have to make do with a photo album."

"Wow...I'm surprised at how much you've already written," Marlène replies as she quickly flips through the many pages, "Now, I also know why you went skiing with me so rarely. Amazing...but you know what, we're going to take the manuscript to the beach, and there I will read it in peace and quiet. What do you think about that?"

"That's fine by me. Let's go!" Naturally, Francesca has nothing against this suggestion. Moreover, she is looking forward to swimming as well. Just when they are getting ready to leave the villa, the phone starts to ring loudly. Despina wants to take a long, leisurely walk and visit them up on their hill in the late afternoon. They are both thrilled with the prospect and are looking forward to it. It will give them a chance to start celebrating Despina's upcoming birthday ahead of time, as Marlène will not be at her party in October.

Once again, the friends spend another beautiful afternoon at the seaside. They swim a lot and lie lazily in the sun.

At one point, while they are leisurely doing the backstroke next to each other, Marlène suddenly asks, "What's wrong? Am I really swimming so absurdly or what?"

Francesca shakes her head surprised, "Hmm...no, why do you ask?"

"George is swimming next to me and he's laughing his head off. I mean it, honestly. He can hardly contain himself!"

Francesca chuckles because she knows exactly why George is so amused, if he is really watching them swim. "Sometimes, when he and I would lark around while swimming and I would try to catch him, he would always escape by doing a swift backstroke, but only because I would start laughing every time he did it.

But that wasn't the only reason...he really was very fast. He had his own special style of backstroke, not like where you alternate, dipping one arm, after another into the water. Instead, he used both arms at the same time. It's just that when he did it, it looked so comical as though he was turbo-charged, the way he ploughed through the water with his long arms, as if they had turned into human propellers. So, he would always power away like a motorboat. I could never catch up with him; and if he is here, as you say he is, watching you paddling around like a lame duck...well no wonder he's laughing his head off." Then, Francesca tries to show her friend, George's special swimming style, which, due to her laughter, is a pitiful attempt.

In between swimming, Marlène continues to read the manuscript. Although Francesca is curious and can't wait to find out what her friend thinks of it, she leaves her alone to read and waits patiently. Finally, Marlène puts the papers aside and looks at her friend who is waiting expectantly.

"Okay, honestly...you have a very interesting way of writing. Really!"

"Uh oh, there's a "but" in there somewhere, isn't there?"

"You're right," Marlène smiles, "but I want to be really honest with you. What you have written so far is a very interesting and entertaining travelogue. Now you have to decide what you want. Should it only be a little book for your sister, or do you dare take it one step further and write a real book that can be read by anyone? I personally think it would be a pity if you didn't do it. Writing has provided you with an outlet that you enjoy; it makes you content and fills up your days. Now, after years, I have been able to detect a subtle change in you, just in the past few months. You are more balanced and have become calmer. And the constant melancholic look has disappeared as well. You laugh more often and you are happier. If you find the courage to publish this book, then, in my opinion, I would say that it lacks the most important thing, and that is *soul*. You *must* leap over your own shadow and fill those pages with your heart. You have to leave a little of yourself in it, only then will you hold something very special in your hands once you finish, not just an ordinary travelogue."

Marlène has barely mentioned the word "soul", and Francesca already knows what her friend is hinting at and trying to say. But to imagine doing this is inconceivable, simply impossible. The idea alone is terrifying. This would mean she would have to open heart and bare her soul, so that everyone could be a part of what she is feeling, what she's been through. That would be far too personal, too intimate for her. Francesca sighs deeply, and while she turns onto her stomach, she holds out the bottle of sun cream to her friend.

"Slather up my back, would you," she murmurs quietly.

Marlène knows exactly how she's feeling right now. But she has to get through this alone, decide for herself what she wants to do.

When they arrive back home in the afternoon, Despina is already sitting in one of the comfortable bamboo armchairs on the terrace, waiting patiently for her friends. Her normally pale complexion is flushed from her walk, which matches her face, giving her a fresh and healthy look. She is wearing sturdy walking shoes and in a small backpack there is an almost empty water bottle.

After a warm greeting, it is time for a cup of coffee and some gustatory pleasures. Francesca and Marlène had stopped by Emerald, a renowned bakery, on their way home and brought back an assortment of the finest flavours from their large selection of homemade ice cream. In this relaxed mood Marlène and Francesca wish their dear friend a, 'Happy Birthday' and present her with the gifts they had chosen together at Zurich airport. She is delighted and moved and expresses her thanks because she had really not expected this.

"But my birthday isn't until October," she remarks haltingly. Although Despina does find it wonderful to be able to open her presents now, she is a bit hesitant, *I hope they don't change their minds and I'll have to wait after all...*

Marlène asserts that they want to celebrate her birthday somewhat earlier because she will not be able to be there in the autumn. Despina looks at her presents with shining eyes. She is thrilled as she admires the Pandora bracelet that Marlène has helped fasten around her wrist. But suddenly she is silent. Completely withdrawn she sits between the two friends and no longer takes part in the lively conversation.

"What's wrong with you, you're so quiet all of a sudden?" Francesca asks with a concerned look.

"You know, this moment out here on the terrace with the two of you is very special to me. I can feel your closeness, your energy and your love. The fact that you have accepted me and allowed me to be a part of this, that is something that doesn't happen a lot.

Francesca feels that the time has arrived when she should leave Despina alone with Marlène for a little while. With a small apology, she gets up from the armchair and disappears into the house.

When she returns a little while later with a jug of water and fresh glasses, she immediately registers Despina's excited condition. But Marlène is already explaining to her, "Despina just told me that she can also see George, and he appears quite clearly. Because she has no experience with supernatural awareness, she was startled and a little scared. There's no one she can talk to regarding such things without being considered crazy."

Spontaneously, Francesca embraces her friend.

"You can't imagine how I envy you for this. The two of you can see George, only I can't...can you see him now as well? Is he here? How does he appear?"

"No, I can't see him right now. But when he appears to me, he's usually wearing khaki or beige coloured trousers, the ones he used to like wearing with a light blue shirt with the thin yellow and orange stripes."

Francesca signals them to follow her and together they climb the stairs to her bedroom. She goes to the closet and without hesitation takes out a shirt hanging on a hanger and shows it to Despina. In a tear-filled voice, she whispers, "Yes, that's it, it's the same shirt that I saw him wearing."

All three are stricken. They are all aware that at this moment they are experiencing a very special and magical moment together.

Despina doesn't stay long. The experience has shaken her too. For now, she just needs to be alone. In harmony, they walk up the path to the wrought iron gate at the entrance to Francesca's property. They would have loved to give Despina a quick ride home, but she waves them off laughingly, "Walking is a good way to meditate, and at the moment my head is full of new impressions that I have to process."

With a deep embrace, she says goodbye to her dear Swiss friends. Then one final wave, and Despina disappears behind an olive tree. Slowly, Marlène and Francesca walk back to the house arm in arm.

It is a sublime and mild evening. After a light meal, they both sit on the terrace reading a book and listening to music. Suddenly, Marlène raises her head and asks with a mischievous smile on her pretty face, "I would really like to experience a totally crazy moment every year when I visit you on Corfu, something I can remember with pleasure when I'm back home. What thrilling thing can you suggest? What can we still do that's exciting?"

Surprised at the unusual request, Francesca cannot come up with an immediate answer. But then she looks at her *petite fée* with a challenging smile, "Alright then, prepare to be surprised. All you need is a towel."

"Brilliant! Where are we going? What do you have in mind?" Marlène asks with excitement, her face beaming.

"How about swimming naked in Dassia. Is that exciting enough for you?"

"What? Are you crazy? It's already dark outside!"

"No, I'm not...and yes...you'll see. There's nothing more glorious than swimming naked in the dark," Francesca replies to Marlène's lame excuses.

Marlène realizes that her friend is serious when she returns with two large beach towels, her eyes glittering with mischief. Nothing can stop her as they both run out to the car in high spirits, full of exhilaration.

It's been a long time since Francesca has treated herself to a midnight swim. But one very special, crazy night in particular she will never forget. Years ago, she and her beloved husband, as well as a close friend, had spent hours dancing away the evening until they were sweaty; afterwards they had undressed and plunged naked into the dark water. For this reason, she is more than looking forward to sharing tonight's experience with Marlène. To have the chance to give her a glimpse of the "old" Francesca before fate cruelly struck and stole all the joy in her life.

Wound up and with high expectations they reach Dassia, a small touristy resort on the eastern coast in between Barbati and close to the bay of Gouvia. Francesca steers the car directly to a small car park that belongs to the last bar on the beach. Beach clubs, *tavernas* and high-class hotels with beautiful gardens line a kilometre-long narrow pebble beach along the waterfront promenade.

Striding quickly, with two fleece jackets tucked under her arm that she always keeps in the car for contingencies, Francesca heads purposefully towards the entrance of the bar from which the sound of pop music is coming. Marlène remains where she is, hesitant, the beach towels pressed tightly to her chest.

"Come on scaredy-cat. Don't tell me you're afraid to walk through the bar. It's just a few steps, then we'll be on the other side, right on the beach," Francesca calls over her shoulder before she continues on without hesitation.

Only a few guests are present. Two elderly Greek men with bushy grey eyebrows that look like shoe brushes are standing at the bar smoking and drinking their ouzo while having a lively conversation. One of them, who is sporting a long grey moustache, is wearing dark trousers and a white shirt with the sleeves rolled up. His friend is out and about in light beige trousers and a blue shirt. Both men are wearing their shirts unbuttoned almost to their navels, so they can display their hairy grey chests – a source of male pride. A heavily made-up, very young, woman in a colourful backless top with matching miniskirt is standing behind the bar swaying her hips slowly in time to the music while she dries off beer glasses.

With Marlène close at her heels, Francesca swiftly walks through the bar with a friendly '*Kallispera*'. Surprised, probably because it doesn't happen often, two pairs of eyes stare in appreciation following the females striding past them.

Outside on the promenade, Marlène starts to giggle, "Did you see those two older blokes with the salt-and-pepper hair? They looked as if they would chat-up anyone!"

Francesca grins. "They would have been hard to overlook. I bet they were hoping to have a holiday flirt, here they call it "*kamaki.*" But take a look...it is so beautiful this evening. The sea literally blends into the darkness. It is pitch black outside."

And indeed, one can only make out the faint silhouette of the nearby hills and bays that surround them. However, the many lights of Corfu and its castle blaze in the night sky. Individual guests stroll along the lighted promenade. Many of the bars have placed comfortable armchairs outside to seat couples or small groups of friends. Music is playing in every bar.

In a carefree mood, Francesca takes her friend's hand. Together they run towards the fine sandy beach that lies waiting in the darkness at the end of the promenade. Years ago, the beach huts of the first Greek Club Med stood here.

The dark shadows cast by an olive tree towards which Francesca is leading her friend, scare Marlène. Haltingly, and with a queasy feeling in the pit of her stomach, she lays her towel next to Francesca's on top of a low stone wall surrounding the tree and sits down. Hints of rosemary and thyme drift in the mild night air. It is completely windless and still. Only the soft swish of the waves coming from the sea and the faint sound of music can be heard.

Francesca lets out a deep sigh, "Somehow I feel like I'm in a void in this total darkness, as if I am the only one who exists on the planet...come on, let's go swimming. The evening is incredibly beautiful. It radiates mystery, something magical."

"I'm not so sure," Marlène says hesitantly, "there are people over there not even 40 metres away. I thought we would be completely alone."

"No one can see or hear us here," Francesca laughs, "it's so dark, I can barely see you."

Shortly thereafter, she runs naked across the cool, wet sand and slips into the velvety water. After a few powerful strokes Francesca has disappeared into the obscurity of the night.

Marlène has never experienced something this crazy. Before her courage fails her completely, and she has to remain on the beach alone in the dark, she quickly undresses and dashes naked after her friend. And how much fun this turns out to be. To swim in the dark, invisible to all so close to the shore. To hear the music and watch the people as they stroll along the promenade or sit in bars along the beach.

Millions of stars shine in the sky with a supernatural beauty. Carefree and happy they swim side by side through the dark water like two mermaids, enjoying the marvellous feeling of being naked.

The two friends continue to swim farther along the beach, at one with the sea and the entire universe, until Marlène suddenly lets out a small cry that interrupts this singular mood. "Quick, quick, turn around..." she shrieks, and without waiting for her friend she swims away frantically. A moment later Francesca sees what has startled her *petite fée*. Someone is scanning the sea with a large searchlight. At first the light only grazes them, but seconds later it swings back and hovers above their heads. There is no use diving under now. They can hear loud hoots and whistles coming from the beach.

"Slow down, otherwise they'll think that something really exciting is happening out here and they'll know what we're doing," Francesca calls out to her.

Leisurely she swims behind her friend. *And even if they do, who cares. Anyway, besides our heads, there's nothing else to see.*

Marlène has long ago disappeared from her sight. Meanwhile, the pranksters have stopped playing with their searchlight and in a moment Francesca is swimming again in absolute darkness.

Marlène reaches the shore finally. She slowly climbs out from the water and scans the beach for the spot where they had undressed and left their clothes.

Halfway between the sea and the wall surrounding the olive tree, where her soft, fluffy beach towel is waiting for her, she sees the glowing end of a cigarette which belongs to a person sitting on the ground. A man is watching her in amusement as Marlène walks past him in her birthday suit whispering a self-conscious, "Good evening," as she stumbles towards her beach towel.

As soon as it's in her grasp, she wraps herself in it tightly like a bandaged mummy then fearfully scans the surface of the sea searching for her friend.

Not a soul in sight, not that I would even be able to recognize anything. Except for this nosy parker. What an absurd situation. Why did I insist on having an unforgettable moment? Now I've got my rush of adrenaline. All alone and face-to-face with a sadist, who's just waiting to pounce on his victim. I'll be the headline in tomorrow's local newspaper "Tourist attacked after daring midnight swim. Found naked and dead on Dassia Beach!" One would think I made this situation happen.

But the man remains calmly seated a bright smile lighting up his face.

Even the moon has become curious wanting to know what is happening down there. All of a sudden it appears from behind a hill that had been hidden in the dark, a giant orange-red disc slowly making its ascent.

Francesca would love to stay motionless for a long time staring up at the night sky. The contrast between the deep night and the over-sized, blood-orange moon that looks as if it has been hung in the heavens is breathtaking. But slowly she starts to worry about her *petite fée* and does not want her to have to wait any longer.

When Francesca arrives where they started out, she slowly and carefully wades the last few metres towards the beach her head tilted up to face the moon. The first thing she can make out in the distance is a large, rectangular, ghostly-white apparition, which, as it draws closer turns out to be a towel that Marlène is helpfully holding out to her. Francesca shivers and goosebumps appear on her as she hastily climbs out of the water and allows Marlène to wrap her in the warm towel.

"Thank you, you're an angel. But it was so lovely, I didn't notice how long I had been in the water."

"My God, where have you been? Hurry up!" Marlène, who has long since gotten dressed, discloses, "About two to three metres away from us is a voyeur sitting on the sand, who's already gotten a good look. Let's not give him another opportunity!"

"What are you talking about, there's nobody there."

"Yes, there is. Now hurry up and put your clothes back on."

Francesca's interest is piqued. She wants to uncover the mystery so she stares motionless into the darkness until she too discovers the cigarette's red glowing tip in the night. Now, surprised that Marlène's assumption has proven true, she focuses intently on their surroundings until she detects a shadowy form sitting in the sand smoking a cigarette.

She almost bursts out laughing.

"There is indeed an ominous figure that almost certainly must have thought it was dreaming when it saw you suddenly emerging from the sea like Aphrodite with long, dripping-wet hair."

"Just go ahead and make fun of me. I really thought I was a goner because of one of your ridiculous ideas," Marlène replies, already forgetting that she was the one who had started this by wanting to do something extraordinary.

In order to expedite dressing, Marlène holds up the beach towel to shield her friend who is finally slipping into dry clothes. Only the leggings are giving her trouble as they are tugged on with great difficulty—and quite a few curses—over her damp legs. While they awkwardly slip into their jackets, they both try to suppress their nervous giggles that are threatening to escape. They swiftly grab their towels and make an almost desperate escape from the darkness as they head towards the bar, which in the meantime has filled with tourists.

Several of the guests are sitting in deep, comfortable chairs on the beach, others are crouched directly at the shoreline and stare mesmerised at the unusually large moon hanging in the dark sky, still casting its fantastic light on the equally dark sea paving a golden path on its surface.

Ignoring their sopping wet hair, they both try to act cool as they make their way across the bar as unobtrusively as possible past a throng of grinning patrons. Just as they were earlier, the two Greek granddads are still standing at the bar, and this time they wave at the girls their eyes full of laughter. One of them calls out in a heavy accent to the two mermaids as they pass, "What a beautiful night, what a beautiful moon, just made for lovers."

For a moment Marlène and Francesca look at each other in consternation until Marlène asks incredulously, "Did that old bloke just wink at us?"

"I bet they think we were a couple of lesbians!"

During the entire ride home the two vivacious night bathers keep breaking out in uproarious laughter as they repeatedly recall their eventful evening, especially the end, when they thought they could escape discreetly.

Back at home, all Francesca and Marlène want to do is take a shower and retire for the night with a cup of hot tea. They are both tired after the evening, which will probably remain etched in their memories forever. Before they turn in though, Marlène gives her friend a loving hug and kisses her lightly on either cheek.

"Thank you very much for this fun and memorable evening. I will never forget this adventure."

14

A nother record-breaking autumn morning wants to indulge the two friends on their last, full day with a cloudless, brilliant blue sky. After tidying up the kitchen and taking the washing off the clothesline, which the gentle breeze has already dried, they decide to drive to the western coast to visit the picturesque sandy beach of Glyfada for a change, in order to take full advantage of the beautiful day.

Francesca is very excited before they even reach the beach, as she notices with a shriek of joy the high waves that are ideal for body surfing.

At the southern end of the beach, at the Louis Grand Hotel, they find two loungers under an umbrella that are still unoccupied. *My goodness, that looks highly dangerous,* Marlène thinks, watching in fear and fascination as the swimmers hurl themselves into the waves, somehow regain their footing, then draw in a quick gasp of air only to let themselves be thrown about by the next big wave.

With a burst of energy and a challenge in her smile, Francesca grabs Marlène's hand pulling her up from the lounger. "Come on my delicate *petite fée*, I want to show you how much fun you can have doing this. It's far better than anything you can imagine. Believe me. Don't look so afraid! In this past week, you have learned to dive and swim like a fish. You even did a "bare-bottomed" handstand in the water. Just look at these gigantic waves. C'mon, c'mon, hurry up! I can hardly wait to jump in."

Marlène at her heels, Francesca runs to the shore where the thundering breakers crash and swirling white foam rolls across her feet. With a whoop that escapes from deep within her, Francesca hurls herself into the depths and disappears immediately.

This is far too risky and treacherous for her friend. But when she sees Francesca shooting up out of the waves waving to her as she sputters and laughs along with all the other carefree swimmers, she feels that she is missing out on something indescribable if she doesn't find the courage to meet this new challenge.

After the first large wave passes over Marlène and nothing happens, apart from her soaking wet hair clinging to her head and suddenly finding herself topless and looking like a fool, she loses her fear. Casually, the bikini top is repositioned in the appropriate place before she surrenders herself completely to this entirely new and fun experience.

While taking a quick break, she observes full of admiration how adeptly Francesca has mastered the art of bodysurfing. First, she fights her way a few metres through the breakers. Then, she searches patiently for the perfect wave, waits until the last moment before throwing herself outstretched onto the breaking wave without hesitation. Seconds later, she is shooting out like a board at high speed towards the beach where she is spit out unceremoniously onto the sand. As she awkwardly scrambles out of the spume, Marlène is waiting with an outstretched hand to help pull her breathless friend onto the beach.

"You absolutely have to teach me how to do that," Marlène exclaims with enthusiasm leaping around Francesca with excitement. "I want to learn how to do this, really! It looks like so much fun."

Bursting with energy and joy, both of them play tirelessly in the high waves. Though they do swallow litres of water and their hair—not to mention other parts of their bodies—is full of sand, they enjoy the experience immensely. And every so often, some bathing suit bottoms wind up hanging around a pair of knees or a top goes missing. Other swimmers are also facing clothing challenges, none of which stops them from enjoying this fun.

But then the moment arrives for the two insatiable women to flop onto the hot sand, with blue lips, shivering with cold. They let the rays of the sun slowly warm them up again.

After their wildly beating hearts have settled somewhat and they have recovered from their tumultuous fun, they sit relaxed at a beach bar scoffing a gigantic hamburger. Along with this, Francesca drinks an ice-cold beer. Cheerfully, she tells Marlène that today she has had the greatest luck of all, because such ideal conditions, like high waves and barely any wind, do not happen often. Animatedly, they watch the others who are still playing, undeterred, as they let the waves toss them about.

Together, they stroll barefoot along the shore to the northern bay, where a beautiful white villa has been built upon a rock outcropping. Francesca describes to Marlène what the place looked like the first time she discovered the beach with George, on their scooters. Back then, there was only the hotel and two *tavernas*. In the past few years, the entire beach had been developed with charming townhouses and two or three larger bars.

"It's actually a pity that the building boom wasn't monitored better. After we visited you for the first time Eddy was very interested in finding a flat in this vacation paradise," Marlène recalls.

By the time they reach the end of the bay, the breakers have already diminished to the point where they now leave behind a trail of beautiful and even wave patterns on the sand. Although the afternoon sun shines down somewhat paler, it still radiates a pleasing warmth. Some of the swimmers have already left the beach. Only a few are still enjoying the late afternoon and the peaceful time of day, which is approaching slowly.

Silently, and with their eyes closed, the two friends slowly wade into the water that is now completely still, until it reaches their necks. When Francesca opens her eyes, and finds herself surrounded by the sea's crystal clear, turquoise water she is reminded of her husband's blue eyes. Her feelings of guilt overpower her with such force that she is unable to conquer them. She stands there with her head hanging, frozen in pain, and her lips trembling. Silently, the first tears begin to roll down her cheeks.

Marlène waits motionless until her friend has collected herself. At first haltingly, but then amid heaving sobs the words spill from her like a torrent, "Right up until the final day, I acted as if everything was going to be all right. I was truly convinced that a miracle *had* to happen. The terrifying illness, this whole situation, it was so surreal, unbelievable. The whole thing must have been a big mistake. This wasn't our life...each and every moment I had hoped to awaken from this nightmare and return to my happy carefree existence, as if nothing had ever happened.

But George also played along with me in order to not scare me, pretending that he would get well again. My heart aches when I think of it. All those weeks I wasn't there for him as I should have been. We did not speak to each other, openly trust in each other or share how and what we were feeling. We should have been more honest and shared our fears with one another. But the truth is that this wicked illness stole its way into George's life. I feel ill even thinking about how he fought back the fear, alone, every second, minute and hour. Never, not one single time, did I ask him what he was feeling, if he was afraid of what was happening to him, to us. Nothing...absolutely nothing...not even in those final days at home, even though there had been enough opportunities."

Helpless, Francesca is caught up in her emotions, and when she is able to speak again she continues, "I stuck my head in the sand fearing the truth, or perhaps out of helplessness and shame because I was unable to help him. I acted as if everything would turn out fine in the end. Even when he once whispered to me as he was falling asleep that he would like his final resting place to be in Corfu, in *Ag. Nikolaos*. Back then I only embraced him tightly, but not a single word of comfort, hope or optimism passed my lips.

During our final 24-hours in the hospital, I only wanted to lie down next to George and hold him tight. But I was so afraid of hurting him, I didn't do it...every day I have to remember that all George must have seen in me, in those last weeks, was a heartless woman without feelings. I am so mad at myself. For so many years we had been open with one another, confided in each other, and then, when the most important, terrible moment of our lives arrived, I failed abysmally."

Francesca is now sobbing openly. Like an erupting volcano, all of her suppressed agony, the self-recriminations at having done everything wrong for the person she loved the most, pours forth.

And suddenly Marlène too is crying. Completely unexpectedly, she feels a terrible ache rip through her heart, almost stealing her ability to breathe. Through a veil of tears Francesca notices, somewhat disconcertedly, her friend standing next to her, looking at her in abject misery.

Sobbing, she tries to explain, "A sudden gentle breeze appeared like a caress. I immediately felt it enter me and in that very moment I could feel yours and George's loss. Normally, I would take you in my arms now and comfort you by saying, 'it's all quite normal.' But this time the gift has penetrated me in the form of a faint breath, I could feel the missing part. There is also this recurring feeling that we are not three individuals, but rather, the three of us are a single entity. We are *One*. This is why, for the first time, I was able to feel the same loss, the pain and the helplessness that *you* feel.

Up until today, I have always wanted to help draw you out whenever you were feeling bad. This time though, I was surprised and unprepared for it. I just mean that instead of trying to distract you by saying, 'come on Francesca, let's do this or that,' the wind showed me how much you were suffering, how much you miss George. I feel as if your heart is beating in my chest."

Their hot tears blend with the sea, which rocks them gently back and forth in a comforting motion. In order to calm down, they swim side by side slowly to the white villa that overlooks the sea from its rocky perch.

"When you lost George, you also lost everything that made up your true existence, everything you created through your great love for one another. After your pilgrimage to Santiago de Compostela, the resistance to your loss and your fear of being alone slowly and gradually gave way to the realisation that you still exist. At first you fought it because you thought it would make you forget George. But in truth, this feeling led you to who you are, along with all that you became through George. This is because George is within you, not outside of you where you were searching."

When Francesca doesn't answer, she continues, "At that point you had two options: resist or give in. The fiery pain gave way to the light of consciousness. If you had resisted, you would have taken on the role of a victim, which would have resulted in anger, and you would have closed yourself off to others. It was a long battle, but then you did give in. You have accepted what is and have allowed peace to enter your heart; you once again opened yourself up to life.

What I find most incredible is that you never doubted my words. Unbiased, and without hesitation or reservations, you followed the path that I showed you. You placed me in the light, and during special moments in our lives the path we walked together was illuminated. And this especially happened during the week-long holidays we have spent together here on Corfu, when we find the time to quieten down and set our innermost feelings free."

For a while they both simply float, lost in their own thoughts until with a deep sigh Marlène says softly, "In these past few years you could have closed your heart and eyes to your inner sun with the excuse that you had lost everything, and you would not have seen me, heard me or felt me. Just imagine what would have happened then: We would not be here to share these unique moments together.

In this life, I have often asked myself what good it does to experience so many things or feel them within, to experience so much upheaval. Now I know. I believe what we consider to be the ultimate test is what enables us to undergo an inner change, so we can return to being who we really are. You, on the other hand, because you trusted my perception, have helped me connect with my roots again, at first to help you find your inner light, but then also to find mine, which was buried deep within me." Exhausted from this exchange of emotions, they swim back to the shore silently.

Glyfada has always held something magical for Marlène, something special. The few times, several years back, when she had visited Francesca and George with her family, they had stayed in the Louis Grand Hotel. Her favourite memory of this wonderful time is when her husband, along with George, buried her son—who was only one and a half at the time—in the sand until only Maël's small blonde head was sticking out of the sand watching all of their nonsense with stoic calm. But today, returning after all these years, she notices to her great disappointment that since then the beach has become smaller and lost a great deal of its magic and charm. However, before, when she was standing in the water with Francesca, she felt transported back twenty years. It has never happened before, but today, here in Glyfada, she feels for the first time a painful loss.

Pensive, and without a sound, Francesca and Marlène drive on the narrow winding road to *Pelekas*, a charming mountain village perched on a rise above the beach of Glyfada. It is the second largest mountain after Pantokrator and offers a panoramic view of Corfu. At the observation point, there is a small *taverna* where the girls take a seat at a table with a grand view of the sea. This little spot is coveted for its unique sunsets not only by couples, but by anyone with a romantic tendency, or those who want to shoot some extraordinary photos. Francesca orders a small bottle of ouzo along with *mezze*, small appetizers. Marlène insists on having a small glass herself making an exception, for she needs a drink after their emotional day. A few stray drops find their way into her glass of water, just enough to turn the liquid a milky colour. A third glass is reserved for George. They both toast with him symbolically drinking to friendship and love.

Slowly, they both feel the energy around them become lighter and the strain of the last two hours slips away, the ouzo has probably helped. Francesca tells light-hearted, amusing anecdotes of the time when she was here with her husband to enjoy the sunset, and the nights they spent in the *Pink Panther,* the local discotheque. Unfortunately, the food hasn't improved since then. But the breathtaking view from up above, across the open sea and spanning the entire island is more than enough compensation.

More and more people start to arrive, some armed with cameras, seeking an ideal spot so they are prepared when the captivating moment arrives. Then it's time...

While the sun illuminates the horizon with its final rays, everything becomes quiet around them. Slowly, the sky changes colour from orange to a deep blue. The air, just like the mood surrounding them, changes, becomes softer. Then the wonderful event happens... the glowing red disc slowly glides deeper and deeper towards the sea, and then in a short, magical moment bids a final farewell to the day as it slips into the sea.

"How beautiful!" they both utter at once with deep emotion. They remain sitting for a while, absorbing the amazing energy and casting a last glance across the sea before saying goodbye to the unforgettable place. Satiated by the day's experiences they hold hands as they walk back to the car and drive home.

15

arlène has already packed her suitcase and stowed it in the car. She is happy that they still have time to go to her favourite beach for a long swim before she has to head back home. A small plastic bag lies on the seat for later, awaiting her wet bikini.

There is not the slightest hint of a breeze this morning. The final day of their holidays promises once again to be pleasantly warm and lovely. Today, they don't linger. Instead, they hurry their breakfast in order not to waste even one minute of their precious time.

The friends swim one last time side by side along the coastline and then once more out to the farthest buoy. Neither wants to spoil the mood by thinking of the impending departure, so they chatter about pleasant things and enjoy every moment.

Suddenly, Marlène's relaxed expression changes, and she looks in earnest at her trusted friend. "George is here. He wants me to let you know that he doesn't understand your feelings of guilt, and that you should finally shake them off!"

Francesca is stricken. *How I long to do just that, but I can't just brush away the feelings of guilt that have torn me apart and followed me around for so long as if they never existed.*

"My dear *petite fée*, just how do you envision me doing this? These feelings have become a part of me; I can't simply shake them off. I will never again receive an answer to all of my questions. And now, to pretend that they never occupied my thoughts? I would so like to believe what you are saying, to know that George does not hold anything against me. These are the very thoughts that are driving me crazy, to think that he might be disappointed with me."

Marlène feels helpless. How can she explain to Francesca that she understands and knows her self-recriminations are unnecessary and pointless? She needs to stop judging and punishing herself with a guilty conscience. She has to finally let go.

"How can you even think such a thing, after all you have experienced and seen, and what you heard from George just now. Have all of our deep conversations and unique moments evaporated into thin air? Have you already forgotten everything? Did nothing stick? Didn't you understand anything?

But, if you are still convinced that you have done something wrong, then forgive yourself for your mistakes and remember all the good things you have achieved in your life."

Today too, they don't emerge elegantly from the water. Instead, they skitter across the rocks on their backsides until, with some "Ows" and "Arghs" they stumble across pebbles on stiff and wobbly legs to their sun loungers and collapse onto them in relief. They thirstily down the cold water that a kind waiter has left for them in an ice bucket. With a contented sigh, Marlène allows her gaze to drift across the calm blue sea, absorbing the view like a sponge.

Slowly, the beach fills with people. Because the weather conditions are ideal today, there is a lot happening at the water sports platform farther down the beach. A non-stop flow of proficient, and not so proficient, water-skiers show off their skills, others are towed by motorboats sitting on an inflatable banana or flailing around in large floating rings until, in a high arc, someone is ejected and lands in the water.

Francesca's eyes suddenly light up with interest, as she observes a parachute being spread out on the platform in preparation for a tandem parasail event. She gives Marlène's arm a gentle squeeze.

"Hey, take a look, wouldn't you like to do that? It would be amazing. Kind of like a super-cool ending to our holidays. It's got to be sublime, to glide high up in the air and have a bird's-eye view of what's below."

"I had my first parasailing encounter right here, more than 20 years ago," Marlène smiles as she recalls her past experience.

Naturally, Francesca can't forget the event because it was the first time that her friends had visited them on Corfu. It had been unfortunate that she and George had to work that day and couldn't accompany Marlène and Eddy on their adventure.

"I was three months pregnant!" Marlène continues, "I will never forget the amazing feeling of happiness that filled me. Since then, I have taken advantage of any opportunity I get to fly, in any conceivable way. Lisa was three and a half, and Maël was six when I took them on a balloon ride."

"Really? You never told me that."

"My family surprised me with a helicopter ride as a 40th birthday present. Along with my brother, my sister and my brother-in-law, we first flew over Icogne, where I was born. Then we continued towards Lens, where my parents were standing on the lawn in front of their châlet waving colourful handkerchiefs. After that, we circled over Crans-Montana, where, thanks to my neighbours, I immediately recognized my flat. For when they heard the noise of the rotors, they quickly ran out onto their balcony waving and shouting like crazy. Afterwards we circled over the ski runs, flew around the 3000m-high *Plaine Morte* glacier then glided down the Rhône valley until we landed back at the airport in Sion, ending the spectacular event."

Busily she searches the bottom of Francesca's beach bag for the sun cream. Finding it, she smears it over her arms and legs while she continues to reminisce about her flight experiences:

"From that moment forward, I knew that I had to find out what it would feel like to actually fly myself in such an amazing "bird", to be the person at the controls. The following year, along with Eddy and my children, I was allowed to take control of a helicopter as an amateur pilot with a flight instructor by my side. Eddy, whom I had terrified with some of my involuntary acrobatic manoeuvres, was completely overwhelmed and swore never to fly with me again."

Francesca laughs out loud as she imagines the scenario.

"Maël and Lisa, on the other hand, accompanied me on one more flight when I had to throw a football from the sky for a birthday party."

"Really? That's incredible. You've never shown this side of yourself before. You kept it completely hidden from me! I didn't know that you were so taken with flying."

Her friend just gives a slight shrug of her shoulders.

"A few years later, I was allowed to take off from the ski run at an altitude of over 2600 metres in a tandem paraglider. It was unforgettable, as I circled a few times towards Crans-Montana, then flew over the frozen lake and landed in the centre of the stadium, right before the eyes of a crowd of excited tourists. It is for this reason whenever I have the opportunity to fly, to experience this feeling of freedom, I can feel myself beginning to grow wings." Marlène laughs, and her brilliant blue eyes light up her face as she smears the rest of the sun cream on her friend's back.

"And you know what, that's going to be my belated birthday present for you!"

Friendly and helpful assistants instruct them in a crash-course of what they need to do, especially when they land. Tightly buckled in and secure they both sit in tandem, each in their own harness. There is not a lot of time for reflection because the parachute is already catching the air as the motorboat slowly takes off. They both give a shriek, then one or two steps, a small jerk, and then with excited cheers the companions are airborne. At first Francesca grabs the bar holding on for dear life, but gradually she relaxes and enjoys the view and the flight.

"This is so beautiful. See how far the view extends from up here. And look, over there, the city of Corfu with its two fortresses...and how small the people on the beach look," Marlène remarks enthusiastically, as she waves to the people down below.

Francesca is thrilled as well. She's flying... weightless like a bird she glides through the air. Far below, the glint of solitary sailboats makes them stand out against the blue of the sea. Her gaze drifts along the Albanian coast and travels farther inland to the mountainous terrain. As the boat makes a slight turn, distancing itself from the shore, the entire channel lies stretched out beneath her. On one side is the coast of Corfu, on the other the Albanian coast. Directly ahead, towards Italy, the blue sea forms a solid blue plane, becoming one with the horizon. Overcome with emotion, she closes her eyes for a moment. *What an extraordinary feeling. I'm flying...how wonderful it would be to really have wings, to be able to spread my arms and fly.*

"Oh, noooo...he's already turning to head back, and he's slowing down. We're falling!" Marlène screams.

And indeed, the sea is rushing closer, as they rapidly make their approach. They laugh and scream as their feet touch the water before the boat slowly starts to pick up speed and, once again, they gently rise into the sky.

"This is sooo cool!" they say simultaneously.

Completely thrilled, they enjoy the last few minutes high above the sea before they slowly and very gently land in the water close to the platform. Once they have released their harnesses, they both climb back into the boat with some help from the gallant captain. Happy and content with their spontaneous adventure they speed back to where they started.

Francesca gives Marlène a huge hug and thanks her profusely:

"What an amazing birthday present! It's something I will never forget. Thank you!" Beaming with joy, she kisses Marlène on the cheek. A short while later they are lying on their loungers relaxing in the warmth of the sun.

Swimming under a cloudless blue sky and having adventures in the air can make a girl hungry. Marlène is starting to become restless with her eye constantly on the clock. Time is rushing by. In two hours, they need to be at the airport. They both rinse the salt from their hair in the showers provided for the guests. After a quick rub of the towel, they jump into some dry clothes and head towards their table that has already been set. The chef had been very understanding and made an exception by preparing their meal an hour earlier than usual. They don't need to wait long until a young waitress brings them a giant plate of mussels. And she did not forget the glass of chilled white wine for Francesca and the glass of iced tea for Marlène. The bright ring of their glasses sounds like a promise, as they make a final emotional toast to each other with small, hesitant smiles.

Once again they find themselves in the middle of the hectic hustle and bustle of the airport. After an emotional and wonderful week, this now feels like a cold shower. Neither of them wants to let it show; they want to be strong for each other.

Francesca can't stop herself and says with a failed smile, ""Welcome back to reality. Adieu, mystical world full of magic and harmony. Hopefully, until next year."

"It's a promise!"

Francesca watches as her *petite fée* walks through passport control, then turns around with a small smile to give her one last wave before she finally disappears around the next corner, along with the other passengers.

So that she doesn't have to feel the sudden emptiness at home, she busies herself with the usual necessary chores in the house and garden. Later, she lies down in the hammock with a glass of wine and absentmindedly gazes at the towels and linen flapping in the breeze on the clothesline. She lets her gaze wander across the garden until it reaches the breakfast nook.

How many things my petite fée has once again taught me this year. It's like a precious present, to have experienced these unforgettable moments with her for an entire week. I could reveal my innermost thoughts and feelings and talk to her about everything, knowing that she understands me. This deep friendship that connects us is something absolutely unique, very special. In addition to this is her ability to act as a medium, to be a line of communication between two worlds. I have to prove to her that I was able to retain something from our week together, and I want to face my guilty feelings and work on them.

Even though she promised herself to be strong, it still happens. Her lips suddenly begin to tremble. She can feel her eyes becoming damp and salty tears begin to run down her cheeks. She is helpless against her emotions and a deep wave of sadness washes over her.

It is not because of Marlène, for she had to go home to her family. No, it is simply because she is once again aware of how lonely she is without her dearly loved husband, who filled every day with his laughter and humour. *Why did you have to leave my life so suddenly?*

For 30 years you enveloped me with your love, made me feel safe and protected, and now all of a sudden, nothing...how does one deal with that? – Now stop with the self-pity! –

Of course, it's not the same. But this week with Marlène was incredible. We surfed a wave together and gained a little distance from reality. She makes me feel so good. She lets me feel her love and care. She gives me strength to continue and believe in the miraculous. I promise myself that I will make the most out of my life as is possible, even if I find it very difficult right now.

Francesca no longer knows how much wine she has had to drink. By now the day has faded into night and the washing has long since been removed from the clothesline. Slightly tipsy she climbs stiffly up the stairs to her room. She turns on the light and opens the balcony door to let in some fresh air. On her way to the bathroom she sees a letter lying on her bed. With curiosity, she takes it and immediately recognizes Marlène's handwriting:

My dear soul sister,

I want to thank you for a very special week.

When I am close to you, I can feel a motherly love, strong and unconditional. The purest love.

This week has been a great gift for me. I realize that I am able to impart all that I can because you are there, paying attention and ready to receive what is given to you. Your heart is now open, you are ready...

Marlène

Part Three

Restoring Trust

16

Despite the lone clouds in the sky, Francesca is greeted by a beautiful sunrise on this very special June morning. *How could it not be?* She thinks with a smile, this evening Marlène is arriving, her dearest of friends, who doesn't want to wait until her usual visit in September. She jumps out of bed full of joyful anticipation and runs briskly downstairs, in her bare feet wearing a faded Mickey Mouse t-shirt to make herself a cup of coffee.

She swiftly opens all the doors leading to the terrace and takes a deep breath of the fresh morning air. Carefully, with her steaming cup in hand, she walks across the grass, which is covered in dew and looks as if millions of shining crystals have been scattered over it. She loves this time of year; spring, when nature is awakening to a new life. She is happy that this year everything around her is blooming abundantly. Seeds and buds are bursting open, plants are sprouting and growing; but best of all the days are getting longer.

She can feel a force developing all around her. She stands there with a dreamy smile and shining eyes gazing at the beautiful, green and hilly landscape stretching out before her. *It really is beautiful here at my place...only George is missing in this picturesque idyll,* she muses sadly, and lets out a deep sigh.

She slowly strolls back to the kitchen where she prepares a tasty thick slab of bread with some freshly made jam for herself. Content, she walks outside into the warm morning sun and lets herself fall into her old, but extremely comfortable bamboo armchair.

I simply must rinse off the terrace and get rid of all the bird droppings from the swallows' nests.

For now, though, she enjoys her moment of complete peace and quiet. As she relishes her bread, she has to think back to her own discombobulated arrival a week prior:

The stress had already started in Zurich. The time in between the connecting flight from Athens to Corfu was extremely tight because we departed an hour late.

With my laptop bag slung over one shoulder and my fully stuffed, heavy handbag hanging over the other, I ran, panting madly and out of breath, behind a very efficient ground staff member, who was clacking down the entire concourse in her high-heels while she constantly called out to me: "Grigora, grigora!" Like a streak of lightning she guided me through the airport, and, with last-minute success, shoved me onto the waiting airplane.

Sweaty and with a beet-red head I managed to squeak out a small "Hello" as I slunk past two annoyed flight attendants, who immediately slammed the aircraft door behind me to make a statement. It was quite an uncomfortable feeling to negotiate my way down the narrow aisle, past all the scornful, and some hostile, looks until I finally found my seat on the aisle, thank goodness. As if the 15-minute delay had been my fault.

Without further incident, we landed in Corfu – but without my suitcase! Because Spiro and Despina were still in Boston visiting their family, Eileen had kindly offered to pick me up from the airport. After excitedly greeting one another, I told her about my suitcase dilemma. "Not a problem," was her laughing response, and she assured me that Alan would be waiting for us outside in the car. So off we went to the Lost and Found office where we got stuck for an entire hour!

Francesca's smile grows as she thinks back to the time they finally found Alan, who was parked in a no-parking zone underneath a taxicab sign, quite upset with a perturbed look on his face. Of course, her first reaction was to think that she was the cause of his annoyance. But it wasn't long before his wife determined that the registration plates on his car were missing. Upset and gesticulating wildly, he explained how, whilst he took a short nap, a policeman had unscrewed and taken the plates...

Even though she had to control herself so she would not burst out laughing, Francesca felt responsible. All of this would not have happened if he hadn't needed to wait for her for so long. But why didn't he park the car in the car park? The welcoming kiss was forgotten, and the mood during the drive was also shot.

Eileen was so angry that she just wanted us to drop her off in town as she was expecting a student at home, to whom she was tutoring English. So, Alan and I wound up driving to the villa alone in a gloomy mood. He was kind enough to try and start my car – unfortunately, with no luck.

The brand new 50-Euro bill in his pocket along with a fat kiss, probably helped ease the discomfort because his face brightened significantly and he said goodbye with a sincere, "Welcome back home."

Then I went to inspect the refrigerator. A gaping void! But of course, Despina's not here! And I hadn't dared ask Alan to stop at the grocers on the way home, so I could at least stock up on essentials. Fortunately, I found an old tin of Rio Mare tuna and a bottle of red wine.

Francesca runs to the kitchen and pours a glass of orange juice. When she has finished her last bite of bread with apricot jam, she gives a slight shake of the head and a short laugh.

That day was really something else. Shortly thereafter, I found out to my dismay that there was no hot water in the house. Right away I stormed out to the gas tank and started hammering on it like mad. To my unschooled ears, it made a hollow sound and so I did an immediate about-face and went inside to call the gas company. The embarrassing thing though, was that three days later when the gas I ordered arrived, I was informed by the delivery man, his index finger raised for emphasis, that the tank was still half full, and the indicator was showing it at 40%! I could have spared myself the cold showers...

The embarrassments continued, when on the following day my kind neighbour Sergio stood in front of my door with his son-in-law, who is a mechanic, ready to help me with my car that still refused to start. Just when they were walking towards it holding the jumper leads, an electric spark jump-started my brain. I suddenly knew why Merky wouldn't start, couldn't start. For the first time, I had forgotten to insert the security stick, which restores the electronic connection before I can turn the key in the ignition.

The look on their faces should have been filmed, as I ordered them in a firm voice not to move from the spot, no matter what happened; I didn't want to hear a peep out of them, or hear any stupid chauvinistic commentary. Seconds later, I was sitting in the car. I turned the key and the engine sprang to life after the first try. The two of them had stood there watching me with dropped jaws. Once they figured out what had happened, they couldn't hold it in and stood there laughing their heads off. Tsk, tsk...how embarrassing. I won't forget this years' turbulent return soon.

But now it's time to get going! You've got more on your to-do list today than sitting around reminiscing while you let the amazing sunny weather lull you into doing nothing. And jumping up, Francesca heads back into the house with long strides.

Sitting in the airplane that is taking her to Greece, Marlène observes the other passengers and ponders: *Is this what connects us all together, the air that we breathe? The air that I exhale is the same air that my neighbour, or anyone else for that matter, is breathing. It is better to keep it pure and charge it with positive energy, so that it has the optimal balance for those who inhale it. All the negative thoughts that I have will pollute the air if I exhale them, and they will burden the next person who inhales them with negative energy.*

The same goes for words that we say out loud. They are gathered in a collective space and have far more impact than one would think possible. The person sitting next to me, who is handing me my meal tray while giving me a gracious smile, is sending me positive energy subliminally, while another passenger, who is constantly nagging the flight attendants and demanding their attention, is spreading discomfort throughout the whole cabin.

Consciousness is what essentially determines who we are. We lose it when we equate it with our expectations, our mental constructs. The key is to observe these mental products vigilantly, to let them pass and return to the centre, so they can reunite with its core.

As the airplane begins its descent towards Corfu, Marlène's thoughts are suddenly interrupted by the pilot, who announces an earlier than scheduled arrival, to the delight of the passengers.

Francesca drives to the Ioannis Kapodistrias Airport in her good old Merky late in the evening, wearing her favourite jeans and a white linen blouse with rolled-up sleeves. Since the nights can still be quite chilly, she has thrown a lightweight blue cotton jumper over her shoulders. The radio is turned up to full volume. While she cruises through the still busy streets, she sings along cheerfully to some of the familiar tunes.

All day long she was running around in feverish excitement. The blue petunias that she bought yesterday have been planted in their specified pots and placed on the wall that surrounds the lawn. The entryway was also beautified with the same white and blue flowers. Thimios the gardener already mowed the lawn two days ago and had also trimmed the dead fronds from the palm tree.

The guest room looks quite lovely, with its new bedclothes and matching curtains that are enhanced by a pastel coloured bird print. The bathroom has also had a face-lift. The old towels were disposed of and replaced with new plush ones in mauve and pink. Francesca has also found the matching accessories. She is very pleased with her efforts and glad that everything is ready and prepared for her *petite fée*.

When Francesca arrives at the airport, she can already see from a distance a woman with long blond hair wearing fashionable denim jeans and a leather jacket, looking lost and forgotten, as she stands alone at the exit scanning the area expectantly. She has to smile when she sees that despite the mild evening Marlène is dressed far too warmly. As she pulls the car up alongside her, her friend's halting look changes and she gives the driver a beaming, relieved smile and her blue eyes shine.

Francesca quickly exits the car and greets her friend with a large effusive hug. "Have you been waiting long?" she asks concerned. "I actually left quite early, so that you wouldn't have to wait."

Marlène waves her off. "It doesn't matter. The main thing is that you're here now. The impossible happened and we landed ten minutes earlier than scheduled!" While she gets into the car, she adds with a laugh, "The gods probably knew that I couldn't wait any longer and were competing with each other to see who could blow the strongest tailwind."

While Francesca stows the suitcase in the car, Marlène admits eagerly, "I would really love to drive into town."

Francesca has to smile at her exuberant friend who is still awake and keen for action, "What? This late in the evening and you're not tired?"

"Not at all, I would love to go and enjoy some of the nightlife."

"Then let's go and have some fun," Francesca replies eagerly. "And I already know where I am going to take you. No, no. Don't ask, it's a surprise...all I can tell you is that it's a wonderful place that you haven't seen yet."

Francesca wants to take her to the Hotel Cavalieri, which is centrally located in downtown Corfu. This 4-storey manor house from the 17th century, which had once belonged to a nobleman, boasts a rooftop terrace with a restaurant and bar. From this vantage point one has a grand, panoramic view over the rooftops and alleyways of old town Corfu, the fortress, as well as the Albanian mountains and the sea, all the way to the airport and Mt. Pantokrator.

But then everything turns out differently. When they arrive at the cricket field on the Esplanade and park the car, they can already hear the very loud, cool music of a rock band that is playing passionately in front of the Asian Museum, the former royal palace. An ecstatic guitar player tries to dominate the bass and drums with his talent as he skilfully races up the musical scale building up to a crescendo of sound that drowns out the other instruments.

The Hotel Cavalieri is momentarily forgotten. Electrified, the two friends race towards the music striding briskly and before long are standing amongst the crowd of onlookers, who are thoroughly enjoying the band comprised of four older members. The audience cheers them on as they toss their long hair and dance with wild abandon to the rhythm of the music, as if they have survived a time warp.

Suddenly, the guitar falls silent. After a brief pause, the drummer starts playing. At first faintly, but then increasing in speed, he works the drums frantically in a wild vortex of rhythm until the entire audience breaks out in enthusiastic applause. Clapping and cheering wildly, they spur him on to an even faster pace until finally, sweating, exhausted and gasping for breath, he stops and bows before them thanking his excited audience, his dripping wet hair plastered to his head.

Fired on by the people, the band resumes playing. Francesca and Marlène are really getting into it as they rock out with the jubilant crowd. Beaming, and with flushed cheeks they clap and dance tirelessly to the compelling rhythms.

Dancing, celebrating and having fun can be a thirsty business. Laughing, Francesca drags her friend away. Close by, at the Liston, they find an empty table outside, underneath a palm tree, and with contented sighs they both sink down into two deep and comfortable armchairs.

The Liston is a long building that lies along the Esplanade with its beautiful arcades lining the street. The French can be thanked for the building which was commissioned by them. The construction took place between 1807-1814. With its cafés and restaurants, it is the perfect meeting point for locals and tourists alike.

On this mild, early summer evening it is teeming with people of every age, who meet for coffee or a drink and sit together in groups outdoors underneath the many shady trees having animated conversations, listening to the music or simply strolling aimlessly on the promenade.

"Wow, those guys are really singing their hearts out," Marlène remarks excitedly, "they played really well. I couldn't have asked for a nicer welcome!"

"I ordered those hot rock stars just for you!" They both laugh and look at each other happily.

"Man, it's almost midnight and the whole town is still up and about. That's just fantastic!"

"Yep...well, perhaps not the whole town, but right here, the Liston is the central pulse of the town— its soul—so to speak, something is always happening here. This is where you can feel the Corfiot "*Joie de vivre*"," Francesca explains proudly.

While the two friends talk animatedly, observing the people and listening to the band that is now playing more quietly, Marlène makes an exception and, to celebrate the day, orders an ouzo for herself as well.

Blind to all that is happening around them, several teenagers sit on the ground their cans of beer beside them, smoking and carrying on a lively discussion. Elderly Greek women all dressed in black stroll leisurely past them with understanding smiles on their faces.

Two boys zip by at breakneck speed on their bicycles, darting in between the pedestrians until one of them comes to a screeching halt, skids and falls to the ground. Grinning, he gets up, grabs his bike and continues on as if nothing has happened, though this time somewhat slower. Here and there scruffy, ragged dogs lie sleeping undisturbed by the commotion happening around them.

The girls enjoy their reunion and the vibrant atmosphere of town at this late hour until Marlène starts feeling so sleepy she almost slips off her chair.

"The spirit is willing, but the flesh is weak," she remarks with a tired smile as she tries to supress an enormous yawn. Francesca is surprised that her *petite fée* has held up for this long because usually by this time she is already in bed and under the covers. Not to mention the fact that she has had a long day.

Marlène suddenly shivers then snuggles deeper into her leather jacket. Now Francesca can feel it too, the temperature has dropped a few degrees and it has slowly become quite cold.

"Brrr, *pame*, let's get out of here," Francesca says shivering, now that the cold is getting to her as well. She stands up clasping her friend's arm, pulls out the correct amount of money and leaves it on the table. Nervous giggles escape them as they briskly make their way across the cricket field to the parked car, which fortunately is warm inside from the sun.

Enormous, white oleander bushes line the drive to the brightly lit villa. The covered entryway is almost smothered by the weight of the bougainvillea's violet blooms. A small squeal of pleasure escapes Marlène, as she slowly exits the car and looks around. Amazed, she looks up to the night sky, which tonight is especially bright and studded with billions of shining stars. "How amazingly beautiful it is. It's almost surreal."

"I know what you mean. I have the feeling that you would only need to reach out your arm, and you'd be able to touch the entire universe, that's how close the stars appear," Francesca replies, equally fascinated.

It is already past 1:00 a.m. Despite being tired, Marlène still insists on unpacking her suitcase before going to bed. Shooing her hesitant helper from her room after giving her a big hug and saying goodnight. She looks at her room taking in the decorative changes with pleasure as she sits on the edge of her bed. It has been many years since she has visited Corfu in the late spring, just like she used to with her family during the school holidays.

She sighs and starts to unpack her luggage looking thoroughly forward to the moment when at daybreak she will catch her first glimpse of the garden with its lavish vegetation, lush from the winter rainfall, the vibrant colours and the blooming bushes with their intoxicating scent. The freshness of the mornings has not yet given way to the dryness of summer, and the brightness that nature brings forth in the spring has not yet faded.

Half an hour later, she finally manages to finish the unpacking. Completely exhausted, but very happy that she gets to spend another carefree week with her friend in Corfu, she falls into bed.

After Francesca has hesitantly and with mixed feelings said goodnight to her *petite fée* giving her a big goodnight kiss, she climbs the stairs to her room to get ready for bed. She snuggles down under the covers and thinks of her busy bee, who, instead of going to sleep, has insisted on unpacking her suitcase despite her exhaustion. *Now my petite fée is here again. A whole three months earlier than usual. This is great! Something unknown has prompted her to come this year in the spring and not September. Regardless of the reason, the main thing is that she's here now!*

And yet, she still can't settle down. Restlessly she turns first on one side then the other. *I wonder what we will experience in this coming week? What unusual and exciting things will happen? What will we discuss, and how many magical moments await us? I have already experienced the most incredible and unforgettable hours and moments in the past years. What spiritual surprises lie ahead? I can hardly imagine that they might be more intense than what we have already experienced. That would be impossible!*

And what will we do, what kind of excursions will we have, what hasn't she seen yet? Are we going to be disappointed because we're expecting too much?

She shakes her head in irritation and takes a deep breath.

Just stop with these stupid thoughts and nonsense. Just let the days play out and enjoy every moment, being normal with your friend, who probably just wants to enjoy a carefree week. Nothing other than that...

And anyway, we had a fantastic start with tonight's impromptu rock concert. We couldn't have asked for anything better. If that isn't a good omen...

Finally, she drifts off to sleep with a small, pleased smile playing across her face.

17

*F*rancesca is torn from her sleep shortly before dawn by the crashing of thunder and the lightning streaking through the sky. The rain is pelting the roof. The cypress trees, as well as the dwarf palm, outside her bedroom, were shaking and rustling frighteningly loudly outside. The tempest, a true Corfiot storm, immediately puts her on alert.

With one leap, she jumps out of bed, quickly pulls on a wool jacket and races barefoot down the stairs into the sitting room. First, she unplugs the computer and the kitchen appliances from their respective wall outlets, for she has already seen the effects of lightning when a surge of electricity had fried her TV. Although the storm is drowning out the sound of everything else, Francesca still tiptoes about in order not to wake Marlène up, even though this would be fairly impossible judging by nature's upheaval outside. With urgent haste, she runs out to the terrace to quickly gather up all the cushions, and she even manages to grab the hammock before everything is drenched by the rain.

Half frozen, but reassured that she brought everything inside in time, she runs on ice cold feet back up to her room and scrambles under her still warm blanket. She hopes to grab even a smidgen of sleep after this unplanned intermezzo, which has taken place so early in the morning. In fact, the rhythmic drumming of the rain, the faint thunder and the rustling of the palm tree outside ease her gently back to sleep.

Meanwhile, Marlène groggily opens her eyes disoriented. "What's wrong, where am I?" Despite the closed shutters, a bright streak of lightning lights up her window sending ghostly shadows dancing across her wall. This is followed by an ear-splitting crash of thunder that shakes the whole room, ensuring that she is now wide-awake and sitting straight up in bed. *Whew, everything's okay. I'm not in the middle of a nightmare,* she smiles in relief, *it's only a storm.*

The rain continues to patter rhythmically on the round glass table that sits outside right below her window. It is the first day of her holidays and already an apocalyptic gloom has settled over it. *Whatever, I'm back in Corfu, together with my island sister, in my home.* Content, she snuggles back down under

252

the cosy blanket. The crashing of the storm raging outside keeps her from falling back to sleep. With closed eyes, she lies on the bed relaxed and lets her mind wander: *George was everything to Francesca, he was her world, her universe, and when he departed it all fell apart. She understands that George is now part of the Whole, that she can find him in the landscape, in the heavens, in an action, and she is able to connect with him not through memories alone, though they tend to increase her feelings of loss that lie right below the surface.*

She is once again living in full awareness. She doesn't let herself get carried away by dwelling on what George and she could have still done together. She just lets those assumptions pass so that she can be free of them and see them for what they really are—thoughts, not reality.

Hours later and fully rested, Francesca runs down the stairs hoping that Marlène survived the storm. Her friend however, is already in the kitchen and looks at her cheerfully.

"Good morning sleepy head. I've never experienced such a storm. It was as if nature was out of control. Fortunately, the weather has calmed down enough so that we can still have breakfast outside on the terrace. Come on, I've already got everything prepared, you're right on time."

"Ah, *ma petite fée*, you are an angel," Francesca gives her friend a kiss on the cheek. "And I am really hungry. It appears you survived this morning without too much terror. I almost expected you to come crawling into my bed for protection," she teases.

Marlène waves her away with a laugh.

"Oh no, I even opened my shutters later so I could observe this amazing inferno taking place outside, and watch this wild force of nature which I have never seen before."

After taking two bites of her toast, Marlène jumps up and runs into the house to grab a warmer jacket. "It's definitely far chillier than September," she remarks with a shiver.

"And it's also the first time we get to have breakfast while we watch it rain," Francesca replies. Although it rarely happens, this morning her stomach is growling, and she ravenously attacks the mountain of freshly toasted bread.

Though the sky is grey and overcast, Marlène stills enjoys the opulence of the surrounding flowers, especially the lush bushes of white and red oleander. "It's so beautiful. Everything is blooming at this time of the year. It's so different from autumn. Yesterday evening when we arrived home, I was already admiring the drive lined with blooming oleander and the lush bougainvillea spilling over the entryway."

Suddenly Marlène stops, her cup motionless in her hand and whispers, "Did you hear that?"

Astonished, Francesca looks at her friend.

"No, what's up?" "Shhh... just listen!" She strains to hear the sound her friend has apparently heard. And then she hears it too. A small, hesitant, *"Meow, meow..."*

They both look around searching and at the same time discover an emaciated, black kitten meowing pitifully as it slowly comes towards them from the other end of the terrace with a hitching limp that gives it a comical sway. When she sees it, Marlène's heart melts, and she carefully approaches the cat, which fearfully stops in its tracks.

"Wait, I think I still have a tin of cat food left over from last year," Francesca adds softly and retreats to the kitchen. Shortly after she returns with an open tin and hands it to her friend along with a fork. The startled kitten has run away and is now peering out from under an oleander bush at the far end of the terrace. While Marlène puts some of the food on a rock, she continues to speak to it softly and persuasively. But only when she returns to Francesca at the table does it launch a famished attack on its unexpected feast.

"Do you see how thin it is?" Marlène exclaims with pity. "And it's got that funny limp."

"Well, at least the poor thing doesn't have to starve today," Francesca adds lightly.

Without rushing or being in a hurry they both continue to enjoy their breakfast and are soon caught up in a discussion about universal energy until they are drawn back to the present. All of a sudden Marlène blurts out, "I can see George wearing a yellow Lacoste t-shirt, standing behind you between the two pillars on the terrace, and he is listening to us and laughing!"

"What...and he's doing it in a yellow t-shirt? He *never* wore yellow! I honestly have to ask myself if he's become colour-blind wherever he is, or if it's simply not important anymore?" They return to they conversation about the interconnectivity of all things. Francesca is still unable to understand why George doesn't communicate with her and asks Marlène why her friend can see George but she can't.

"The dead are all around us," her friend explains, "and it is possible to contact them through clairvoyance. One can see them, or details they want to point out to us, so that they can send us a message.

Clairaudience is when an inner voice is imparting words to us. And that lucid feeling, *clair ressenti*, is when you can somehow perceive the imparted message within your body. This is how mediums work. Every one of us would be capable of doing this, if we were able to listen to our small inner voice.

If George made himself known to you, it would be difficult for you to discern between what it is you want to hear, and what he is actually trying to communicate to you. The division between the two is very subtle. In this case one would need objectivity, and this is difficult if someone is personally affected. However, I know that you can feel him within you."

This all makes sense to Francesca. She can understand it, reason with it. She stares off in the distance, pondering.

Suddenly an idea comes to mind that she can't shake off. "If everything is connected and we are *one* with it all, wouldn't George need to form himself from atoms and molecules in order to be seen by you? Who knows, this may be the reason why you can see him..." She gives a short shrug and looks at her friend questioningly before she calmly continues, "you have a unique talent, it is an extraordinary gift to be able to see what remains hidden to others."

Marlène is surprised by Francesca's spontaneous interpretations, and with joyful blue eyes beams at her friend, who, on the other hand, gives a light shake of her head, as if she were trying to free herself from something. She wasn't prepared for this sudden outpouring of inexplicable thoughts that confuse her terribly. Normally, it's her *petite fée* who tries to find the right explanations for her arcane questions.

Meanwhile, noon has arrived. Both of them hadn't noticed the cloud cover slowly lifting, and now the sun is shining down warmly. It is right about time that they cool off their heated discussions with a dip in the sea.

In an upbeat mood, they grab their swimming things and speed over in old *Merky* to their favourite beach, Barbati. Although, Francesca has to throw a denim jacket over her shoulders, she supresses a grin when she sees that her friend has taken along a jacket, a pullover and short pink socks as a precaution, so there is no way she will get cold.

Marlène sits silent and contemplative next to Francesca—who keeps stealing worried glances at her—she can't help but notice the budding nature all around her, which she is experiencing for the first time on Corfu. The blazing red and dark violet bougainvillea growing partway up the slender cypress trees. Very large oleander bushes in pink and white line the roads. Blossoming patches of yellow gorse shine between the contrasting green of the olive trees and brush transforming the island into a vibrant paradise.

Marlène has already changed into one of her attractive vivid coloured bikinis, smeared herself with sun cream and braided her long blonde hair into a plait. This accomplished, she lies stretched out on a sun lounger close to the water and waits for her friend, who is taking an unusually long time today. Relaxed, she lets her gaze drift across the sea and along the Albanian coast. She observes a seagull with interest as it glides in search of a tasty meal over the surface of the sea, which is choppier than usual today. Despite the loud rush of the waves rolling in, she can hear the crunch of pebbles and the sound of approaching steps.

Awkwardly, Francesca stands before her friend presenting herself, somewhat embarrassed, in her brand-new bikini. But Marlène claps her hands with enthusiasm, glad to see that her friend has finally overcome her reluctance and gathered enough courage to once again show herself in a two-piece swim suit, which happens to look very good on her.

"You look smashing in it. Simply fantastic! You see, I was right. I just hope that those boring black swimsuits no longer exist," Marlène remarks spiritedly, and gives her friend the most beautiful smile.

"Shh, shh...not so loud, people are already looking."

The two best friends spend the entire afternoon at the beach in Piedra enjoying the warm sunshine. This is the place that makes them feel the most as if they were vacationing in a 4-star hotel, with its white umbrellas and comfortable sun loungers, where a fantastic DJ plays his rhythmic music selections all day long.

A lot is happening. Many Greeks spend Sundays here with their children. Young couples enjoy the final day of the week or recover from a wild night at the disco.

Quiet and relaxed, they recline side by side when Marlène, who is reading a book by James Redfield, *La Prophétie des Andes* (The Celestine Prophecy), suddenly sits up, looks at Francesca with earnest eyes and says the following: *"Einstein's entire life's work was aimed towards proving that what we perceived to be solid matter, was in fact only empty space. The same applies to our own bodies."*

She looks at her friend intently, but Francesca does not have any idea about the point she is trying to make. "This statement," she explains impatiently, "reminds me of our discussion this morning. He wrote almost the same thing that you spontaneously brought up, when you were explaining how you thought George was able to make himself visible to me!" she says, giving Francesca a meaningful look. "How often have you complained about how frustrating and unjust it is that I can see George but you can't? Then, this morning, out of nowhere, you just blurted out that it's probably due to pure energy, atoms and molecules which can reassemble at a point where I am able to see him!"

Two brilliant blue eyes lock into hers with a fixed stare. Francesca suddenly feels hot and starts to sweat. "I'm sorry, but I suddenly got very warm all over. I think I have to go cool off first." She treads carefully across the pebbles and down to the beach where she slowly glides into the water.

With powerful strokes, Francesca swims for some distance then turns onto her back to float as she catches her breath. She tries to make sense of what Marlène has just said, but her mind remains empty. *Why did that just upset me so much? I should actually be happy that, for once, I got an answer, a suggestion, to one of my arcane questions. Perhaps, it's the surprise effect which has me so agitated. I don't even know why I said what I did this morning. It just came to me. What do I know of cosmic energy and molecules? Anyway, if I try to picture it...it simply surpasses my imagination.*

And why are you bothering yourself with all of this? Up until now, you have never questioned what Marlène has been trying to explain to you for all these years. She already told you that there are certain forces and effects at work which exist beyond the scientific realm. You have always accepted the fact that certain spiritual and metaphysical correlations cannot be explained, so do the same thing now. Slowly, she swims back to where Marléne is still waiting patiently at the same spot without having moved an inch.

There are times when things are normal, and then there are times when the hours and minutes don't count. Then time stands still and one loses track of it, and life—real life—seems to have withdrawn. For quite some time now the two friends sit silently, side by side, without taking note of the beach life happening all around them. Both are caught up in their own thoughts until Marlène hesitantly asks, "How is it that you have an unwavering belief in me, that you see me as someone special? You have an unbiased acceptance of all things arcane, and you believe that I am a fairy princess even though I continually doubt myself?"

The question comes as a surprise to Francesca. She would never have thought that her *petite fée* suffered from so much insecurity, she, who always has an answer for everything.

She lies back on the lounger, laces her hands behind her head and closes her eyes. An impish smile appears on her face.

"Do you remember that winter many years ago in Crans-Montana, when we were sitting on a bench at the ice-skating rink, freezing, while we watched people skating to the music across the ice, some far more elegantly than the others?"

She doesn't see Marlène give a slight shrug and shake her head. Because she receives no response, she continues with her story, "It was there you hesitantly shared with me the incredible event you experienced with an acquaintance, who told you calmly and with conviction that you were the princess of the fairies."

Francesca can barely suppress a giggle. "Of course, I was blown away. I was confused, and thought you weren't quite right in the head. I was seriously concerned about your mental abilities. You don't hear such a fantastical story from your best friend every day. I know I must have sat there for a moment with my mouth open because I needed time to digest this piece of news. But then when you looked at me so innocently with your big blue eyes, I had to think to myself: *And why not...*"

There are so many things between heaven and earth that no one can explain. Why shouldn't there also be fairies? I remember when I was a young child that I was so enthusiastic and would devour countless books about them. So why shouldn't I believe in them as a grown up?"

Francesca sits up, touched to find a tear coming off Marlène's eyelashes and slowly sliding down her cheek. Because her *petite fée* still isn't responding and sits there in silence, Francesca picks up where she left off, "You know I've always trusted you. To me, you were like a butterfly, a little fairy...I don't know why. But you would somehow always manage to find the right words for me.. You would bring order to all my chaotic emotions, and explain so many things that were completely foreign to me in a way that was clear and understandable. And well, you know me...hours later I had forgotten everything. And still, I was able to experience moments in which I was convinced that I had understood at least part of the big picture. You have always been a good teacher to me. You helped me develop spiritually, especially after George's sudden death, something I would have never thought possible a few years ago."

Marlène's big blue eyes stare at her friend with an indefinable look.

"What's going on, ? Did I say something wrong?" Francesca asks in concern.

"No, no," Marlène gives a slight shake of the head. "But the fact that you didn't question my dubious confession back then, that really stunned me. That you could envision me as a fairy, something I had never before seen in myself. It was as if the veil had suddenly been torn. For a brief moment everything was bright, almost an enlightenment. I think that I understood everything all at once. Everything that we have experienced together up until now has had its reason.

I now know why I simply had to go to Germany when I was nineteen years old, not England like everyone else. The German language had a subliminal importance for me, so I would be able to read what you would write at a later point in time. It had to be this way, where you first had written your book, *James*, before you could dare try anything else. I was so certain that the next book would be about George and your life together. But that would mean it would have to skip the second part of a trilogy. First you would have to write about why we met, why we were set upon the same path. And it was in this one, very brief, moment that I also understood many more things. When we met, the many years you had to wait for me, for our, this, very special magical moment..."

Francesca takes her friend by the hand and pulls her to her feet with a smile.

"Come, let's take a walk along the beach. The sound of the water and the gentle breeze will help calm our emotions."

Together, they stroll along the shore trying to avoid the waves that wash up onto the pebbles. They both take in deep breaths of the fragrant air. Every now and then, one of them stoops to closely examine a stone before she throws it back into the sea. Suddenly Francesca is holding a beautifully smooth, white stone with a black circle in her hands. "Oh, look at this, the circle of life." Beaming with pleasure she gives the stone to her *petite fée.*

Marlène feels like having some ice cream. For this reason, they stop at the end of the day at a renowned bakery, Emerald, which has the best and most exotic assortment of ice creams. Marlène wants only one scoop. Her friend, on the other hand, can't decide on a flavour, so she chooses a variety of the irresistible treat.

They sit on wobbly barstools at one of the tall tables outside. Marlène watches in amusement as her sweet-toothed friend stuffs one full spoon after the other into her mouth, all the while making smacking, unintelligible sounds, each ending in a contented sigh.

"What?"

"You look like a little, happy child with your dark chocolate-covered mouth. Even your nose has some!" she remarks, unable to suppress an amused giggle.

"Go ahead and laugh, it's because you're constantly whining, 'I have to have an ice cream.' Yes, that means eating one, not just smelling it! You're poking around in yours and spooning up teeny little bites that can only be seen with a microscope."

Marlène really is tasting her ice cream like a little bird.

"This, my dear, is called *e n j o y i n g*!"

"Nonsense...this is what real enjoyment looks like," Francesca remarks as she sticks a heaping spoon of dark chocolate, baklava and strawberry ice cream into her mouth rolling her eyes with pleasure.

Since it is too windy and cold to sit outside on the terrace that evening they enjoy their meal hunkered down in *Mumsie's Corner*, a cosy, sheltered nook on the west side of the villa, wrapped in warm jackets and leggings and surrounded by the glow of the storm lanterns. Unfortunately, it gets too chilly and uncomfortable rather quickly. The cold creeping in and the sudden wind drive them away, so they have to hurry back inside in surrender. Francesca fetches some wood from the garage and in a short amount of time a fire is burning in the fireplace spreading a pleasant heat. While the fire is being lit, Marlène is in the kitchen preparing aromatic tea. The jazzy strains of a Nora Jones CD play softly in the background. Relaxed, the friends sit together and play a game of Yahtzee.

"Do you know that in all these years, we have never needed to flee from the cold. We have always been able to spend our evenings outside. But it's nice to see the moody side of Corfu as well and make use of your sitting room."

Francesca smiles and is glad that Marlène isn't bothered by the weather. But the game is like a curse.

Even though she howls with joy and is confident of her win, as the dice land in a very rare Yahtzee combination, Marlène's dice trump hers, and she throws three more Yahtzees, the dice jumping merrily on the table.

"It's impossible, there's got to be foul play here," Francesca says with a forced laugh and demonstratively packs the game back into its box.

"I've had enough. It's getting late. Would you like some more tea?"

18

On this morning, Francesca wakes up to bright sunshine spilling into the room. The rays tickle her nose and elicit a loud sneeze, as they dance their way through the half-closed curtains. She slowly opens her eyes and indulges in a deep stretch as she continues to lounge in bed. *Ahh how nice...today is going to be perfect for swimming!* A quick glance at the clock tells her there is no time for dawdling, as she has an appointment for physiotherapy for her arm which she broke ice skating in a spectacular fall whilst showing off in front off her seven year old niece. Hurrying down to the kitchen where Marlène awaits her with an cheerful, "Good morning!"

"I'm sorry *petite fée*, but I have to leave right away."

Carefully, she takes a sip of the steaming hot coffee from the mug her friend has handed her. "Thank you, you're an angel. I'm already late. I completely forgot to tell you I have an appointment at 9:00 a.m. with the physiotherapist for my arm, but I'll be back in an hour."

While Francesca grabs her handbag, Marlène calls out to her, "It's such nice weather, I'll probably take a walk and go up to see George."

"What a splendid idea. Put on sturdy shoes, and make sure you don't step on the tail of a snake," she says as she walks out the door.

"Whaaat!"

"No worries, I'm only joking. But you should wear sturdy shoes. You never know. Bye, see you later," Francesca gives her friend another smile, and then she is gone.

Marlène butters herself a piece of bread and prepares a cup of tea to take out to the terrace as she cannot function without breakfast. She observes some swallows that have built three nests beneath the sheltered eaves of the roof with fascination. They are now tirelessly feeding their young, twittering and chattering to them loudly as their small open beaks poke out from the nests. Every now and then a small 'plop' can be heard when one of them hangs its small bottom over the nest and ejects some droppings. Francesca has placed some cardboard on the spot below the nests as a preventative measure, so that the stone surface won't have any lasting stains.

She keeps scanning the landscape, which is now in full bloom, allowing her gaze to drift down to the sea. She is filled with boundless joy knowing she will spend yet another week here in this beautiful, quiet place with her best friend, far away from all the everyday worries.

Before long, she hears the same pitiful meowing as the previous day. She doesn't have to wait long before the same black kitten limps towards her armchair. Today as well, it will not let her stroke it. However, she places the left over cat food on a plate and is glad to see the kitten devour it. *I had better keep this sweet little incident secret.*

But then Marlène stands up and is raring to go. She carries the dishes into the kitchen and quickly gets ready. The words of her friend are still ringing in her ears, so she makes it a point to put on sturdy shoes, which she has brought along especially for hiking. As a precaution, she closes all the doors and in the best of moods trudges away through the olive grove to the small cemetery, *Ag. Nikolaos*, that lies farther up on a peaceful elevation.

For the first time, Marlène walks alone on the path, which winds through the olive trees and takes her to the small cemetery where George has found his final resting place. She hesitates when she comes to a spot where the path branches off then decides to take the path on the left. Although, she continues on, she continually wonders if she is on the correct path.

She comes to a marvellous old well made of stone and stops for a few moments in wonder. *It reminds me of the well that my sister, Nicole, and I admired, at this very time last year, on the Way of St. James,* she says to herself and can't help but smile. She continues on for a few more minutes, completely lost in her thoughts as she remembers the unique moment the two sisters had shared together.

A further fork in the path brings her up short. *This place doesn't look familiar at all. I've never been here before...I think I'm lost.*

She looks around and tries to pinpoint something that can help her. There is no one about. In any case, the Greeks that live on this part of the island barely speak any English. The sun has reached its zenith and it is getting increasingly warmer. She is already drenched in sweat. She starts to feel uneasy. *Perhaps, I'm not as far away from my destination as I think, but just lost in nature without knowing how I got here. Do I cut through the trees? But which path? The trails in this area all look the same.* She is gripped by a sense of fear. "George!" she says out aloud. "If you want me to stop by and say hello, then send me a guide. Otherwise I'll be wandering around lost for hours in this place."

Not long after, the call of a cuckoo can be heard, and so she marches off towards the sound. In a short while, she spies the tower of the small chapel located inside the cemetery. Out of breath, she pushes open the entry gate and climbs the steps that lead her to the white marble slab which marks George's grave. In her mind, she thanks the bird that led her here.

From the frame of his picture, which is secured in a niche above the gravesite, George fixes her with his blue-eyed stare. Marlène lights a candle that Francesca has left there, so she can communicate with him through its flame.

Suddenly, it is as if George's smile in the picture contorts and transforms into a grimace. *Oh no, George. Not here in the cemetery, it's terrifying! What's wrong?* The response comes to her immediately.

"*My hair, my clothes, the photoshopped picture,*" he conveys to her.

"Would you like us to change the photograph in the marble frame?" she asks out loud.

"*Francesca can find one where I no longer have this tired smile on display,*" he answers immediately.

Marlène replies to him in a small voice, "Give me a sign to confirm that this really is your wish and not just a figment of my imagination." She remains for a while at the grave of her friend who died far too young, then makes her way back home. All the way back, she puzzles over how she can share George's message with Francesca, that is, if the requested sign will even appear.

She is halfway home when a yellow butterfly suddenly appears and begins fluttering around her, then flits ahead of her until she reaches the entryway to the house. Marlène enters the villa and closes the door behind her. She quickly crosses the sitting room, and full of curiosity walks out onto the terrace. The butterfly is waiting there, settled on a white blossom of one of the oleander bushes lining the property. There can no longer be any doubt. First the cuckoo, then the butterfly, the sign has definitely been sent.

Hunched over, Marlène sits at the table on the terrace in deep concentration as she furiously writes something down in a blue notebook. Her long blonde hair hangs in front of her lovely face like a curtain. She is so engrossed in her work that she doesn't even raise her head when Francesca stands next to her and touches her lightly on the shoulder.

"Hey, what are you doing?" she asks quietly, so as not to startle her friend. Two large, bright blue eyes stare at her in momentary confusion, as if they were being transported back from a different world before lighting up seconds later in cheerful recognition.

She jumps out of her chair almost knocking it over. Francesca has never seen her so agitated.

"Hold on now, slow down, what is going on?"

"George told me he cannot stand the sight of his photo!"

"What? How?"

"You have to destroy it!"

"Okay now, just take a deep breath and start slowly from the beginning."

Then Marlène tells her about her incredible morning.

Without interrupting her friend, Francesca listens and her jaw drops. *This is really one of the most hair-raising stories my petite fée has ever confronted me with. Could it possibly be true? Did this really happen at the cemetery? Is George really so upset about his photograph? Can he even get upset in the place where he is right now?* Now Francesca does have to smile, for her husband did always pay great attention to his appearance. *It's the photo that was taken at Mum's belated birthday celebration, at the end of January, she remembers; and one month later he found out that he was ill. But this totally outlandish tale isn't coming from someone who is schizophrenic, but from my petite fée.*

"You do know how this unbelievable, crazy story must sound to me!"

"But it all happened exactly as I told you. It surprised me as well and I was completely shaken. Something like this has never happened to me before either!"

In her mind Francesca can see the photograph and starts to describe it haltingly to her upset friend. "In the photo, his smile really isn't relaxed and open as it usually used to be, it appears forced." She is now completely fixated on the picture as she continues to remember. "I don't think it's due to the hair, but rather the dark rim at his hairline, where one can easily see the lighter skin. Up until now I had thought that it was due to the cap that he always wore in the summer. But now when I think of it, his darker skin was one of the first signs of his illness, not the sun that was starting to leave its mark."

"Yes, of course! When someone comes to visit him, he naturally doesn't want a photo that shows his illness, instead, he would like it to portray how he really looked. Now you already have two answers, and what's with the photoshopped picture? He told me quite clearly that he didn't like it."

"You're actually right about that too," Francesca has to admit.

"It was taken in a restaurant. I didn't want other people's backs or heads in the picture. That's why I had it cut out and pasted onto a neutral background."

A relieved smile appears on Marlène's face. "You can't believe how happy I am that all this has been cleared up because I didn't feel good about telling you such an outlandish story. And it was a very special, but almost uncanny experience for me."

"There certainly are some strange and unbelievable moments in life. Now I really must exchange the photo for another one."

"That is his message delivered through me." Marlène is beaming once more.

"Come, it's about time I made you a cup of coffee."

While Francesca sips her hot beverage with pleasure and replays the whole incredible story in her mind, Marlène jots down the rest of her notes.

After the emotional morning, they drive to the sandy beach in Glyfada on the west coast. The sun shines down brilliantly from a cloudless sky. The only drawback is a cold, northwest wind that makes them both shiver in their bikinis, even though they have found a sheltered spot to spend the afternoon. Despite this, Marlène wants to swim. It is only with the greatest effort and a honeyed tongue that she can finally convince her friend to brave the ice-cold water; slowly, step by step. It doesn't take long before Marlène's entire body breaks out in goosebumps, and in the shortest amount of time she looks like a small and freezing plucked chicken. Francesca doesn't have time to worry about her trembling friend because she has her own problems.

"Tell me, are we not quite right in the head, or are we a bunch of sadists? This is insane. I can no longer feel my legs!"

"At least I can say that even today I went swimming in the sea." Marlène replies, teeth chattering. "But I think it would be better if we turn back now before we are frozen solid and land up in the intensive care unit due to hypothermia."

They have never changed so quickly out of their wet clothes. Wrapped in large bath towels they take a long time rubbing themselves dry. Marlène pulls on some leggings and slips on a warm pullover. Her friend however, after putting on a dry swimsuit, simply drapes a cotton cardigan across her shoulders. They jog barefoot for a short distance across the sandy shoreline in order to warm up, but it doesn't take long before Francesca gives up gasping for breath.

"What's wrong?" Marlène asks amused. "I thought that you would be in great shape after all your swimming."

"Well...that's the privilege of getting older," Francesca replies airily once her heartbeat is back to normal. As they continue the walk at a slower pace, they have time to leisurely observe the diverse activities taking place on the beach. Every now and then in between all the oiled and tanned bodies sunning on the beach—some reading, others sleeping—a topless woman stands out, her bare white or already reddened breasts starting to burn in the sun.

They not only dodge around teenagers playing Frisbee, but small children as well, who are whooping and yelling as they dash into the breakers under the close watchful gaze of their parents. They carefully step over sandcastles that have not only been built by children but by adults as well, who have constructed them with amazing patience and imagination.

The feeling of sand sifting between the toes and the now warmer wind tousling their hair is sublime. They walk past brightly coloured motorboats and paddle boats that come with built-in slides, though today there is not a lot of demand for them due to the windy conditions. When they arrive at the hotel, the waves tower high and thundering breakers crash onto the shore. The turbulent sea has changed to a dark green contrasted only by the white spume, which has been whipped up by the waves. It is incredibly beautiful, this endless expanse. No barriers, no obstacles, not even a fishing boat is braving the tempestuous sea.

They finally arrive at the south end of the bay with its picturesque rock formations. Overwhelmed by the sight they watch as the waves crash against the rocks, the wind depositing millions of fine droplets of spume on their face, when suddenly a naked man appears from behind a rock, taking both women completely by surprise. Apparently oblivious to the two female onlookers, he starts to leisurely apply sun cream to his penis. The smell of coconut quickly wafts their way.

Both pretend not to notice, as if this event is nothing out of the ordinary and continue to walk for a few metres, trying hard not to focus on his midsection. But then they can go no farther. Enormous, sharp rocks prevent anyone from clambering over them, except for the very brave.

Once they have recovered from their surprise they start to giggle uncontrollably like a couple of teenagers.

"Did I just see what I think I did? That bloke actually slathered sun cream on his finest member," Marlène remarks, completely stunned.

"I really hope so. Otherwise it would mean that the horny bastard is in the process of pleasuring himself! In all the years that I've come here, I've never seen something like this happen," she sputters in reply.

They laugh so hard that they have to hold each other up, until Francesca raises her head and risks a quick glance over her friend's shoulder.

"You know what, you can no longer call this an *innocent* application of sun cream because he's now switched into high gear," Francesca hisses beneath her breath.

"Whaaat...oh nooo...come on, let's get out of here quickly!"

"Just play it cool sweetie, something like this should be a cinch for two old hands like us."

Because they don't want to go anywhere near the man they have to wade through the water for a few metres. Once they are level with where he is standing, they break out running, splashing water in all directions as their buoyant laughter mingles with the loud rush of the surf.

After a while, when they stop to catch their breath, they watch as a silhouette slowly wades into the sea until, shortly thereafter, it disappears from sight. Marlène remarks dryly, "That idiot really needs a cool-down."

The entire way back until they reach their spot, they joke and laugh as they recollect the incident. Then Francesca calls out, "Come on, last one in the water is a rotten egg!"

They hastily strip off the cardigan and pullover and make a mad dash into the water.

The rest of the afternoon passes by quickly. Even though it is still rather windy, the brilliant sunny weather has contributed to warming up the atmosphere. Marlène has her nose stuck in the book by James Redfield, while Francesca gazes dreamily at the sea, which has calmed down and traded in its former dark colour for an intense blue. Idly, she casts a glance at the people all around her until the gentle sound of the rushing of the waves start making her drowsy, her eyes close and she falls fast asleep.

She awakens abruptly and looks dazed into the smiling face of her friend, who is soaking wet and standing over her, cheerfully splashing her with water. "You've got more than enough time to sleep at night. If you still want to go in the water, now's your chance because it's getting quite late."

Francesca has no real desire to get up. She executes an expansive yawn and stretches idly on her lounger.

"Hmm, don't be in such a hurry. Please let's not get all stressed out."

But Marlène has already stripped off her wet bikini, stepped into her jeans and pulled on a long-sleeved sweatshirt. Unimpressed with her lazy friend, who is still lying there motionless, with her eyes demonstratively closed, she packs up her belongings. With a sigh, Francesca finally rises and also stuffs her things into her beach bag. She knows when she is beaten and, resigned, stomps back to the car behind her stubborn *petite fée*.

This evening as well, she has no desire to sit with a cold nose out on the terrace all bundled up in thick jackets. Francesca shows Marlène how to prepare *spanakopita*, a spinach pie, which they later enjoy by candlelight in front of the fire listening to music. While Marlène brews herself a cup of hot tea, her friend is feeling more like a glass of exquisite red wine. It is extremely cosy and comfortably warm. Both are lost in thought as they watch the licking tongues of flame that have an almost hypnotic effect on Francesca. She has to think back to this morning, which unexpectedly releases an assault of guilty feelings. She breaks the silence in a soft, trembling voice, "This morning you were very animated when you told me about George, how he can't stand the picture at his gravesite, and how I should destroy it. I simply can't comprehend how he could get so upset over something as trivial as a picture, but he never mentions to you how disappointed he is with me. How I abandoned him during his most difficult days. I pretended as if he would get well again, that in the end everything would turn out all right. When he needed me the most, I let him down with all of his doubts and fears. If he would just complain to you about me, that would be understandable. But no...he gets upset over a stupid photo. I would so like to know if he has forgiven me...I can't even forgive myself," she finishes choking back her tears.

"The only way to find peace with yourself is to do it right now. Start with it step by step. Forget the notion that you could have done something differently or changed something in the past. It is what it is. Naturally you will fall back into your usual pattern, you will doubt yourself and your grief will get the upper hand. But keep your eyes on the goal you have set for you: To be at peace with yourself."

19

It is early in the morning and Francesca is already standing in the garden dressed in her old, torn jeans and a t-shirt with a hose pipe in her hand giving the young citrus trees a thorough watering. Each one of them is closely inspected, as she looks for signs of bugs or any other rodent or pest. She is pleased with the many small trees that have grown during the winter months. It is amazing how hundreds of miniscule green fruits developed from the white blossoms, which not too long ago gave off a strong and heady fragrance. *I hope they don't all fall off again like they did last year before they can ripen into oranges and lemons,* she muses.

Suddenly, she discovers that Marlène is standing behind her ready to go in her pink shorts and matching top. Her long blonde hair has been pulled back into a ponytail.

"I've been looking for you everywhere in the house!"

"Hey, good morning, you're up already." They give each other a cheerful hug.

"I'm almost done here, it won't take too long."

"Go ahead and finish your work. In the meantime, I'll walk around the property and say hello to my old gnarled friend, the olive tree. That's why I wore my sturdy shoes," she raises her hand in salutation and tromps off.

She walks towards her favourite olive tree so she can greet it and absorb some of its energy—something she does every time she comes to Corfu. As she draws closer she stops, and looks at the tree in amazement. *Oh no! From this angle, it almost looks dead. Part of the trunk has died.* She walks around the tree and on the other side she finds it looking just as she had pictured it. Relieved, she wraps her arms around it, feeling the energy generating from its bark, the pulsating life force that flows from its roots all the way to its branches.

Leisurely she strolls around the tree once more. Viewed from the south, it is made up of three separate parts. First, there is the trunk that is growing to the right, and then another that is growing to the left, and growing out from that one is a third part, which has been cut off about one metre above the ground. A rock sits in the divide of the two living trunks, right where a human heart would be.

Shortly thereafter, Francesca hears her name called insistently several times. She immediately turns off the water and runs in the direction of where she assumes her friend to be. As she comes closer, Marlène waves her over excitedly.

"What happened, did you find a snake?"

"Nonsense!" Marlène places her arm around her worried friend.

"That over there is my olive tree, right?" Francesca can only nod her head not comprehending.

"Yes, and...?"

"A few years ago, you showed me this tree, which I consider to be my little part of Greece within your home. It has fascinated me since I saw it for the first time, without knowing why. Now I can see the big picture. Do you notice anything in particular, especially if you take a closer look?" And indeed, now Francesca can see what has gotten Marlène so excited.

"That's you and George embracing: one side is dead while the other is alive and covered in soft moss. I am the third part, by both of your sides, and we all share the same roots, but are separated by this rock; I don't interfere with your love for each other, but I am bound to both of you by an immeasurable friendship."

Francesca has walked past this tree countless times and never noticed anything out of the ordinary. Only today, once her friend has made her aware of it, does she see the obvious. The olive tree is not only composed of two trunks that have grown together, but there is also a third—dead—trunk wedged in on the northern side that had been cut back some time ago—a small stump protruding from the gnarled tree trunk. Francesca immediately sees Marlène's point.

"Amazing!"

"And now I understand the incredible experience you had last year, when you felt as if the tree were trying to suck you in." Excited, she looks her friend in the eye.

"I didn't have such a powerful experience as yours by far. I could only feel its energy, its life force. That's why it was never just *my* tree; it has always been *ours*! You, George and I all come from the same root source, together we are one and the same trunk."

Francesca is speechless. What an extraordinary statement.

Later, during breakfast, which they are finally able to have on the terrace, they have a long and animated conversation about the morning's unusual discovery while Ermioni tends to the household.

"I don't believe it," Francesca suddenly cries out and frowns as she walks towards the garage. "The black, limping cat has actually managed to bring along two more starving companions today."

Marlène gives an amused laugh.

"I guess the word got around quickly that there's good food to be had here."

"This isn't a sanctuary for ugly and disabled cats," Francesca says grouchily.

While Marlène runs to the kitchen to fetch the last tin of food for the poor starving creatures, she chuckles softly to herself. *She'll get over it; I know her soft heart.*

"For goodness sakes, do you have to do that? If you don't feed them they'll try their luck somewhere else," Francesca says impatiently. But she knows her friend far too well. She has a hard time saying "no". The more forlorn the creatures look, the more they move her enormous heart. The three unfortunate-looking felines have chosen the two women to be their providers, so they can stuff themselves for the foreseeable future without having to rely on thin air and the occasional mouse. Somehow, they know they'll be fed gourmet food. While Marlène feeds them, she comes up with names.

The older ginger and white-striped male, who has probably used up most of his nine lives, is christened 'Bum Ear'.

The old female one-eyed tabby receives the name 'Cyclops,' and the third one, the black kitten that swings its hind leg as it walks, she calls 'Limpy.'

"There's no helping you; and afterwards I get stuck with this group of ruffians."

"You should be glad. Now, you have a large, extended family. And because they look so bold and daring, they'll protect you from any burglar." The three new members of the household pay no attention to the back and forth teasing and continue to devour their food. Who knows when they will get their next meal.

After they have fed their new, wild-looking friends, the two women drive into town where they are meeting Despina. They take their clueless friend and steer her through the entire town with pleasure until they stop in front of the Pandora shop's display window. One after the other the happy trio enter the shop where they are greeted by a chubby and effeminate, but very friendly male clerk, who recognizes them from earlier visits to the shop. Heads bent over the showcases, they admire the newest arrivals. Marlène would like to give Despina her birthday present now because, again, she will not be there in October to celebrate her 60th birthday. Therefore, she asks the lucky one to pick out a charm for her bracelet. After a great deal of indecision, Despina chooses a charm of a mask representing the Greek theatre with its two faces: one comic and one tragic. Happy and with a big hug she thanks Marlène for the unexpected surprise.

In the best of moods, the three of them enjoy a delicious lunch at a newly opened eatery. They discuss and philosophise enjoying one another's company and deep friendship. Despina reflects a little surprised, *I'm sitting here across two modern-day "Heidis" and have to ask myself how people from different countries, cultures etc., who are brought together through unusual circumstances, can have a spiritual connection. It didn't take long to determine that by saying a single word or the name of a very special loved one out loud, an entire spiritual realm is revealed that can carry human relationships to levels beyond the imagination. I treasure the time we get to spend with each other, and I am curious and looking forward to finding out more about myself after all the valuable discussions we have had.*

Marlène makes the spontaneous suggestion to travel to Glyfada to go swimming because the beautiful sandy beach is only a short drive away. Despina is hardly enthused with this unplanned event. Unimpressed with her friends' howls of protest, she graciously says goodbye and takes a taxi back home.

When the two remaining friends arrive in Glyfada, they take a relaxing walk along the beach until they find a suitable spot. On this late afternoon, the western coast has an almost mystical charm. The muted light floods the entire beach. No wind is blowing—it is completely still; the mood is divine.

The endless sea is crystal-clear today as it lies before them. Haltingly, Marlène dips one foot in the water and immediately sucks in her breath. In shock, she looks back to Francesca, who is standing behind her waiting. "Brr, the water is still ice-cold. It hasn't warmed up one bit since yesterday."

Francesca has to laugh, "Well, you really can't expect it to happen that quickly!"

But today they don't let the cold water discourage them. Francesca looks on in amazement as within seconds her *petite fée* dives beneath the surface and then rapidly swims away. She doesn't want to be left standing there all prim and proper, so before she can change her mind she jumps into the water as well, and with a loud shriek hastily swims after her friend. It doesn't take long before they overcome the cold shock and feeling euphoric, they swim out to the elegant villa majestically enthroned on a large rocky promontory, which overlooks the bay.

Later on, after changing out of their wet clothes, they relax on their loungers. Marlène looks like a schoolgirl. Her long hair has been braided into two plaits, which she has fastened on top of her head with a hair clip. In her beach bag, she has discovered her old, faded purple hat made of woven straw that no longer has any shape to it. While anyone else would look ridiculous wearing it, she looks just as beautiful and fetching as always. Clutching a book in one hand and a ice cream lolly in the other which she licks with delight. The sun lies low on the horizon, gilding the water with its diminishing warm glow.

It is early in the evening when they arrive in Gouvia. Before they return home, they want to go shopping and have a little taste of the nightlife. They quickly make their rounds through the resort.

"Hey, stop it with the yawning," Francesca remarks with a laugh, and gently nudges her friend on the side with her elbow.

"It's high time for an aperitif. There's a nice little bar directly on the beach with a view of the marina, Komeno and the little island with the small chapel, Ipapanti."

Not long after, Francesca is enjoying sips of a delicious mojito while her foot taps to the beat of music. Marlène, on the other hand, is drinking an iced tea while she watches in amusement as a dog runs along the shore trying to shake off her two admirers. Although dusk has already set in casting a soft glow, it is still light outside on this June evening and it is pleasantly warm. The bar is soon filled with cheery, sunburned people conversing animatedly. Some are standing around with a chilled glass of wine, others are holding an ice-cold beer or nursing cocktails decorated with colourful umbrellas. At first timidly, but then more daring, a few children start to dance to the reggae rhythms of Bob Marley, encouraged by their proud parents. The two friends sit and enjoy the relaxed atmosphere while they chill-out gazing at the sea observing solitary boats as they slowly pull into the marina for the night.

Much later at home, seated at an elegantly set table with lit candles that bathe them in warm light, soft music playing in the background, they enjoy their evening meal in complete harmony. They talk about this and that, when Marlène suddenly asks her friend, "Hey...have you given any thought to what kind of tattoo you'd like to get? We've spoken about this a lot in the past few months, how cool it would be if we would each get a tattoo."

"Honestly...I've never really wanted to because I thought it would be inappropriate at my age. You know, slack skin, gravitational challenges etc. I really don't want to have this black droopy mass in a few years," Francesca laughs. But then with a short apology she excuses herself and runs upstairs to the first floor. Marlène watches her retreat in surprise.

Does she always have to exaggerate like this? Coward! She doesn't need to puzzle over this for long though, for a moment later Francesca hands her a clear view folder that she has retrieved from her office. Carefully Marlène removes a page.

"What is this?" she asks perplexed.

"I found this among my personal things a few days after George died," Francesca says in a faltering voice. "He must have drawn it during his final days when we came home from hospital and then hid it in my drawer."

Her friend studies the page with astonishment. A symbol has been drawn on it with a red marker pen.

"This looks like a Star of David with indecipherable signs in its centre and symbols encircling the outside. Written below it are the words, *"Good Luck!"* It's an emotional thing to be holding the final words that a man has written to his wife."

"Yes, it is...but what does an Orthodox Greek Christian have to do with a Star of David? Unfortunately, I never asked George what exactly this emblem means. I could only feel that this was something of great importance to him, and I assumed that to him it simply meant *Success* and *Protection*, that it was some kind of good luck charm."

"It's a pity the symbols surrounding the star are indecipherable, or do you know something more specific about them?"

"Unfortunately, not a lot. But those initials in the centre of the star that are intertwined with each other are our initials."

"That's right...now I see it too."

"That's why this is the only image I would want for a tattoo. For me it has a very personal meaning, I feel strongly connected to it." Francesca traces the star's contours with her finger in a faint caress and then stops at the initials as she ponders, "When I was certain that I was really going to go through with it and get a tattoo, I did a search on the Internet to educate myself on the star's meaning as well as the unusual symbols."

"Okay, don't keep me in suspense. What did you find out?"

"It's actually a hexagram, and among other things, it is also considered a symbol for the macrocosm. In alchemy, it is a symbol for the four elements: fire, air, water and earth."

Marlène follows her friend's explanations and studies the drawing with interest. "Fantastic! And look closely—it is a six-pointed star composed of two triangles. It represents the connection between The Creator—where the triangle points down and its base faces up—and Human Nature, where the triangle points up, and its base is at the bottom. It is an illustration of the formula: "That which is above is the same as that which is below." It is considered as a divine sign and bearer of a spiritual influence. It is a guiding star and embodies the goal to be achieved."

"That's a beautiful representation, I like it."

"Do you already know where you want to put the tattoo?"

"Well I can't put it on my shoulder because I'd no longer feel balanced. What about between the shoulder blades? It wouldn't be noticeable in a dress or t-shirt, it would be more discreet."

Marlène shakes her head. "You should have it done below the neck because that is where the energy point is, the door between heaven and earth."

"Okay, cool, that's how I'll do it. Thank you, *ma petite fée*. Now I'm quite certain that this will be the perfect tattoo for me, and in the perfect place."

"You still haven't explained the symbols surrounding the star to me because that's very important. You can't have something tattooed on you when you're not quite sure of its significance."

"I did do my research there as well and found out that the symbols represent different planets. But why George drew them, I'm not sure."

"So just leave the planets. Even without them it is still very beautiful and special," Marlène's blue eyes light up. "I can't wait until winter when we go on our tattoo adventure."

Francesca has to smile at her friend's enthusiasm. "You shouldn't catapult us into the future, we need to live in the here and now!"

"Yes, yes, I know, but I'm still glad that you finally gave in. And we are going to reserve a full day for this outing. Lunch, shopping, tattoo…a real girls' day."

20

It is only 9:00 a.m. when Marlène and Francesca drive off after breakfast, well prepared for the beautiful sunny weather. Marlène looks gorgeous in her white lace skirt and faded top. A white cotton pullover is draped over her shoulders, and at the moment her vibrant pareo with the fish print is being used as a scarf.

Francesca also happens to be wearing white. It is a simple, loose dress that emphasises her even tan. A fleece jacket in white, as well as one of her many hats are lying on the back seat of her car.

Cheerful and looking forward to the day, they drive down the gravel path to the main road debating whether to head north or south for the day's outing. Merky's blinker points left. The decision has been made; they drive to Arillas, on the northwest end of the island.

Nature in June shows itself at its most beautiful. Entire avenues of oleander line many of the roads, some growing as large as trees. Marlène is delighted and can barely get enough of this floral abundance.

Arillas is a small, quiet spot for a holiday, with a few inns, some cafés and *tavernas*. Before them lies a long, narrow sandy beach that extends all the way to the end of the bay, which is lined with blue loungers and umbrellas that at the moment are still unoccupied. The small island, Erikoussa, can be seen just off the coast. A flimsy pier, with a bench at one end, leads out into the sea. They are two of the first people there this morning and quietly look around observing their surroundings. Marlène especially takes time to absorb this beautiful picture because she has never been here before.

"Do you see what I see?" she suddenly asks, grinning. Francesca knows her *petite fée* too well. They both take off at a run. Out of breath they arrive at a white Bedouin tent and, amidst giddy laughter, they let themselves fall onto two loungers with violet mattresses and pillows. A small wooden table with a bucket of ice and a bottle of water stands in between the loungers. The tent is enveloped with soft, white tulle—it is simply heavenly, made for princesses!

The calm sea lies just a few metres away from them. A lone house sits enthroned above them like a watchman on the north end of the bay at Cape Kavo Kefali. A light breeze stirs the air. After they have liberally applied sun cream, they both head north to take an exploratory walk as far as the shoreline will allow them.

Recently, very harsh winter weather stirred up the sea to the point where it flooded over large portions of the beach and swallowed up the sand, leaving only large rocks in its wake. With a little luck, the sea might disgorge all the sand back on the beach in the following year.

Lady Luck is on the friends' side because before them lies a long, stunningly beautiful sandy beach that runs along the very steep coast. The last few winter storms have contributed to the erosion of the sand and clay-streaked rock, much to the joy of the beachgoers, for it has resulted in the narrow beach growing wider and more accessible.

The farther they walk along the cliff, the more protection it provides from the wind, which is increasing in strength. To their delight they find ideal-sized chunks of clay that they break off and stick in crevices to collect on their way back. The clay here is considered a valuable remedy, which nature provides in abundance. First, it is moistened to make a paste, then the paste is spread evenly over the entire body and left to dry. The two women are already familiar with this procedure and do not want to pass up the pleasant opportunity, but they first want to continue with their walk.

Meanwhile the wind has let up completely and because of this it has warmed up considerably. Without a care in the world they stroll down the beautiful beach along the steep coast, continuing casually past the nude beach with all the naked bodies—in all variations—on display, both of them trying to act as natural as possible. They find it hard, though, not to bite back a few comments and fill the self-conscious void with their loud giggles.

At the end of the bay, however, there is not a soul in sight and the beach is strewn with an abundance of bright, colourful stones. It is absolutely still and sublime, all around them only sand and the heavenly, inviting sea. It has gotten too warm for Francesca... water splashes in all directions as she whoops and leaps into the sea. Soon she stops and out of breath turns around and looks about for her friend in astonishment.

"Why aren't you getting in? It's heavenly!"

Marlène does not look too enthusiastic. "My bikini will get wet, and I don't want to have to walk back in my wet things."

"We're hanging out around nudists, aren't we?"

Francesca strips off her bikini with a mischievous grin. Her *petite fée* follows her lead haltingly. But then, with increased courage and a feeling of joy, she runs after her friend. It is a wonderful sensation, and it doesn't take long before they are caught up in a playful water battle. They can hardly believe that now they too have suddenly "outed" themselves, as they relax into the pleasurable feeling of swimming naked.

Despite all their larking about they don't fail to notice how the once empty beach has now increased with activity. A growing number of naked beachcombers are bent over as they search for stones, approaching the exact spot where Francesca has left her conspicuous red bag with her money, car keys and Ray Bans, in addition to their bikinis.

Two newcomers, with an impressive display of exposed white skin that is already showing patches of pink reminiscent of two little piglets, stride slowly and majestically into the sea. They make a beeline for the two mermaids, who had hoped to enjoy their newly discovered nude tendencies alone and undisturbed in this deserted end of the bay.

They can barely contain their amusement succumbing to bouts of laughter, especially when they realize that all the Adams and Eves on the shore are not only watching in interest, but have also begun to wade out towards them in order to get a closer look at the 'fresh meat'.

"Seriously? They have almost the entire beach to themselves and they still have to come here!" In order to scare them off, Francesca executes a handstand and several tumbles in the water, which promptly seems to work. The two pink admirers, who have been waiting close by for a while, wade side-by-side back to the beach insulted when they determine that there will be no sensible conversation with these two. As their large round bottoms, which are practically the same size, emerge from the sea Marlène bursts out in hysterical laughter.

After calming down a little, she explains breathlessly, "To me, their bums looked like two pink piggy banks waiting for someone to stick a 2-Euro coin in the slot!"

"You are totally insane and have a bizarre sense of humour!" Francesca cries out as she shakes with laughter.

After this uncontrolled behaviour, they manage to calm down again. Demure and civilized, they slowly emerge from the sea, change into their dry bikinis and spend some time searching for beautiful stones as if nothing has happened. Meanwhile the others are lying farther away from them and have resumed working on their seamless tans.

When they eventually return to their Bedouin tent and lie down in the sun, the light breeze has turned into a stiff wind. Even though, Marlène has tugged on her pullover and is wearing leggings underneath her lace skirt, she trembles with cold. Francesca had originally wanted to spend all day in Arillas with her friend. Then years ago, when she and George had explored the island, they had wound up here and spent an unforgettable evening together. In a *taverna* right by the sea, they had eaten spaghetti with lobster. Later on, they had sat cuddled up on the beach and watched an unforgettable sunset. Then, sheltered by the dark they had bathed naked. At some point her husband had been able to find a small room where they had spent the night together, in each other's arms.

Unfortunately, the incessant wind increases. "Are we destined to endure this here, or can we drive somewhere else where we're more sheltered from the wind?" Marlène asks in a wavering voice, as she huddles deeper into her beach towel, her frozen form a pitiful sight to behold.

"We don't have to stay. Let's pack up our things and get out of here. We'll drive farther north towards Sidari or Roda. We can eat something there instead of here." Before Francesca can even ease out of her lounger, her friend has already packed and is running towards the car. Inside it is deliciously warm from the sun.

Marlène has soon forgotten her earlier "almost-frostbitten-parts" and is back to her cheerful, lively self as she gazes out the window admiring the many scenic villages they are passing through. An abundance of white and pink oleander is blooming all around them. In this verdant, hilly region purple bougainvillea adds its attractive, colourful punctuation in the form of artfully shaped trees or draped over entryways in lush, intoxicating arches.

"Isn't that Sidari down there?" Marlène remarks suddenly.

"Yes, but it's no longer a lovely place, they have made it unsightly over the last few years. Let's just continue on to Roda," Francesca suggests.

"Is there something special to see there?"

"The most impressive and beautiful things about this place are the sandstone cliffs and the deep fjords that extend along the entire northern coast, especially the legendary *Canal d'Amour*. Young boys would jump off the cliffs into the sea then fight their way back up on a rope to the top."

As Marlène looks over at her friend, she can see how her lips are pressed together in irritation.

"Unfortunately, the fishing village of the 80's and 90's has turned into an overcrowded, ugly tourist development, and the charm that used to surround this place has been lost."

While they continue the drive towards Roda, Marlène can't help but feel deep in her heart that they are putting distance between themselves and a unique village, and if she doesn't visit it, her explorations of the island will never be complete. She finds it hard to believe that the encroaching tourist industry has completely smothered the special energy associated with the place. This region is an integral part of Greek history. She is filled with a sense of unrelenting battles, piracy and intrigues. She feels like she absolutely must go there. And yet, a magical influence is at work once more...

Francesca starts to feel selfish. Just because she is bitter that in the past few years the inhabitants of this village have turned this once untouched region into an overcrowded tourist trap, this doesn't give her the right to prevent Marlène from visiting it. She should draw her own conclusions. She has barely finished this thought before Marlène asks shyly, "Can't we turn back and at least take a quick peek at Sidari? We don't have to stay; we can still drive to Roda to eat."

Her friend is already turning the car around and quickly drives the short stretch back to Sidari. Bars, travel agencies and cheap souvenir shops line the main street, which winds its way through the entire village. The former natural charm of the village has truly vanished. They ask their way through a labyrinth of streets until they are headed in the direction of the *Canal d'Amour*.

The sun shines down warmly from a cloudless sky. The rocky coast that winds past Sidari protects them from a cold, north-westerly wind. Francesca wraps a red, sun-bleached pareo casually around her hips and puts on a hat while Marlène dispenses with her leggings and seconds later is standing next to her friend in her white lace skirt. Her pullover, she has tied around her hips. It only takes a few minutes to walk single file up a steep path until they reach the cliff top. They stand side by side and look out in silent wonder at the imposing sandstone cliffs that rise up from the deep blue sea. Boats slowly chug by leaving white foam in their wake. The Albanian coast is visible from here as well.

"Wow...what a unique, fascinating view from up here, what a panorama! It's simply magnificent." Marlène inhales deeply and reaches out her arms as if she were embracing the world. "It's so beautiful. You can even smell the island's fragrance."

"I had erased the untamed beauty of this place from my memory, after coming here for so many years," Francesca replies, just as overwhelmed. "It's just a pity that there is nothing left of the former charming fishing village. But when you're up here, you can forget everything."

A pleasant stroll along the estuary takes them straight to the *Canal d'Amour*. "Oh my...how this place has changed in these past few years. I can no longer recognize anything. It's such a shame that the *Canal D'Amour* has fallen victim to erosion. There can be no other explanation for it."

"It's still uniquely beautiful, something very special," Marlène replies. She is completely fascinated by the sandstone cliffs, which nature has shaped into incredible formations over the course of millions of years. Her eyes round in wonder, she absorbs as much as possible of her surroundings. She takes countless photos running back and forth in excitement, so that each and every spot can be immortalised. When she places her hand against the cliff wall, she realizes in astonishment that it is as smooth as velvet. She can feel her hands become one with the rock, the sea and the sky. Her heart begins to beat faster in her chest as she feels herself melt into the surrounding nature. Her feet are rooted to the ground, the sun caresses her skin and she inhales the smell of the wind and the waves that roll in from the sea and crash against the rocks.

"Look," Francesca points to a small cove with a sandy spot of beach. She interrupts her friend's flow of thought bringing her back to reality with a jolt.

"Sidari is surrounded by cliffs that reveal impressive rock arches carved out over the course of millennia by wind and water. And, by the way, according to legend every young and unmarried woman who swims through the *Canal d'Amour*, will supposedly find the perfect husband."

"That's sweet, well...it would no longer apply to us!" she replies, laughing.

They walk right up to the cliff's edge and peer over the ridge at the turquoise, crystal clear water below. "Over there you can see the other two islands, Othoni and Mathraki. The third island, Erikoussa, you were able to see this morning from Arillas."

"You know what, my stomach's really growling. I am ravenous."

Francesca laughs. "No wonder, it's already past 2 p.m. Come on, let's go look for something edible."

They both walk across the terraced rocks until they happen upon an inviting fish *taverna* with a breathtaking view of the sea and the cliffs along the coast. It doesn't take long before they are enjoying delicious calamari and octopus. While they digest their food, they rent a pedal boat with a collapsible sunroof so they can investigate the cliffs and small coves from close up. They put some serious energy into it and pedal away at a mad pace. For an hour, they admire the bizarre rock formations from the water.

"That's so wild, there's a cave over there that you can swim through," Marlène points out as she steers the pedal boat towards the entrance.

"I love it! And look over there, the smooth chalk drawings on the walls. And doesn't that wall over there look like a gallery with its water-eroded chambers? Like stalagmites in a cave!" Francesca points excitedly to a bizarre rock formation. Over the course of time, small holes in the chalky rock have grown into larger caves or elongated galleries, such as the one here.

The girls are smiling up a storm. They are more than pleased with their spontaneous outing. Francesca is especially happy that she has been able to show her *petite fée* yet another new and mysterious side of Corfu.

"Seeing that we're already hanging out in the north end of the island, what if we drive to Roda and go swimming there? To be honest, the beach is probably less busy there judging by all the loungers lined up here. What do you think?"

After a short drive along the coast, they arrive in Roda which is a quiet, picturesque village surrounded by lush fields and fragrant olive groves. They only have to cross the street to arrive at the long beach, which is sheltered from the wind. There are only a few visitors, who are enjoying the last rays of the setting sun. The pareo and lace skirt drop to the sand, and quick as a wink they are both running into the warm, shallow water. They have to wade out quite far until they are finally able to swim.

"Can you walk along the coast all the way to Sidari from here?" Marlène asks as she floats on her back.

"I think so. If you have a lot of time, it's a lovely walk."

When they emerge from the sea, dripping wet, Francesca presses a chunk of clay that she brought from Arillas into Marlène's hand. Eagerly, they smear themselves from head to toe with it, paying no attention to the occasional curious onlooker. Until the muck dries, they walk along the beach and search in vain for seashells or a pretty stone. Even though it is late in the afternoon, it is still comfortably mild outside. In order to rinse off the now dry clay they sit in the warm, shallow water. When Francesca stands up, Marlène points to her backside and exclaims, "Careful, there's something hanging from your bikini bottom!"

Startled, Francesca turns around to look at her backside. And there, indeed, is a brownish-grey starfish helplessly clinging to her bum. She carefully removes the poor thing, who just had a house sit on it, noting with relief that the unlucky fellow is fortunately still alive. She carefully places him in deeper water on the seafloor a few steps farther away, and as a precaution covers him with sand.

"It's been a long time since I've seen a starfish," Francesca laughs, "and now there's one hanging onto my bum!"

An older woman dressed in black and wearing a kerchief is selling a variety of fruits from an old hand cart. The friends buy some cherries and peaches to eat at the beach until they slip into some dry clothes, pack up all their belongings and walk back to the car.

They drive along the winding coastal road towards Corfu until Francesca suddenly turns off the road.

"Hey, what are you doing?"

"Surprise!" Francesca drives down a steep, tortuous road hoping to reach the small fishing village, Agios Stefanos, in time for them to see the sunset. The village is located in north-eastern Corfu. It is enclosed by steep slopes studded with gnarled, silvery-green olive trees punctuated only by tall pointed cypress. The view across the strait to the bare Albanian mountains is stunning.

"Well, did I promise too much?"

"No, it is quite beautiful." *Does she have to drive so fast on this narrow road, and why aren't there any proper safety barriers? Hopefully, her foot is resting close to the brakes.* "For that, I am officially inviting you out for a drink."

They find a parking spot and stroll around the village, which lies right by the sea and has been developed in the shape of a horseshoe. They take a seat in inviting chairs in front of a café and watch the sun as it dips below the hills.

"It's too bad I can't offer you a sunset like the one in Arillas, where the sun sets into the sea like a large red globe."

"You'll show me that another time. Right now, I am going to enjoy this beautiful place. Francesca has ordered a gin and tonic, and Marlène toasts with her with a glass of iced tea."

"*Yamas*...isn't that how the Greeks say cheers?" Francesca has to smile at her friend's enthusiasm and simply nods in reply.

"*Yamas, Yamas*..." they raise their glasses and make a toast to a beautiful day.

Tired, but feeling fulfilled, from this long, day they finally drive back home, each one lost in her own thoughts. Along the way they stop by Emerald bakery for some ice cream, and full of contentment they enjoy their refreshing treat under the clear, starlit sky.

21

By the time the rooster crows in the morning, the temperature is almost as high as in the summer, though dark threatening storm clouds hang low in the sky. Neither of them is in a hurry to climb out of bed in this dreary, wet weather. When they finally do meet in the kitchen later on, they greet each other with sleepy expressions.

"What a depressing morning, so dreary and wet," Francesca remarks from behind her hand as she yawns. "No wonder I feel so sapped of energy."

"But let's still have breakfast outside. Afterwards we'll be prepared for the day and have so much energy that we'll be able to uproot trees," Marlène replies unconvincingly.

Their good mood returns as the two friends, who are still in their pyjamas, devour their food especially when Marlène spies the three derelict cats roaming around at the far end of the terrace.

"Look over there, it's Limpy and Bum Ear."

"And over there, peeking out from behind the oleander bush is the old one-eyed tabby that looks frightened," Francesca replies amused.

"That's Cyclops," Marlène corrects her. She quickly breaks off a piece of bread, which she first smears with butter before she slowly, so as not to startle them, approaches the cats. In vain she tries to coax them to come closer in a soft voice. The three of them wait warily at a safe distance until their benefactor has placed their food in a bowl on the ground and is sitting back at the table. Only then do they attack their food ravenously. Cyclops, however, pauses at regular intervals to cast a suspicious glance in their direction.

In vain, the sun tries to penetrate the cloud cover to send a few of its rays to earth despite the dark, rain-filled clouds that are growing deeper.

"How do you feel about exploring the town while it's raining and storming?" Francesca asks with a wink as she looks at her friend challengingly.

"That's a super idea. There's no way we can go swimming, and we don't want to be sitting around the house all day."

"I'll even lend you a pair of leopard print wellies, so at least your dainty little feet will stay dry," Francesca grins.

Marlène beams and gives her two thumbs up. Straight away they take their cups and plates back into the kitchen then zip up to their rooms to shower and change. Francesca puts on a pair of jeans and a t-shirt and chooses a waterproof windbreaker with a hood. Her feet are enclosed in a pair of bright red Wellington boots decorated with cute little monkey heads. Marlène decides on faded, dark green designer trousers paired with a pink cotton pullover; a jacket gets tied around her hips. They quickly collect the cushions from the terrace and close all the windows and doors before they head out prepared for every weather. Then they drive off in an upbeat mood.

Without mentioning it beforehand, Francesca makes an unannounced stop at the post office. Before her friend can say a word, she has already hopped out of the car and disappeared behind the door. It doesn't take long before she reappears with a broad smile on her face holding a flat parcel in her hand. She makes a mad dash to the car and drops into the driver's seat just before the sky opens up to release a torrential downpour. While the rain pounds the roof of the car and a cascade of water flows down the windows, Marlène inquires in a loud voice in order to be heard over the din, "What's in there...why are you acting so mysterious?"

"I wanted to surprise you with it. I have been waiting all week for the first copy of my book to arrive from my publisher, and, drumroll, here it is! It was in my mailbox today."

"Wow! Let's see. How exciting. I am so proud of you. I'm looking forward to reading it."

"It's a pity that George can't experience this incredible moment with me." Francesca's eyes fill with tears. No! She will not destroy this very special moment, and she quickly wipes her hand across her face.

"It is the first complete edition that they have sent me for a final review before it is released for print and distribution," she says, as she swallows the last of her tears. With a racing heart, she tears open the parcel, and moments later she reverently holds her first book in her hands. Her baby. Born in pain. Full of emotion, she softly reads the title, "*James: Diary of an Adventurous and Emotional Pilgrimage Through Spain.* Imagine that, my first book. Amazing..."

The windscreen wipers are running at full speed, as Francesca navigates the partially flooded roads at snail's pace following some equally crazy drivers who are out in this weather. Unlike her *petite fée*, she has experienced these storms in Corfu quite often. Marlène looks out her window with a fixed stare watching the water on the road continue to rise, as it is unable to drain fast enough. Slowly and cautiously the cars in front of them drive through enormous puddles spraying fountains of water on either side. In between, she casts a glance at her friend, who is trying to distract her with amusing anecdotes of other storms that have taken place in the past.

Without any noteworthy incidents, except perhaps for a few cars that have pulled off to the side to wait for the worst to pass, they arrive in town safe and sound. After parking the car at the fish market, they hurry beneath the protected arcades and through streets and alleys that have been washed clean by the rain, sheltered only by a pitifully small, collapsible green umbrella. In a brief period of time they are soaking wet—only their feet remain dry.

Laughing, Marlène drags Francesca into the Pandora shop in order to have a short respite from the pouring rain. After shaking themselves off, they fasten their eyes on the tempting displays of beautiful and original jewellery. Marlène's attention is drawn to a silver feather entwined with a delicate, black leather band and finished with a round clasp, which is also made of silver. It is the perfect present that she wants to give Francesca to symbolically commemorate the arrival of her first book. Francesca is touched by this unexpected, very special, gift and immediately lets her friend secure it around her right wrist.

For herself, Marlène wants to purchase *The Eye of Greece*. Francesca places an arm around her shoulder and takes the charm from her to inspect it closer.

"According to legend, in order for the eye to protect someone, it has to be offered to that person by somebody else. So, for this reason my dear, I give this eye to you to add to your bracelet, to commemorate this unforgettable, once-in a-lifetime day, and I hope it will always protect you."

The sales clerk is touched by this gesture, when she sees the two friends embrace and thank each other for their unexpected presents.

It is still pouring buckets outside. Carefree, they stroll arm in arm beneath their tiny umbrella through the almost deserted town, where the water is streaming along the side of the curb down to the harbour, singing jauntily: "We're singing in the rain, just singing in the rain, lalalala..." A few of the pedestrians, who are hurrying through the streets ducked low beneath their umbrellas look at the two silly women and shake their heads. Every now and then, the friends stop off in one of the many boutiques in order to get out of the rain. They eagerly try on clothing and shoes, while outside the town looks like an automatic car wash, with bubbles of foam floating everywhere on its streets.

Meanwhile, they have both become hungry and are sopping wet. Just as they enter a *taverna*, they hear a loud splash right behind them...startled, they stop and turn around. It is as if all the Greek gods had emptied their bathtubs. In seconds the sidewalk is flooded. At the same time, countless streaks of lightning illuminate the sky and the thunder that follows makes the *taverna* tremble.

"Wow, we made it just in time, a moment later and we would have been washed away," Marlène laughs and looks at Francesca with relief. They take a seat at an empty table and both order a hot tea to warm themselves up. Afterwards they bury their noses in the menu and decide on a classic Greek specialty: grilled aubergines and moussaka. An old radio plays music, which is completely drowned out by the elements raging outside.

"It's really quite original, this minimalistic *taverna* with its solid tables and chairs made from a light wood," Marlène remarks, "Something different for a change. It's great."

"I was completely taken with it as well when Spiro and Despina invited me here one day. The food is superb and prepared by the chef with love and great attention to detail," Francesca replies. Slowly, with a thoughtful expression she lets her gaze travel across the spare, but tastefully designed interior and remarks softly, "You know what troubles and scares me, is that lately, I don't think of George as much as I used to. Especially when I'm spending these days with you. We have never spent such fun and carefree holidays together as we are doing now. Never once did I even ask you about him."

Marlène looks at her with amusement. "Have you noticed that this year we have mostly been living in the moment and have gratefully accepted every minute that these past days have had to offer?"

George is no longer omnipresent because we no longer need him every time we turn around. We no longer need to say, "George, look at what's happening to us! What would you do in our place, in this situation?"

And you...you are now taking your fate into your own hands. In the meantime, you already speak fairly good Greek, you drive like a Greek and you live on this island as if you were born here. You have achieved a remarkable serenity, you have rediscovered your spontaneous smile, your eyes are shining with joy and your heart is filled with love for Corfu and its picturesque little corners."

"You have to stop exaggerating..." Francesca replies with a small embarrassed cough.

Marlène continues undeterred, "You want to share with me the best this beautiful place has to offer, each and every moment of our holidays."

"Thank you," Francesca whispers moved, "you always find the right things to say to me to put me at ease."

They both relish the delicious meal, and watch the storm rage outside through the open door, waiting for it to subside and move on. Their clothes have also had a chance to dry in the meantime.

In the afternoon, the sky finally relents. Although it is still overcast, it has at least stopped raining. Neither of the women feel like hanging out at home right now.

"You know what," Francesca suggests, "despite everything, it's still very warm outside. And we do have some of our swim things stashed in the car, so why don't we drive to the beach at Ipsos and go swimming?"

Marlène looks at her friend not sure if she is joking.

"It'll be super. It doesn't matter if it starts to rain again, we'll be in the water and wet already."

"That is such a crazy, but equally brilliant idea." Marlène starts to feel adventurous. "And don't forget that the beach is practically on our way home."

They splash down the wet streets full of exuberance, stomping in deep puddles like boisterous children until they arrive at the fish market, where Merky awaits them washed clean by the rain.

To go swimming on such a day, when storm clouds hang threateningly in the sky, is a new experience for Marlène. One doesn't need sun cream, umbrella or a hat, and there are no overcrowded beaches.

So, when they arrive in Ipsos, the coastline, which is covered in driftwood, kelp and other nondescript objects, is entirely deserted. There is not a single dry spot to spread out a towel.

"My god, what happened here?" Marlène asks in dismay.

"The storm this morning must have raged dreadfully. The waves must have been so violent that they washed into the street and flooded the entire beach."

Francesca has already seen how strong storms can destroy even the most beautiful beach. Afterwards, it takes days to clean it up and return it back to normal. She tries to downplay the ravaged view for her friend and explains that things look far worse than they really are. She does not want her *petite fée* to be frightened and miss out on a pleasant experience. At the moment, the sea lies flat and calm before them. Only the normally intense and lively colours have given way to a fluid sliver, reminiscent of mercury, which spreads along the coast and far out to sea.

With a little encouragement Marlène is cajoled into braving the water. They can't help giggling as they stumble around in one of the small beach huts where they are changing into their bathing suits whilst hanging their clothes on a rusty old nail. And then, once again, it starts to rain.

Unperturbed, they quickly pick their way through the washed-up debris on the beach and run down to the water, which has unfortunately turned the colour of mud due to the churned-up sand. It is wonderful though. The water is relatively warm, and the rain is falling softly on their faces. Full of exhilaration, they swim leisurely along the coast. They feel free and are one with the sea, the rain and the entire universe.

A small group of plucky tourists who have forsaken the bar, dressed in colourful rain coats, are walking along the quay snapping photos of the crazy women swimming in the sea.

"What an amazing experience; it is such a huge pleasure to swim in the rain...simply fantastic!" Marlène's face is beaming with joy. "My hair is completely wet, I don't even need to dive under," She says with a laugh.

They are fortunate that day. Thunder and lightning are absent, only a continuous light rain patters on the water, making interesting patterns on the surface.

Francesca closes her eyes. What a sublime feeling to swim with her eyes closed and feel the raindrops splash upon her face.

She doesn't notice the passage of time until Marlène suddenly gets cold. Shivering, they run back to the little hut and tear off their wet swimsuits without hesitation. Giggling, they grab their clothes and run back to the car wearing only their towels. They toss their things onto the back seat, which is already covered in boots, bags, jackets and shopping bags. This time, without making any detours, they take the shortest route home.

"Well, I have to tell you. Nothing is ever boring with you. Now I am sitting here in this car, stark naked except for a towel wrapped around my body. What happens if we are involved in an accident, or even cause an accident?" Marlène chuckles, despite the fact that she is freezing.

This makes Francesca laugh. She is glad that she could offer her dear friend another lovely and unusual experience today in spite of the rain.

As they turn off the road and continue onto the gravel path that leads to the villa, Francesca does feel some concern.

"I'm interested to see if there is still a passable way to get to the house after all the heavy downpours. Hopefully, the road hasn't been washed out."

"Are you trying to scare me?"

"Of course not. But each time we get this much rain more soil gets washed away and only rocks remain. It will be difficult for me to continue up the hill with Merky because he rides so low, and I could possibly damage him."

But it turns out better than Francesca feared. Slowly and very carefully, she drives over sharp rocks that have been exposed by the rain. Only twice does she set the chassis too firmly on the ground. Marlène throws her a concerned look.

"Don't worry, everything's okay," she says calmly with a confident smile. "Several years ago, I had a big problem when a sharp rock perforated the oil tank. In the repair shop they went ahead and installed a metal plate like they do with taxis. It protects and really helps."

"But now what is going to happen with your drive? All the people that come to visit you, your friends, everyone who lives around here ruins their cars."

"Unfortunately, that happens a lot when we have heavy rainfall, especially in the winter. The local authority has no funds, so money is collected from the residents, and the road gets a makeshift patch until the next time it happens." Francesca gives a shrug and laughs. "Don't look so distressed. We're not living in

Switzerland. You get used to it. The main thing is that we made it to our house."

In their respective showers, they let the hot water revive their lost spirits. Francesca finds one of Hillary's pre-cooked gourmet meals in the deep freeze, which they hungrily devour by candlelight and soft music on the terrace in their warm tracksuits. Her book, *James*, lies next to Francesca. Marlène smiles at her understandingly, "Knowing you, you're probably going to start reading it in bed."

With her hand, Francesca caresses the book's cover.

"Don't you think that the cover is too conspicuous?"

"Absolutely not! It's perfect. I think the caricature of you and your sister is really fitting." She takes the book and slowly fingers through it.

"I wish I had more time, so that I'd be able to read it as well."

"You take it, this way you can start reading it now."

"You'd really let me do that?"

Francesca only smiles and nods her head. Even though her fingers are itching to start the book, she would happily let her *petite fée* have the pleasure.

Outside in the obscure night, three very slender four-legged shadows slink about close by, keeping an eye on the two friends inside.

22

*F*rancesca loves to keep her eyes closed for a while after waking up. The sun rising beyond the Albanian mountains is already spreading its glaring white light. Silly that she forgot to close the curtains before going to bed. But the cloud cover had lifted last night revealing a night sky studded with millions of stars. It was truly blissful to leave the door open when she went to sleep, to breathe in fresh air, everything washed clean by the rain. She shifts a little to her side, so that the light will no longer bother her despite her closed eyes.

She is glad that the sun is shining again today, and that they can spend the day at one of the lovely beaches. She blinks her eyes for a moment and then looks at the clock. It is rather early, but trying to sleep is out of the question. The early riser shoves a pillow behind her back and slides up the wall until she is sitting comfortably. She grabs her laptop, which is always lying within reach on her large bed. When she opens it up, a pink post-it note is stuck to the keyboard. She immediately recognizes Marlène's handwriting:

5 short messages are hidden around your house. Never give up your dreams, for only if you believe in them will they come true. Thank you for being my best friend and my island sister. I love you, Marlène.

Francesca is very touched. How kind of her *petite fée*. Where could she have hidden the other four messages, and what will they reveal to her? It promises to be an exciting morning.

Shortly after, Marlène awakens from Morpheus' arms and has to smile when she thinks about Francesca finding her little notes, which she has hidden around the house thanking her for showing her the wonders that Corfu has to offer. She is grateful for their unbreakable friendship. She is also happy that her friend has opened her heart wide to her new existence, one that is completely different from the life she had shared with George, but despite everything is still exciting. Accepting life's magic, with all its small, daily moments of joy can only be seen by someone who pays attention. It is a blessing to be able to treasure every moment, the good as well as the bad by accepting things as they happen—just as they are— along with all the lessons they have to impart.

She climbs out of bed and after completing her daily yoga routine she goes out onto the terrace dressed in a white tunic with gold sandals on her feet and Francesca's book in her hand.

The weather being so delightfully warm, Francesca selects an airy beach dress under which she is wearing her new two-piece swimsuit in an aubergine shade of purple. After tidying up, she grabs an armful of dirty clothes, takes them downstairs and stuffs it all in the washing machine. She wants to take advantage of the beautiful weather and hang her laundry outside in the sun before they head out for the day. As she steps onto the terrace to string the line between the pillar on the terrace and the large palm tree, she sees Marlène sitting in one of the old bamboo armchairs looking at her with a beaming smile.

"And a good morning to you too. It appears the sun has coaxed you out of bed as well."

Marlène places the book, *James*, which she has just been reading on the small table next to her and stretches luxuriantly.

"It's so nice to feel the warm sun on my skin and listen to the chirping of the birds after all that rain. Let me help you with the clothesline," she says, and jumps up to help her industrious friend.

While they are attaching the clothesline, Francesca remarks, "By the way, I woke up this morning to an exceptionally lovely surprise written on a pink post-it note. Thank you, you are such a treasure. When did you write the messages? And there are supposedly four more of those. How exciting!"

Marlène is very happy that her surprise is such a success.

"Come on, let's get some breakfast, you're probably hungry as well." While she is preparing their toast, and setting an inviting table, Francesca fetches the milk from the refrigerator. Inside, another bright pink note awaits her. Happily, she waves it in the air and runs outside. As she drops into the chair next to her friend she reads out loud:

Thank you for the wonderful week that we are enjoying under George's benevolent watch. It makes him happy to see us laugh, and the only thing he wonders about is why the exchanges between the three of us make us cry considering all the joy and togetherness we share.

"You are a true poet *ma petite fée*," Francesca replies, and looks at her friend lovingly.

Later, when they are hanging up the fresh washing, Marlène is the first one to notice their three new friends.

"Look, over there...our three derelicts are already waiting impatiently."

And indeed, Limpy, Cyclops and Bum Ear are slinking around at the end of the terrace, as they do each morning now, waiting for Marlène to bring them something tasty to eat. Today, they even let her pet them. Only Bum Ear is playing hard to get. Her attempts to entice him have no effect, and he casually waits at a safe distance until their benefactor turns back to her washing.

Unfortunately, clouds slowly appear and inch teasingly past the sun obscuring the blue sky. With a frown creasing her forehead, Marlène looks up at the sky with concern.

"Why don't we pack up our swim things and drive to Boukari for lunch. It's wonderfully warm outside, and you already know the scenic drive along the eastern coast towards the south. And at our destination, the most delicious, aromatically grilled fish awaits us," Francesca says eagerly, as she rolls her eyes in ecstasy.

Marlène is thrilled with the idea. Her beautiful face lights up again as she runs to her room to collect her beach bag, along with socks, leggings and a thick warm fleece jacket.

Meanwhile, Francesca is looking warily at the almost dry washing. It would annoy her if it got wet and dirty again. She quickly decides to remove it all from the clothesline and then discovers the third pink note sticking out from between two towels. She reads:

This fleeting note relays a message from the words of Saint Exupéry: The Good, one can only see with the heart. The things that are important are invisible to the naked eye.

My *petite fée* is so right: But why is this in particular so difficult? Why is it so much easier to let your eyes deceive you instead of listening to your heart?

While they are driving more clouds gather together in menacing clusters. At the same time, the colour of the sea and the surrounding hilly landscape starts to lose its intensity. The mood is unique. After almost an hour the friends arrive in Boukari in high spirits. It is a small, enchanting fishing village that lies in a quiet location on the south-eastern end of the island. Immense boulders protect the small, picturesque harbour, its vivid painted fishing boats rocking gently in the water. Oblivious to the world, a fisherman sits on the quay mending his nets. A grey tabby cat sits close by appearing bored, but watchful as it licks its paws.

The friends first stop off at the *taverna*, which lies directly on the beach, and greet the young owner whom Francesca has known since he was a child helping out his father on the days when he didn't have school. They receive a hearty welcome in the kitchen by his mother. In a business-like manner, she shows them the large selection of fish lying on ice from which

Francesca knowledgably selects a gilthead sea bream weighing almost 2 kilograms, which will slowly be grilled to perfection on the barbecue. In the meantime, they plan on going for a swim to whet their appetites.

They leave their bags in the *taverna* taking only their towels with them. As Francesca opens her beach towel, she discovers the fourth pink message. She cheerfully shows it to Marlène and reads out loud:

We are the five words engraved in your heart. FRIENDSHIP, RECOGNITION, JOY, EXCHANGE, LUCK. This should encourage you to have that guiding star tattooed on the back of your neck. George will stand behind you and watch over you.

Francesca smiles, "I will take it to heart. Now all I need to find is one more message. I hope you still know where you hid it."

Marlène just grins and, with her friend at her heels, walks down to the small beach that is deserted today. One has a perfect view of Corfu from here with its green surroundings. As they spread out their towels on two of the few blue and white striped loungers, a window opens in between the thick black clouds, and warm rays of sun are shining down upon the two contented women. Greatly pleased at this unexpected gift from nature, they jump into the placid water and swim away slowly enveloped in a wonderful stillness.

After a while, Francesca notices in the distance small whitecaps forming on the waves, but here in the bay they are still sheltered from the wind. Unconcerned, they swim side by side along the coast, which is almost uninhabited save for some enormous olive groves, which characterize the region. "I simply can't believe it," Marlène remarks after some time. "Heaven's window is still open and allowing rays of sun to pass through, while the rest of the sky is obscured with thick, black storm clouds."

They lie on their backs and float while they observe in fascination how the cloud masses constantly shift and change into new formations, passing by rapidly above their heads. All the while Francesca keeps a watchful eye on the sea to recognize the first indication of a storm, so they will be able to swim back in time.

"It is a completely new and unique experience for me to swim in such inclement weather. But now I'm concerned that our fish is going to get over cooked if we delay any longer," Marlène remarks, expecting her friend to make some kind of cynical comment. However, Francesca appears to be relieved.

"Finally! I'm starving."

When they emerge from the water the atmosphere outside is one of a kind. The formerly quiet sea has taken on a deep, emerald colour. As Marlène goes to her lounger to dry off, she realizes her spot is already taken! A large, striped tabby cat is lying there, spread-eagled on its back with its tongue hanging out. It refuses to be disturbed by them, even when they start snapping some funny photos of it.

The sky suddenly takes on a threatening hue, as the entire area grows dark. The waves, which had just recently been their friends, now look menacing and are tipped with whitecaps. Then, a sudden burst of wind closes the single opening in the sky smacking it shut. Wind gusts tug at the sails and rigging of individual sailboats. Dust and sand swirl into the sky. An old, forgotten paper tablecloth becomes airborne, carried out to sea by the wind. With their towels wrapped tightly around them, they make it back to the shelter of the *taverna* just in time before the storm releases with a fury and opens its floodgates.

The temperature drops suddenly and it becomes unpleasantly cold. Exhilarated, the shivering women who are covered in goose pimples quickly change out of their wet clothes. Blissfully warm and cuddled into their fleece jackets, they are the only guests in the *taverna* seated at a well-protected table with a front row view of the tremendous storm.

The sea continues to build up until the waves crash upon the pebbled beach and wash up against the few deserted loungers. In the meantime, the cat has most certainly fled to a safer and much drier hideout. The wind increases rapidly. It is already whistling all around whipping up dry sea grass and tossing it through the air. Meanwhile, the sea and sky have taken on the same dark hue, so one can no longer determine where the sea ends and the sky begins. All colour has been leached from the area, what remains is a picture in black and white.

The roaring of the breakers and the storm, which sounds like the temperamental finale to a powerful allegro played by a 200-man orchestra, accompanies them as they enjoy their delectable fish. Completing this feast are marinated sardines, an abundance of grilled vegetables and herbed garlic bread. Along with this, Francesca treats herself to a large glass of chardonnay.

"What a priceless moment, what an experience... it is simply too beautiful for words. We have never before experienced something like this together. It's fantastic!" Marlène beams, and looks at her friend with joyful blue eyes.

"It is a fantastic thing to watch a storm like this while sitting safe and dry and scoffing down the best-prepared fish on the island," Francesca laughs.

Where only a half hour ago the sea was still and smooth, high waves now crash angrily against the shore and even try to devour the path along the beach. The sound of cascading rain mixes with that of the sea. Just a few metres away the wind whips the rain through the streets. In the small, protected harbour, fishing boats are being tossed about by the wind, bobbing back and forth on the waves, as if trying to out dance each other.

When the weather finally subsides in the late afternoon, the two friends drive back home along the coast with joyful hearts and full stomachs. The radio is blaring at full volume, and their spirited accompaniment fills the car. Fortunately, Francesca is very familiar with these parts, so she can easily negotiate the detours around the areas, which might have been flooded by the heavy rain. Suddenly, she reveals to Marlène, "You know what I'd really still like to do, and I hope that you support me in doing it?"

"Whatever you want, I'm all for it!"

"I would like to drive to Paleokastritsa, up to the Monastery, and from the highest point I want to deliberately toss George's picture off the cliff and into the sea. I'm certain he would approve because he loved the place."

"What a great idea, let's do it. That is, if it doesn't rain because then it would be too dangerous to climb over the wet rocks."

The gravel path up to Francesca's villa looks far worse than yesterday. Portions of it are like a riverbed.

Slowly, she drives cautiously and fully concentrating up the embankment so as not to damage Merky. Suddenly she stops.

"What's wrong?" Marlène asks, worried.

In the middle of the drive a tortoise is making its way laboriously across the rocks and gravel.

"Ooh, let's take it with us!" Marlène is completely beside herself and quickly jumps out of the car. She picks it up carefully, but then a long stream of fluid shoots out from between its legs. Marlène has the presence of mind to hold it away from the car. They both burst out laughing at the startled tortoise's misfortune.

"We'll call it *"Yassou"*, which means "Good Day" in Greek—one of the few phrases I know," Marlène blurts out eagerly. When they arrive at the house, they welcome Yassou to his new home by feeding him bite-sized morsels of tomato, which he readily enjoys. Francesca kneels next to him in the wet grass watching his wide-opened mouth greedily devour each piece.

It is still very cloudy, but the temperature has risen again following the storm, and now in the early evening it is still pleasantly warm. The marble frame containing the laminated laser engraving of George is lying in a bag on the back seat of the car, as Francesca and Marlène—both wearing jeans, sturdy shoes and a warm jacket tied around their waists—drive to Paleokastritsa.

The hilly locale lies nestled beneath steep green slopes replete with olive trees. The monastery, which dates back to the 12th century, is built on a high peak of a peninsula surrounded by the deep, blue sea. The existing buildings date back to the 18th century. A museum has been established in one of the monastic cells to exhibit the precious icons and relics.

"How impressive and noble the monastery looks enthroned up high."

"Just wait until you stand in front of it. It is singularly beautiful and you have a breathtaking view of the island from up there."

They park the car in the village. Francesca slings the bag containing the marble frame over her shoulder, and together they climb up the steep path with its magnificent view of the surrounding, picturesque landscape, and the ever-present Ionian Sea; they walk past countless flowering oleander bushes until, out of breath, they reach the monastery. And the view from up there is truly stunning.

Marlène is immediately caught up in the spell of this harmonious, magical place. The monastery with its whitewashed buildings is impressive and its gardens are very well maintained. They slowly stroll through the interior courtyard, past the former cistern, which today serves as a wishing well.

"It's so incredibly beautiful here. I can feel the peaceful atmosphere all around us."

"Come on, the most glorious sight for me is still to come, you have to see the monastic chapel."

As always when Francesca walks beneath the clock tower, which is overgrown with bougainvillea, she is overcome by a sense of peace and stillness. Marlène admires the romantic garden with its pots of fragrant basil. Ancient grapevines are growing all around, and even more flowering bougainvillea. It's almost certain that the many native cats lying curled up in their dry places feel the peace and quiet as well, since they ignore everyone who passes. Moved, the two friends enter the chapel.

For a moment, Francesca closes her eyes and breathes in air redolent with the smell of incense and candlewax. Then she lights a candle that has been placed there for visitors, and places it in its awaiting holder in the sand. With a smile, she hands one over to Marlène, who silently copies her actions.

One after the other they slowly approach the altar, which is framed by holy icons. Everything glows in silver and gold. Remarkable biblical frescos adorn the walls and the ceiling. They solemnly move from one silver-framed icon to the next, most of them finished in wood with pictures of saints rendered by hand. "Come," Francesca whispers and walks quietly ahead of Marlène through the empty rows of chairs until they reach the farthest corner and sit down on a bench in the semidarkness.

The candles, which cast a faint light in the dark, bathe the room in a warm and calming light, as if nothing evil has ever disturbed this holy place. Francesca starts to ponder: *How often have I escaped into this still and tranquil place in order to find inner peace and comfort, and to think about so many things. There was a time when all I did was cry, and I was so full of anger and despair that I could have killed all those saints who were looking down on me with their stoic peace and understanding.*

Since my painful farewell I have walked a long road until I found my inner peace and trust. Sometimes it is easier, sometimes more difficult. Today I think that my soul was already familiar with all the pain that I had to endure, that this enormous love precipitated something much larger. My soul knows me best, it knows everything about me; how I feel health wise, knows my wishes, fears and longings. My soul understands why it is here. It also knows when it must leave. But why does it not tell me what it knows? Why did I have to suffer through all of that damned pain?

Perhaps it is because we would otherwise never have these experiences that are part of the path that we need to walk. I no longer want to fill my life with bitterness and resentment. I am thankful for all the beautiful things I am allowed to experience each day. I have grown through my hardship; have changed. I have learned to accept myself as I am.

I still try in vain to reach my innermost self, to speak to my soul, though I usually fail. Perhaps I don't have enough patience to listen to my inner voice? It should in fact be there, but up until now there has been no dialogue. Over and over I continue to come to this mystical place, where I feel welcomed and protected, where I hope to one day actually be able to have an inner dialogue with myself.

For a while now, Marlène has been sitting motionless next to Francesca on the hard, uncomfortable bench observing her surroundings with interest. What a wonderful, magical place. If these ancient walls could speak...it is only now that she notices an elderly woman sitting across from them, who is dressed entirely in black from head to toe bowing her head in deep prayer.

My poor island sister. Though I can't make out your face in the dark, I can feel your turmoil. Please don't revert back to your former sorrow and despair. You have learned so much in these past few years, you know

344

now that George will always be with you in your heart and that he has never really left you. So, accept this knowledge with gratitude.

A monk enters in his long, black robe. He has hidden his youthful face behind a beard. He first bows devoutly before an icon bordered in silver before mounting two large, white candles to either side of the alter, which he then proceeds to light.

Still moved by the powerful moments they have just experienced, they exit the monastery through the portal with lighter hearts.

"Now the big moment has arrived. I want to climb up there with you to that rock, the one with the large iron cross, and honour George's request," Francesca says cautiously.

Carefully, due to the wet rocks, they walk along a steep precipice until they reach the rock with the iron cross. At this highest point, they are exposed to the brisk wind from all sides and quickly don their jackets. The fabulous, giant rock formations jutting out from the blue sea far below them are remarkable. They can hear the crashing of the waves and the screech of seagulls flying over their heads.

"Look, with the monastery over here; and just across from this wonderful vantage point we have a magnificent view of the castle *Angelokastro*", says

Francesca, pointing with her finger towards the top of this incredibly steep and rocky terrain. She eagerly explains this to Marlène, because she loves this view and often travels here to enjoy it in solitude. Up here between the sea and the sky one feels free and unfettered from all of life's problems.

"Wow, it is stunningly beautiful, what an incredible view. I will be eternally captivated by this place."

Francesca smiles warmly at her friend. She knows this feeling only too well.

"So, now it's time…" She takes the marble-framed picture with the photo of her husband and looks at it for one final time. She gently strokes her fingers across his eyes, nose and lips. *You will get another photo, I promise.*

"I'm glad that you're here with me as well. It's somehow a weird feeling to go and toss him down into the sea where he will be smashed upon the rocks."

"Just get on with it. He can't feel anything, and we are only respecting his wishes."

"Okay, on the count of three…one, two, three!" Francesca holding her breath, with the frame held high above her head, hurls it as far as she can over the edge of the cliff into the abyss below. Two pairs of eyes follow its trajectory in silence until it disappears between the rocks, where it will settle in the sand on the seafloor forever and always.

"I can just imagine one-hundred years from now, how a very young, lovely girl, searching for sea urchins or squid suddenly spies something shining in between the craggy rocks covered in slimy algae and kelp," Francesca muses, as she places an arm around her friend's shoulder. While they both gaze dreamily at the sea she continues, "Carefully, the young girl takes the piece of white marble in her delicate hands, and with her thumbs rubs away the smeared dirt. Full of curiosity, she inspects her discovery through her diving goggles. She soon discovers a handsome man's mouth smiling back at her. *Perhaps I'll find more of these rocks lying around here?*" Excited she starts searching every centimetre of the surrounding rocks. It doesn't take long for her to be successful, and she gathers up all the white marble pieces she can find and places them in a small sack that she always carries with her. Later, when she steps back onto the shore, she tips out the rocks and spreads them on the warm, fine sand. Patiently she begins to piece the puzzle together until she is finally looking at an extremely attractive man's face. "*Who are YOU? And when and where did you live?*" She is immediately mesmerised by this elegant face. "*This is exactly how my future prince must look,*" she whispers with a smile before she presses her lips to the cold marble."

"I see the two of them, him, as he looks at her from eternity, and she, how she smiles at him with shining eyes," answers Marlène in a subdued voice. "A moment of connection, a bridge between two worlds where they have met fleetingly and which she will remember for a lifetime, never realizing that the curtain that divides these worlds has opened briefly to allow the magic of life to shine through."

In the meantime, the wind has driven away the clouds, they have moved on. Now the horizon is glowing in varying shades of red. It is crimson in the spot where the sun kisses the sea, farther up it glows a more intensive red and above them the sky is blue.

Reverently they stand next to each other and watch the red disc until it has disappeared completely below the horizon.

"Come now, you little dreamer. It's already twilight and late," Marlène says with a note of concern in her voice.

Francesca has to close her aching eyes for a brief moment. She is enveloped by a deep sense of security. When she looks up to the sky for one final time she says in a pleased voice, "Look up at that light blue streak in the sky, it is shining faintly, the first star. I am sure it is a goodnight greeting from George."

Feeling pleased and at one with the world, they pick their way very carefully across the rocks, which are still wet and slippery and return happy and content to the waiting car. By the time they arrive it is already pitch-black outside.

"What do you think, should we make a quick stop at Emerald for some ice cream?" Francesca asks her quiet passenger.

After an indulgent yawn, she answers in a small voice, "I think they'll have to do without our visit tonight."

23

The wind that flared up quickly during the night appears to have exhausted itself and stilled. The final day of their holidays begins with a clear, blue sky.

Yawning heartily a tousle-haired Francesca, who is up quite early this morning, opens the doors to her balcony and shuffles outside wearing an oversized t-shirt, her bare feet shoved into a pair of worn out sneakers. *How splendid, the weather is perfect. My petite fée will be so glad. One last time to lie in the sun, relax and swim—just be lazy.* She sits down on the low wall of her balcony and, as she always does when she sits here, enjoys the view of the peaceful and idyllic landscape.

From somewhere, a donkey brays his good morning greeting at full volume. Here and there a dog pursues its favourite pastime by chasing and barking at cats that don't make a break for it fast enough. The neighbour's rooster adds his "cock-a-doodle-do" to the morning concert. *Our final day...time must have wings because there is no other way the week could have passed so quickly.* A brisk breeze makes her shiver. She can feel the chill gradually creep up from her feet to her legs. It has only just turned 8:00 a.m. What has happened to the sun all of a sudden?

In a dejected mood, the two friends sit out on the terrace for breakfast. The conversation stagnates; it is hard to stretch out.

"Okay, that does it, otherwise we're going to spoil our last day with this dismal mood," Marlène says resolutely.

"You're right, it would be a pity after such a fantastic week; and your family will now be looking forward to your return this evening. We know that all good things have to come to an end."

Broad smiles appear on their faces and Francesca continues, "It's only our thoughts that are playing tricks on us, every one of them. With each thought, we create our own reality, instead of living in the moment. We should be happy that you don't have to leave in the morning." And then, as their three new and peculiar tenants show up together and pace impatiently back and forth at the far end of the terrace, all the sadness at leaving is forgotten.

Marlène makes an extra special effort today to win Bum Ear's trust, which finally happens to her great delight when he allows her to stroke him. With whispered endearments, she says her goodbyes to Cyclops and Limpy, her three conspicuous wards, who brush around her legs with their tails upright purring devotedly, as if they can sense their benefactor's imminent departure.

"Be sure to continue feeding them!" Marlène looks at her friend imploringly. "I know they're no beauties, but their fur is already healthier and better looking, and they don't look as neglected as they did a few days ago. They've also rounded out a bit so that you can no longer see their bones."

"I promise *ma petite fée*," Francesca assures her. "Who was it that remembered to stop at the minimarket for more cat food last night on the way home?"

After the cats, who are more trusting now, have been fed, the two friends gather up their swimming things and drive one final time to the beach in Barbati. The wind has calmed down now and is blowing a gentle breeze through their hair, as if it were saying farewell.

Marlène wants to get comfortable on her sun lounger, leisurely lie in the sun, observe people, be lazy and do absolutely nothing, for the week has been quite intense. They drove around a lot, though they discovered many new and interesting parts of Corfu.

Before Francesca loses her courage, she slowly enters the sea, which has cooled off considerably after the many storms of the past few days. She promptly loses her balance on some stones and falls into the water with a pointed shriek. After she recovers from the cold shock—actually being the best way to get this torture over and done with—she swims a few strokes then turns around and yells, "Hey! Come in here as well. The water is refreshing, it's fantastic."

Marlène shakes her head with a smile, and waves her off, as she lies back down on the lounger and stretches out with a blissful sigh.

Meanwhile her friend is swimming with strong even strokes far out to sea and soon disappears between the waves. Out of breath, she turns onto her back and lets the water carry her. In her mind, she is completely connected to her husband and imagines him warming her with the sun's rays and carrying her gently, now that he is part of the sea.

Suddenly, out of the blue, a question comes to mind: *And what if this new life philosophy that Marlène has taught me these past few years isn't true? That George is sitting next to me with an ironic smile, as if to say "You both have no clue!" What if all the theories and theses that have given me new courage in life, that console me and help me through the day aren't correct. The beautiful hypotheses we like so much, that sound good; what if they are impossible? Perhaps there is no other spiritual realm that lies parallel to ours. Is everything untrue that he or other helpers from the intangible world —such as angels—support me in my existence, and that Marlène is mistaken and only imagines that she has a connection to this ethereal world?*

Perhaps, my belief in things that lie beyond the tangible has always been there, and I simply had no access?

And is it even important to have to know everything so definitively? No one can be one hundred per cent certain before crossing over into that realm themselves one day. NO, everything is good the way it is. She dives deep below the surface and swims along the seafloor completely detached from everything until her lungs start to burn, and she is forced to resurface with a powerful thrust.

Marlène gives a sigh of relief when she discovers Francesca swimming deliberately back to the shore. Undaunted, she now enters the water as well and swims towards her friend. One last time they swim alongside each other following the shoreline, each of them silent and lost in thought.

"I somehow feel like a balloon right now that has deflated," Francesca remarks apologetically.

"I think that in these past few days we have had so many intense conversations and philosophised over so many things that we have been able to close the circle," Marlène replies, and stretches her neck as far as she can to avoid the pesky whitecaps that are constantly splashing in her face, which is very unpleasant.

"Come on, I don't want you to remember Barbati as a dull place," and without warning, Francesca wriggles out of her bikini and laughing, ties it around her neck. Marlène is taken aback. Then she is filled with a sense of *déjà vu*, and seconds later has slipped off her own bikini as well. But what to do with it? While she is pedalling with her feet and trying to swallow as little water as possible, she quickly threads her top through the bottoms and ties all of it around her hips. They splash and lark around boisterously until they both start to get cold. Demurely, they put their swimsuits back on and swim leisurely back to shore where they stumble back to their loungers, giggling.

Later, after putting on dry bikinis, they sit on the beach and let the rays of the sun warm them. Small waves lap gently around their feet, as they tuck into the club sandwich that they have ordered. The vivacious beach life continues all around them oblivious to who comes or goes. Marlène casts a glance at her large, turquoise wristwatch and sighs, "I think we have to leave, it's already late."

They both accept the inevitable and quickly pack up their things. Francesca ties on one of her colourful pareos, and Marlène puts on her light blue shorts and a t-shirt. For a moment, she lingers at the shore gazing at the sea and whispers, "I can feel your high and low tide inside of me. You live within me. Engraved on my skin are the wind's caresses, the soft rays of the evening sun and the extraordinary light at the beach as the day draws to a close. I absorb all of this inside me so that any time I want, I will be able to remember this perfect merging together of Corfu, Francesca and George, as well as myself." Her eyes bright with emotion, she turns around and follows her friend across the pebble beach to the car.

They needn't have hurried with the packing and showering because Marlène is one of the first passengers to check in. Now they have more than an hour to kill, which isn't an interesting option at the small airport. So, Francesca spontaneously drags her heavily protesting friend back out to the car.

"What are you doing, have you completely lost your mind? We're not allowed to do this."

"Oh rubbish, nobody's going to even notice," Francesca grins challengingly. "Until you have to go through Customs, we'll have long since returned. This is only going to be a short little outing to get our adrenaline going. Better than dying of boredom here, right?"

Despite a fluttering in her stomach, Marlène lets her incorrigible friend convince her. As they leave the airport behind them, she starts itching for an adventure as well, and is greatly looking forward to one final thrill together before she returns home to her daily routine.

The two crazy individuals arrive in town in a fantastic mood and then proceed to stroll through the streets. Francesca remarks that Marlène is constantly looking around for something. "What's wrong, are you looking for something in particular?"

Marlène admits that the last time they were in town, a very cool tattoo and piercing shop with a unicorn logo over the entrance had caught her eye. She would like to find it again.

"Don't tell me you want to get a tattoo on the fly, or god forbid, get a piercing?" her friend asks aghast.

"Yes, exactly. For years I've wanted to get my navel pierced, and I think that right now before I return home is the right time to go through with it. What a lovely symbol to remind myself of the incredible moments we have shared here together. What do you think?"

Francesca can only shake her head but helps her search. After ten minutes of searching, and being no closer to finding the unicorn, a young Russian woman approaches them on the street and asks if they would like to rest their feet for a while and be pampered in a fish spa. Francesca's eyes take on a mischievous gleam, and she is already approaching the friendly woman. Marlène follows her and asks fascinated, "Do we still have enough time for this?"

After a quick glance at her watch Francesca replies airily with a grin, "We still have 40 minutes. It takes only 5 to get to the airport. So, there's more than enough time to try an alternative pedicure."

Shortly after, the girlfriends are sitting side by side and let their feet dangle into a large basin, watching in interest as small, voracious fish nibble diligently at the dead skin on their feet.

"This is far more fun than waiting around in an overcrowded airport for hours on end, wouldn't you say!" Francesca grins.

"But it tickles so much," Marlène giggles, "though it really does feel incredibly good."

For one blissful, relaxed moment they have both forgotten that one of them has to fly home, until Marlène finally looks at her watch. She breathes rapidly as she tries to keep her panic in check, "You know what, we really need to leave."

This time Francesca nods in agreement. Nervously they dry their feet, which are now as soft and smooth as a baby's, and hurriedly put on shoes and sandals. Out of breath they arrive at the car. Indeed, after five minutes they are back at the airport.

"You see, we're still early enough to wait among all these sweaty people smelling of sun cream. At least we had a blast," Francesca says brightly.

"Thank you, it really was a super idea," Marlène replies enthusiastically, "But please, go home now. I don't like extended goodbyes."

"You're right," Francesca admits. Gone is the exuberant mood from their adventure just a moment ago. This, here, is reality. Francesca will go back to her car and return to her villa alone. Marlène will get on the airplane and hopefully, land before midnight in Geneva where Eddy will be waiting to embrace her.

As they both say their heartfelt goodbyes, Francesca firmly admonishes her friend, "I don't care how late it is when you arrive, but please, send me an SMS, so that I know everything is okay."

"Of course! I don't want to be the cause of you losing out on your beauty sleep."

One last time they kiss each other on the cheek, then Francesca resolutely turns around and pushes her way through the relaxed crowd of people, as she heads towards the exit. When she looks back for a final glimpse, her *petite fée* has disappeared from sight.

Marlène briskly clears the restricted area, and to her dismay discovers a very long queue of passengers waiting in front of passport control. She gets in line and thinks back to the last hour she spent in town. A voice from the loudspeaker echoes throughout the airport ripping her from her reverie. She hears her name being paged along with a sentence in Greek. She looks at her watch and discovers to her horror that there are only twenty minutes left until departure. This means, "Move it!" She races past ten people waiting in the queue in front of her and stops at the counter in front of a customs official, who is giving her a severe look while the other travellers are looking at her stunned and unable to comprehend her audacity. She shows him her documents and stammers, "They're paging me, I think my flight is leaving without me."

With incredible calm, the official only rolls his eyes, sighs, but then lets her pass pointing her in the general direction of the gate where her flight is boarding. She runs over to it and arrives breathless only to find out that it is closed! She turns around runs back in the opposite direction towards the Customs official and the passengers, who are still staring at her in astonishment. With difficulty, she explains to the official—who only speaks broken English—that her flight is taking off in five minutes. And then something miraculous happens. The official grabs the phone, one of the ground staff arrives and escorts Marlène to a small car that is parked on the opposite side of the departure gate. The car races across the tarmac and deposits her at the foot of the stairs leading up to the aircraft. Taking four steps at a time while dragging her pink suitcase behind her she finally stands face to face with a stewardess, who is eyeing her coldly. The pilot growls, "It's about time!"

Marlène timidly adopts a shaky smile. The stewardess points her to a seat at the far end of the airplane. *Well isn't that great, right next to the loo. But I won't complain.*

Dozens of eyes follow her in annoyance and she catches snippets of comments, which are directed at her in a loud tone of voice: "Some people like to draw out their holidays until the very last moment...guess she's not in much of a hurry to get home...go ahead, take your time...Swiss punctuality doesn't count in a foreign country..."

She has barely reached her seat when an announcement is made from the cockpit: "Good evening, this is your Captain speaking. The passenger who has delayed us has finally decided to grace us with her presence, therefore we will be departing fifteen minutes late."

All heads turn to look at Marlène who sits in her seat completely still and mortified. If only she had a magic wand and could turn herself into a little mouse in order to flee the accusatory glares.

A few minutes later, once she has her emotions back under control, she sees the levity in the whole situation. She feels something start to build in her, which she is unable to control and bursts out laughing. With tears in her eyes, she tries to hide her face in an open magazine and remains in this position in order to catch her breath and return to some semblance of earnestness.

Two hours later when the plane lands in Geneva and her tears of laughter have already dried, she waits until all passengers have exited the cabin before rising and walking to the airplane door.

It is pitch black outside. The sky is filled with millions of shining stars as Francesca arrives back home at 10:30 p.m. When she opens the door, and walks into the sitting room, she is surprised at how still the house is. She stands there for a moment, motionless. *Strange, now I'm actually imagining that I can hear the silence.*

Exhausted, she lets herself fall onto the sofa. The remote control for the television lies untouched before her on the coffee table. Somehow, she doesn't know what she wants; sit in silence and see what develops, or fill the void with some mindless film or television show.

A close acquaintance—who also happens to be a psychologist—urged me years ago to set a date in my calendar and make an appointment with myself and keep it. This would be the only way I would take time for myself, learn to take myself seriously and give in to my needs. I was to have a dialogue with my innermost self. The result of these appointments could be very surprising, if I would accept the responses.

Now, I've been sitting in the dark for at least half an hour, and still nothing has happened apart from the rushing in my ears, which still hasn't subsided. I probably don't possess enough sensitivity to listen to my inner voice. Perhaps I don't have one? I'm probably just an empty shell; too arrogant, too impatient. It's best that I just shut up, turn off the constant thoughts and don't think of anything.

With a suppressed sigh, she stands up and finally turns on the light and the television. She fetches butter, ham and a few leaves of lettuce from the refrigerator and makes herself a sandwich. The disjointed voices coming from the television give her a headache. She turns everything off again and goes up to her room, sandwich in one hand and glass of wine in the other. She puts on a jacket and steps out onto the balcony, where she sits down on the wall with a cushion before taking a hearty bite out of her sandwich.

An owl hoots at regular intervals. Undefined noises are coming from the palm tree. A dog barks in the distance. The stars shine even brighter than before. Francesca is happy at this very special moment. No thoughts are forced upon her. There is only herself, the sandwich, a glass of wine and the universe.

After showering and getting ready for bed, she lies down with her book, *James,* and tries to read. Her thoughts are with her *petite fée*. She knows how her friend hates to be out at such a late hour, especially on an airplane. All the while she fights the drowsiness that threatens to overcome her. Finally, at 1:00 a.m. she receives the following SMS:

I just landed, even though that wasn't so certain up until two hours ago. I was paged and driven by car to the waiting airplane, where I rushed to my seat followed by hostile stares and then weheaded for our departure ... you and your spontaneous ideas!!

Francesca is now wide awake. At first, she is shocked. But then she reads the SMS again and breathes a sigh of relief because the way it is worded, Marlène must have arrived in Geneva and that is all that matters. Poor *petite fée*...all of a sudden the muscles in her cheeks start to hurt. Only now does she notice that she is massaging them with her fingers because she has been sitting there the entire time with a huge grin on her face.

When she imagines Marlène, this delicate, lovely person with her enviable long blonde hair, how she timidly made her way to her seat, her blue eyes downcast, while she walked past all the nosey parkers and the disapproving flight staff, she can't help but laugh. She sits on the bed holding her stomach.

When she finally calms down and has wiped away the last of the tears, she stands up. *I have to enter this message in my journal right away before I forget a single word of this delightful intermezzo. What a week; what a finale!*

When Francesca opens her diary, a pink post-it note flutters out. With joy, she holds her fifth message, the final one, in her hand and reads:

Message from George:

Take a joyful approach to your path in life. I will always be at your side.

I thank you for being with me until I took my final breath.

You have always done your very best.

I will continue to be your sun and envelop you with my warmth.

I Love You Forever